THE TAIL OF THE DRAGON

THE TAIL OF THE DRAGON

A Novel

ROBERT L. WISE

&

WILLIAM LOUIS WILSON JR.

THOMAS NELSON PUBLISHERS

Nashville

Published in Nashville, Tennessee, by Thomas Nelson, Inc.

Published in association with the literary agency of Alive Communications, 1465 Kelly Johnson Blvd., Suite 320, Colorado Springs, CO 80920.

Library of Congress Cataloging-in-Publication Data

Wise, Robert L.
    The tail of the dragon / Robert L. Wise and William Louis Wilson, Jr.
        p. cm.
    "Janet Thoma books."
    ISBN 0-7852-6983-5 (pbk.)
    1. Political corruption—United States—Fiction. 2. Nuclear power plants—United States—Fiction. 3. Conspiracies—United States—Fiction. I. Wilson, William Louis. II. Title.

PS3573.I797 T35 2000
813'.54—dc21
                                                                    99-047929
                                                                    CIP

Printed in the United States of America
3 4 5 6 QPV 04 03 02 01 00

DEDICATION

To our wives, Marguerite and Connie

OTHER BOOKS BY ROBERT L. WISE

All That Remains
The Fall of Jerusalem
Quest for the Soul

with Paul Meier
The Third Millennium
The Fourth Millennium
Beyond the Millennium
The Secret Code
Windows of the Soul

with Mike Evans
The Jerusalem Scroll

PROLOGUE

January 16, 1994, 11:30 P.M., PST

The last of the midnight shift hurried through the front gates into the San Onofre Nuclear Generating Power Plant. Cold Southern California winter winds blew in from the ocean and discouraged lingering outside. As the workers drifted into their places, supervisor Ron Holland switched on the public address system, instantly reaching every employee in the facility. "Listen up, people," his deep bass voice rumbled across the concrete walls. "I have an important announcement."

"Big mouth up there loves to hear himself talk," one of the maintenance men quipped and leaned on his broom. "Probably going to embargo eating doughnuts tonight."

His coworker laughed.

"As you are aware, we've been under a seismic alert for the past two weeks," Holland explained. "This evening we received another report from Washington, D.C., putting us in the exact center of the high-risk zone. I want all personnel to review emergency shutdown procedures and evacuation plans. Most importantly, keep your protective equipment close at hand, and be prepared to respond at a moment's notice."

The maintenance man looked at the other cleanup worker in surprise. "Hey, we don't get them warnings from Mr. Big Time often! Sounds like he means business on this one."

His friend shrugged and started sweeping again.

Ron Holland turned off the system and spoke to his first assistant. "George, I'm assigning you oversight of the spent fuel pond tonight. If we have an event, get that protective gear on and immediately find out what it's done to the fuel storage area. Should any containers be compromised, get out of there quickly."

"You bet." George nodded his head enthusiastically. "I've been through a dozen of these alerts since we started in '83. Every time I worry a little more. If one of the thousands of pounds of spent fuel leaks, we're talking goodbye, Southern California." He scratched his head and rolled his eyes.

"Thought these places were built to withstand anything the San Andreas fault could dish out," said the secretary. She looked over her shoulder with an "I-told-you-so" look; Jan was well known for her irreverent and often dangerously flippant remarks. "That's the PR the Washington bosses been putting out for years anyway."

Holland eyed her disdainfully. "This isn't the evening to be cute. The place was built before the U.S. Geological Survey discovered how many minor faults crisscross the L.A. area. Jan, you'd best worry about your backside rather than be smartmouthed. One crack in this place, and Los Angeles will be a dead city for a century. So pay attention tonight, okay?" Holland stomped out of the office.

"Thanks for the evening gloom-and-doom report," Jan quipped to George. "Ole Ron's a little on the chapped side tonight, don't you think?"

George walked out without comment.

• • •

Miles away in the Northridge area of Los Angeles, Alberto Martinez stirred in his small apartment. Pushing himself up on his elbows in his bed, Alberto looked out the window at the bright moon. From the third floor, he had a complete view of the sky and the foothill mountain range behind the L.A. basin. Living on the third deck of a five-floor apartment building gave his wife, Maria, problems climbing the stairs everyday with their six-month-old baby daughter, but it was the best home they had ever had, especially since being smuggled in from Mexico.

Alberto felt the bed move slightly and looked at the alarm clock. 4:15 A.M. *Way too early to be awake,* he thought. *Need to be on the job in three hours. Got to rest.*

"*¿Que pasa?*" Maria asked dreamily.

"*Nada.*"

"You work too hard," Maria mumbled. "The pick and the axe make you too tired."

Alberto tried not to answer. They might wake the baby. The bed wiggled again, then shook. He felt them inching away from the wall.

"Alberto!" Maria sat straight up in bed.

A small chair suddenly flew across the room and hit the end of the bed. Before Alberto could reach his wife's hand, they seemed to be flying up toward the ceiling. The shaking room was accompanied by a splitting noise that escalated from a cracking sound to a deafening roar. Plaster fell in large chunks onto their faces. Hissing pipes and spewing water erupted from the walls. The smell of natural gas filled the room. Everything turned black.

• • •

An hour later, experts in the Washington, D.C., Earthquake Prediction Center pored over the information being received from seismographic printouts as well as two weeks' worth of data from the Acoustical Research Center in California. Phones rang incessantly; computer operators furiously pushed the capacities of their machines. Employees scurried in and out of the room.

"Looks like the thing lasted about fifteen seconds under the San Fernando Valley," a computer operator told a government geologist. "I'm predicting a lot of people have been killed."

The geologist nodded his head solemnly. "Probably. Any sign of what happened in the south by that nuclear power plant?"

"It's undetermined, but looks like the impact went completely north," the technician said. "Don't think we've got problems in the San Onofre area."

"Listen to this." A radio operator turned up the volume on a recording. "We've picked up these really unusual noises that coincide with the quake."

"Tectonic subterranean plates rubbing together," the geologist answered. "They started the quake."

"Maybe," the radio operator answered but shook his head, "but I don't think so. Never heard anything quite like it. More like some low-frequency message or something."

"Got to be the earth," the geologist dismissed the idea. "You think men from Mars started this thing?"

CHAPTER 1

Six Years Later

Unusually heavy traffic clogged the Beltway on Tuesday, September 5, 2000, irritating Dr. Greg Parker. Hordes of summer tourists had finally evaporated, but Washington's rush hour traffic hadn't improved. Because he was a pilot, the pace inevitably made him wish he could fly in to work. As he had done weekly for the past thirty-two years, Parker sipped a cup of coffee and wound his '89 Pontiac through the exhaust-filled maze, hoping his radio might provide a pleasant distraction from the inevitable waiting that bumper-to-bumper traffic would provide. He could easily afford a new car, but this one was reliable and at this point in his life, Greg wanted continuity.

When the ever-dependable strand holding everything together in Greg's life snapped more than two years earlier, Greg was left strung out and struggling with depression. His usual happy, hopeful self was still displaced somewhere in the back-wash of everything that had occurred in the past couple of years—though it seemed like a couple of decades. His normal professional demeanor disappeared when he left the National Security Agency office building and didn't return until he came back to work the next day. He glanced at the clock above his radio. The trip downtown was taking too much time today. He turned up the volume.

After an update on road conditions, the announcer launched

into national and international news. Middle Eastern turmoil had not subsided during the past forty days, and still no one claimed responsibility for the bombing of Haram es-Sharif, the Temple Mount in Jerusalem.

The announcer barked his report in quick, staccato tones. "This morning Arab Wakf officials again attacked Israelis, evoking memories of the Jews' massacre of Moslems in Hebron's great Mosque, the site of the tombs of Abraham and Sarah. The Wakf claim only the Israeli Defense Force could have blown up the Dome of the Rock Mosque, although they offer no evidence. Publicly they blame the state, but privately are confounded because Israel had everything to lose from the attack. Tension continues unabated," the newscaster concluded, "and the political earthquake rumbles on."

The word *earthquake* hit Greg's buttons, and instantly he thought about the California quake in '94, his constant obsession. In fifteen seconds, sixty people died, more than seven thousand were injured, and twenty thousand ended up homeless. Then, that young couple came to mind. Although he had never met Alberto and Maria Martinez, he felt as though he was their godfather, or maybe their avenger. They put faces on the statistics.

When the California earthquake was investigated, pictures of the dead Martinez family had been left in the packet sent to his office. Greg had opened the sealed envelope without the slightest hint of the bloody gore inside. Pictures of the father, mother, and child seemed to leap off the paper, burning forever their images in his mind. Dr. Greg Parker had vowed to do everything in his power to prevent such a tragedy from happening again. The Martinez family became an icon, a symbol, of his task—to stop suffering.

Even though six years had passed, Greg still thought about them. Their three-story apartment building in the Northridge section of Los Angeles was typical California "cram 'em in" housing. Concrete slab construction, stucco exterior, palm trees in front, a little communal swimming pool in back. An inexpensive place to start working on a future.

After three years of marriage, Alberto and Maria had gone to bed one evening, anticipating leaving for work early the next morning, their six-month-old daughter sleeping in a tiny crib at the foot of the bed. Good job. Good things ahead. Good future. But when the earthquake hit in the middle of the night, the ceiling fell straight down, smothering them and smashing everything like a pancake. In an instant, *good* was gone forever.

The pictures were still in the office files, but Greg didn't need a pictorial nudge to remember. When the Martinez family departed this world, they left behind a mission for him. Someone must vindicate their obscene deaths.

"Don't know why and how they set it off . . . but *our own people* triggered the earthquake," he fumed.

Because he'd been preparing his final report on the Northridge quake, that singular thought preoccupied his entire Labor Day weekend, pushing everything else aside. He didn't read the *Washington Post* stories on the ruckus in Israel or even review his usual pile of work from the office. The terrible truth still tied him in knots.

"I still can't believe it," he mumbled under his breath. "Sold out by our own people!" The line of cars abruptly halted, and he slammed on his brakes.

Greg caught a deep breath and fought the impulse to hit the horn. Alice never liked him to honk and always said something funny or distracting to help the moment pass. *Alice would have said* . . . Suddenly, the memory of her completely pushed the Martinez family out of the picture.

Realizing he was speeding, Greg slowed down. *Has it really been two years?* he thought. Two long years since the car wreck. *If I'd known the roads were slick, I would have driven her myself. Gladly. Anytime.*

The pain still felt as fresh as the day the policeman appeared in Greg's office doorway. "Did you know an Alice Parker?" the man asked in a polite and professional way, holding his hat in his hand. He remembered the shock of the man saying *did*, not *do*.

Did he know Alice Parker? Alice was everything. The sky, the sun, the moon. Everything for thirty-three years. She was so good for him; she kept Greg on an even keel—calm, together.

Traffic picked up again. A state trooper was working a two-car collision ahead. Greg looked the other way; any accident was too vivid a remembrance for him. And as always happened after he remembered Alice, he thought of Sharon.

Greg sped up. He reminisced with bittersweet heartache. *It's been two years since I've seen Sharon or even heard from her . . . I wonder where she is, and if she still blames me for Alice's death.*

Suddenly, Greg felt like he might weep and struggled to hold back the tears. *We always seemed to irritate each other. I don't know why. I wonder what Sharon's doing this morning.* He wiped his eyes and grew annoyed with himself. *She's probably vacationing on some beach in California.*

A red Saturn suddenly cut into his lane of traffic, barely missing Greg's fender. He started to hit the horn, but Alice's voice rang in his mind, and again he didn't. Greg grumbled under his breath and stared straight ahead.

He glanced out of the corner of his eye to make sure the seat *was* empty—guaranteeing that Alice hadn't appeared to lecture him. Instead, it was guilt that rode to work with Greg every day, sitting on the passenger side, hindering his efforts to forget. Maybe he should have told Alice about the anonymous calls, the voice that threatened something would happen to Greg or one of his family members if he didn't drop the inquiry into unofficial commercial use of a spy satellite. Apparently it hit a big nerve somewhere.

No question about it, with oil companies playing the angles and investigating possible oil regions once controlled by the Soviet empire, satellites were the key to their success. At least four trillion dollars in crude oil waited for the first industrious group with access to the latest satellite technology. It could give an unidentified American megacorporation the edge over its competition.

Guilt pushed Greg's silence aside. Did Alice's car skid on a rain-slicked highway or slide on a four-trillion-dollar oil slick? Maybe everything was in his imagination. Maybe. Greg gripped the steering wheel more tightly. He couldn't let himself go there anymore.

Everything made the drive from Arlington, Virginia, seem interminably long on this brisk fall morning. Unexpected road construction didn't help Greg's attitude. Twenty minutes behind schedule, he found his usual parking place two blocks from DuPont Circle where he always caught the Metro to the National Security Agency offices. Although the stagnant summer humidity had faded with September's cool promise of fall, Greg didn't feel so well today. His head hurt.

• • •

The subway swarmed with government functionaries, scurrying toward official anthills to drone away another day on behalf of tneir Uncle Sam. The mood of the masses often varied with the headlines. Today, they seemed grim and determined, reflecting the *Washington Post* banner headline: "Israel Cracks Down: East Bank Remains Sealed Off." Greg looked over the shoulder of a woman next to him and scanned her *Wall Street Journal.* A weird story about religious fanatics in Israel. The next column counted. Military machinery was gearing up for an impending battle. Arabs were making progress in signing up heavy hitters for their new shooting team. Not good news. Greg had a sudden sinking feeling. Maybe he'd had too much coffee. The subway slowed down.

Greg exited at the Constitution Street stop and hurried out the exit, habitually looking over his shoulder. National Security Agency (NSA) work in third-world countries conditioned him to always be aware of his surroundings. More than once he had dived in an alley barely avoiding a violent end. But foreign terrorism wasn't what scared him now.

Financial terrorists lurking in the halls of Congress were far more dangerous. Better known as lobbyists, these expensively dressed employees of the "Dragon"—the industrial complex majoring in the clever and devious—always came with carefully crafted names that sounded good on the New York Stock Exchange's big board. You can dress them up, but they were no less capable of "putting out human contracts" on their opposition, as they had done on him. Years of controversial investigations about questionable government contractors and the perpetual fear of being blindsided by some revenge-seeking bounty hunter made the tall, graying, consummate insider cautious. Greg had danced with the Dragon one too many times.

Because of his work in domestic security and his involvement in several agencies, Greg had friends in every sensitive area of government; he even knew their unlisted phone numbers. Greg Parker could be trusted with the keys to both the front and back doors; his honesty was as legendary as the hostility of his enemies.

He stopped and looked in a large store window. Countless hours of undercover work had shaped Greg's appearance. A plain gray suit and conservative blue-striped tie stamped him as one of the innumerable public servants in the nation's capital, an impression that proved deadly when corrupt politicians failed to take him seriously. The Establishment knew Greg could bring down the big boys no one else would touch.

Greg tried to concentrate on edging through the crowd, but other memories erupted, like when the CIA arranged for a top PLO official and notorious terrorist to spend his honeymoon at Disney World in Florida. Greg tracked down the annual three-million-dollar retainer the CIA bankrolled to Ali Hassan Salameh despite his participation in the massacre of Israelis at the 1972 Munich Olympic games. Greg was too young then to make much of a stink, but he never forgot the role a young man named Alex Majors played in making the arrangements in Florida.

Greg mumbled as he hurried across the street, running around a swerving taxi. "I'm not sure how Majors and the CIA started that quake in California, but they did! I know they did." A motorcycle buzzed past a pedestrian, barely missing Greg. "Watch out!" he shouted after the driver. "Ought to sign up with the CIA," he muttered, hurrying across the street.

Walking faster, Greg thought about how Majors was cata-pulted to the top in the mid-1960s because of his role in destroying the Zairian economy and pushing Mobutu into the presidency. At more than one cocktail party, he boasted that he and the CIA did the deed for the good of GOD and country. He would laugh as he explained his GOD was "Gold, Oil, and

Diamonds." Majors's career had nearly ended when he hinted at possibly acquiring a diamond necklace for a senator's wife at the expense of several Africans' lives. Thereafter, he became considerably more circumspect.

Ten minutes later, Greg caught a crowded elevator up to the third floor. "Morning," came the customary greeting from the woman running the elevator. "Nice day."

He smiled politely but said nothing. His thoughts once again drifted to Sharon and her whereabouts.

An attractive young woman brushed by Greg as she got off on the second floor. "Have a good day," she said to everyone before directing her comment toward Greg with a glance.

The good-bye and look went unnoticed. Getting off on the next floor, Greg hurried down the corridor. He needed a mirror; he had to make sure his professional face was in place.

CHAPTER 2

The smell of death hung like a haze over the Dead Sea. With the ferocity of an estranged couple locked in a heated custody battle, the ancient quarrel between the sons of Abraham continued relentlessly, sending shock waves that reverberated worldwide. Sharon's job was to get the blow-by-blow story.

Sharon Parker arrived in Jerusalem on August 15, 2000, one day after the worst riots in Israel's history erupted in Hebron. Getting the assignment hadn't been easy. Although she was twenty-seven, Sharon looked twenty, an attribute she considered a definite detriment to her career. That and the fact that possibly she was too attractive for her own good. Her superiors at Associated Press tended to discount the fact she had graduated with honors from Columbia. Sharon assuaged their reservations by showing up an hour early every day and staying long after quitting time. The sheer force of her tenacity made it difficult for AP management not to pay attention. This story was important, but Sharon had also wanted to get away, out of the country, and a war in Israel sounded like the opportunity she needed.

August's sweltering heat made for hair-trigger tempers in the Palestinian controlled cities, their residents languishing in squalor and discontent. Tension increased with every sunrise. Every so often, a gunshot ricocheted through some forlorn back street. On August 13, as the sun was setting over the West Bank, the powder keg went off. The explosion echoed like a trumpet announcing the prophet's call for a jihad, resounding from mosque to mosque, rolling across the desert and into the wilderness. An Arab uprising erupted like a spark in a gasoline can. Within hours funeral dirges began and requiems followed. Big stories were there for the taking. Sharon was ready.

Now the svelte brunette looked at her watch and glanced down Jerusalem's Bab en-Nasir Street. It was Tuesday, August 22. Despite centuries of wear and tear, the narrow stone boulevard hadn't changed since Suleiman the Magnificent rebuilt the Holy City in 1539. But Sharon's expected guest was nowhere in sight.

Even though she'd only been there a week, Sharon knew the Arab section of the Old City wasn't the best place to meet Rabbi Eli Goren, but she wanted to see how a pious Jew reacted in this environment. The run-down old coffee shop was only a stone's throw from the Dome of the Rock Mosque, and Moslems ran the place. The waiter kept smiling at Sharon with a big toothy grin while serving the sidewalk tables. Her jeans and black leather jacket hooked him. Out of the corner of her eye, Sharon caught one of the locals several tables over trying to get her attention with frequent little waves. Her red silk blouse got his attention. She looked the other way. Par for the course. Happened all the time.

Sharon pulled her dog-eared manuscript out of her bag, along with a notepad. She began reading the carefully crafted words for the fifth time, checking the details for brevity. The facts were simple. Last night, behind Hebron's marketplace, an Arab had stuck a knife in a Jewish yeshiva student's back. Jewish

THE TAIL OF THE DRAGON

settlers retaliated with a full-scale attack on Arab merchants. Gunfire followed. A bomb exploded. Children died. The war was on. Brief. To the point. The way things occurred here.

At the last minute, the "boys" at the front office had assigned her the religious angle in reporting the conflicts. Sharon still fumed when she thought about the implications. It was obviously a ploy to keep her out of real action on the front lines. Not a chance now. Everything was a religious story.

Several of the Washington-based AP editors hadn't been enthusiastic about her working in such a volatile situation because she was small, slight, and young. They mistakenly read reticence into her resistance to her assignment of covering the religious community. The memory made Sharon laugh; she wasn't afraid of anything.

A glance at her notepad confirmed that Rabbi Eli Goren should have arrived five minutes ago. She turned back to the story one more time and frowned.

I wonder how Daddy might like this. Oh, who cares what he thinks? I've got to get over it—and him.

Still, I wonder how good old workaholic Dad is doing today? Sharon thought as she closed the notepad. *Probably worked until 10:00 P.M. on Labor Day and was up at the crack of dawn, trying to prevent some natural disaster no one . . .*

"Sorry I'm late."

Sharon jumped.

A small man with a scraggly black beard and round gold-rimmed glasses walked around from behind her. "Hard to get a taxi this morning. Everyone is afraid of riots." The round black hat and long coat made their statement. Eli Goren looked every inch the Orthodox Jew she expected.

"Thank you for coming." Sharon started to stand but noticed

the rabbi was already seated and hardly looking at her. "I am a journalist writing about the Israeli conflict for American readers," she began. "My latest assignment is to cover the current conflict from the religious point of view."

"I usually don't speak to women," Goren interrupted. "Not Gentiles. Certainly not in private. That's why this place is acceptable, although I wouldn't normally come here." He glanced nervously at the thoroughly Arab clientele. "I'm not afraid of them," he said defiantly. "What do you wish to know?" he asked abruptly as he looked down the street beyond her. "Madame, you *are* a reporter?"

Sharon bit her lip and inhaled deeply. "I am a professional," she said to herself as she smiled thinly. "Yes, I'm a journalist for the Associated Press. People across America read my stories. That's the bottom line. We'd like to know how your particular religious group is reacting to the riots still going on in Ramallah and Bethlehem." She cleared her throat. "Of course, I also desire your opinions on the bombing and who you believe is responsible. I understand that the highways into Jerusalem are sealed off this morning. The television media says this war started because Jewish settlers fired on the Arab merchants."

The rabbi pulled at his black beard and pursed his lips. "We are only a peaceful people, living exactly like the Holy One instructed Israel to do," he began slowly without making eye contact. "Misunderstood by most."

Sharon tapped her pencil lightly on the notebook. *Oh great,* she thought. *A war is raging over the entire West Bank, and I'm listening to one of the outstanding male chauvinist pigs in the world pontificate about his righteousness. The Arab two tables down wants a date, and this guy is afraid I'll entice him to sin.* Sharon shuddered at the ridiculousness of it all. *There's probably a really big story unfolding somewhere else in this town, and I'm stuck here with Rabbi ben Boring.*

• • •

A few days earlier, twenty feet beneath where Sharon was now seated, three men had hustled down a narrow dark tunnel, winding toward the Dome of the Rock and bringing death next door to the Bab en-Nasir coffee shop.

Four years earlier on Wednesday, September 25, 1996, war had broken out at the same locale because of the existence of a similar passageway. Everyone from tour guides to taxi drivers knew about the decades-old excavations along the Western Wall. Archeologists had tunneled down to the massive stone foundations of the two-thousand-year-old wall and extended their dig along Herod the Great's buttress used to reinforce his expansion of the Temple Mount. Israeli experts burrowed down the wall toward the Antonio Fortress, Rome's ancient command post and residence of the procurator, Pontius Pilate. The controversial excavations proved to be an archeologist's dream and a politician's nightmare.

When the shaft eventually surfaced just a few feet from Bab en-Nasir Street, opening into the Via Dolorosa, East Jerusalem Arabs had read the handwriting on the wall. The tunnel was the open defiance of Prime Minister Bibi Netanyahu's government, thumbing its collective nose at the Palestinians' claims to sovereignty in that sector. When Israelis opened the underpass for tourist inspection, Arabs went into orbit.

For three days, Israeli soldiers had battled it out with Palestinian police. When the smoke cleared, seventy-three lay dead. No one knew how many had been wounded. Tensions had not lessened in the ensuing years. Everyone knew about the passageway, but few knew that it was the least significant project going on under the sacred compound.

Then, Jewish archaeologists, seeking to find the original foundations of Solomon's Temple, built a secret network of tunnels meandering under Haram es-Sharif, the sacred mount itself. At one point the dig accidentally came up in the basement of an Arab home. Apologies were made and promises offered.

The matter had died down and the work had continued. The archeologists eventually abandoned the project. Case closed . . . almost.

A man named Kamel Hassan had done the grunt work for the secret dig, carrying wheelbarrow loads of dirt out of the tunnels. No one took the seemingly mentally-retarded Israeli Arab seriously. Although unusually stout, he was small with large thick hands. His bushy black moustache made him look like a remnant of Turkish domination. Kamel couldn't remember what to do from day-to-day, much less comprehend the nature of the project. Dark and swarthy, Kamel had perfected a blank stare, which gave others the impression that he was on drugs or had an IQ of 50. But behind his mask was a master terrorist who had accomplished one of the most remarkable infiltrations in the history of Arab-Jewish espionage.

Like a ticking time bomb, Kamel had waited patiently for the right moment before he used his considerable knowledge of the tunnel system. When the assignment came, he recruited his cousins Uday and Ahmed, a couple of petty crooks with their own brand of radical politics. An expert in espionage, Kamel carefully trained his hotheaded relatives in the use of explosives. For these human moles, day and night no longer mattered.

Dressed in black, the three men lugged bricks of C-4 plastic explosives and primer cord through the dark tunnel in the early morning hours of August 18. The deadly materials often popped up in the Middle East as terrorists' weapon of choice. Because C-4 can be twisted into any shape, the pliable explosive offered endless possibilities to the inventive Kamel.

Following the circuitous route that wound through the Temple Mount, the trio entered the shaft that surfaced at the sidewalk's edge next to a grassy area just off the promenade connecting the Dome of the Rock with the El-Aqsa Mosque— the same place where King Hussein's grandfather had been assassinated.

After storing the explosives at the bottom of the shaft, the three men settled, napping and resting up for the night attack. At 3:00 A.M., a wrist-watch alarm clock sounded. Kamel rose silently, and the final stage began.

"What ya think?" Uday called up from the bottom of the shaft.

"We're right on target," Kamel answered. "Get the conveyor belt running. Dirt's coming down." An electric motor quietly started the swirl of subsoil moving into another corridor.

For the next ten minutes, piles of clay and sod tumbled down. An electronic auger broke large clumps loose and hurled the pieces in all directions. Lateral burrowing under the concrete created a cave large enough for two of the men to work in. Dust filled the long chasm as dirt tumbled down the shaft onto the makeshift conveyor.

"I'm right on the edge," Kamel called down. "Get everything in order. Once I make the breakthrough, we've got twenty minutes."

"We're in place and ready," Ahmed answered. "Go for it!" Kamel beckoned for his cousin to hand him the C-4 up through the shaft.

Uday and Ahmed quickly passed the bundles of destruction

to Kamel, where he embedded primer cord in each hunk. With only the aid of moonlight, he placed chunks in a pile on the edge of the sidewalk.

Twenty minutes later, the bomb looked like a two-thousand-pound pile of clay barely distinguishable from a big rock. The brothers ran for their lives while Kamel put the infrared motion sensor in place. Should anyone trip the switch, detonation would be irreversible. The next guard to walk across the top of the Haram es-Sharif would never realize he just made history.

Kamel hit the activation button and disappeared down the shaft, which was lined with plastic explosives to ensure the bomb's crater imploded, sealing up the tunnel. He paused and looked up the shaft one last time. "You finely educated boys still think I'm a dummy?" he shouted into the darkness. Then he laughed and ran after his cousins.

Ten minutes later, a guard made his nightly rounds. Two seconds after the bomb exploded, the guard and Haram es-Sharif, the Temple Mount, disappeared in a cloud of smoke. A wave of fire instantly reduced the surrounding trees and grass to charcoal. The great Dome of the Rock Mosque disintegrated, the exterior gold roof turning into powder. Walls fell into tangled piles of broken rock. Once a symphony of mosaic and marble, the exquisite octagonal building crumbled into a chaotic blend of ugly, jagged concrete pieces.

• • •

Sharon was asleep in her room at the Seven Arches Hotel. She had chosen this place because AP management promised a room that overlooked the Old City. She could look down on the ancient town and watch the sun glisten on the golden Dome of the Rock while she ate breakfast in her room. The view was so breathtaking that the sight was nearly a spiritual experience, although Sharon had little interest in religious things these days. A frequent Sunday school student as a child, she had learned the Bible stories about Abraham, David, Jesus, and Jerusalem. The vestiges of those memories gave the view a mystical aura.

A few feet from the hotel entrance, the traditional Palm Sunday pathway wound down the Mount of Olives, across the Kidron Valley, and up to St. Stephen's Gate. The narrow passage made for quick access to the city. The location was perfect.

But the picturesque view and sacred pathway were soon extinct when Kamel Hassan's bomb exploded at 4:10 A.M., shattering the picture window in Sharon's room. Glass shards sprayed across the carpet and filled the curtains. The roar echoed around the room like a muffled cannon volley. Screaming as she leaped out of bed, Sharon tripped and fell to the floor.

"We're under attack!" she sputtered and huddled close to her bed. Sharon inhaled and coughed. "Fire!" She stood and staggered to the broken window. Off in the distance the smoldering ruins of the Temple Mount sent circles of smoke into the black sky. Trees blazed and fires dotted the smoking terrain, illuminating the skeletal remains of buildings. "My God! The mosque is gone!"

Although every instinct demanded that she grab her camera and notebook and run for it, Sharon stood mesmerized by the incredible sight. Finally, she broke free of the spell of fire and fury, gagging at the unmistakable smell of smoke from plastic explosives, and dressed quickly. She threw her press identification card around her neck and ran for the ancient Palm Sunday path to the city.

Sharon was among the first herd of reporters inside the devastated area. When anyone protested, she stuck her ID in that person's face and pressed forward. The Dome of the Chain, what was thought to be the original model for the mosque, was smoldering rubble. The front of the El-Aqsa Mosque had apparently collapsed when its support pillars crumpled. Remains of El-Kas, the cup-shaped ornamental cleansing fountain, had fallen into the abyss left by the blast. Chunks of the sidewalk stood upright while other pieces had slid into the twenty-five-foot crater that yawned like an angry giant's mouth. The entire thirty-acre rectangle was a smoking ruin.

The Arab Wakf, responsible for policing the holy site, screamed and charged across the area, shouting unheeded instructions. Sharon's press ID did its job. She snapped pictures until the film ran out. Only well after dawn, when the Israeli soldiers sealed off the area, did she return to the Seven Arches. Covered with dust and smelling like smoke, Sharon immediately called Washington. Suddenly, she garnered the attention of her reluctant editors. Sharon had scooped the biggest story of the century. Now the stories wouldn't stop coming. Sharon Parker was in the center of the firestorm, loving every minute of it.

CHAPTER 3

Mary Morgan saw Greg leave the elevator. She started to call to him but hesitated so as not to be obvious. Since his wife's death, she'd done everything but send him an engraved invitation to dinner. Mary watched him slip away down the hall toward his office.

"Still got your blue eyes on him?" her secretary noticed and giggled. She glanced at Mary's signature crested white blazer. "You look good enough to go grab him. Labor Day weekend must have put you in good spirits."

"Really!" Mary gave her a look of mock consternation.

"You may be his superior in this agency, but you'd obviously settle for being at the door every evening with his slippers in hand."

"Lou!" Mary frowned. "My gosh."

"Don't blame you, Miss Morgan. Parker's a hunk. Why did everyone get into calling him Duke?"

Mary Morgan continued walking toward the back stairs leading to the executive suite of the NSA's director, Allen Jones. "The name came out of an old John Wayne Vietnam war movie. Greg caught up with a billion-dollar scam and was going after the contractors with a passion. Everyone knew they might try to kill him." Mary laughed. "Greg took on that 'Ah, shucks, ma'am, we're just doing our job' attitude. Didn't seem to be afraid of the devil himself. Somewhere along the way the name stuck."

"He's always polite. Up and Up. No funny stuff in the office. Is Dr. Parker a religious man?"

"Don't know. We haven't spoken on that subject, but he's certainly a person of integrity."

"The Duke's a good-looking guy. We're all pulling for you."

Mary noticed that Greg Parker didn't look fifty-five. The square jaw and heavy eyebrows blended a chiseled nose and well-defined lips into the masculine terrain of his tanned face. He could easily pass for forty-five. Plain clothes didn't hide an uncommon face.

"Time to see what's on the big man's mind," Lou nodded toward the executive suite.

"Yes." Mary stepped out into the hall. "Jones seems to be in a lather over something big coming down from the White House."

• • •

Dr. Greg Parker turned the key in the lock and disappeared into his personal nook within the vast office building. The department's receptionist obviously hadn't arrived yet, but he didn't give her delay much thought. *A little too much Labor Day.* His personal secretary took care of everything anyway.

Although Greg was the head of the Geological Research Department of the NSA, his office still had a government-issue look. Seniority gave him the right to personal touches like the room-dominating picture of him and his wife shaking hands with the previous president of the United States. On the other side of the desk, the signed picture of the current Speaker of the House with his arm around Greg's shoulders was positioned to catch the eye of anyone entering the office. Just the right touch to command extra respect from the boys on the floor below.

As usual, the morning papers waited on his desk. Nancy, his ever-efficient secretary, never missed, but Greg already had heard enough depressing news. He tossed the *Post* in the trash and sat down. The perpetually paper-covered desk had been reshuffled again by his secretary into an appearance of order. Only one file wasn't touched. She knew better.

Greg stared for a moment at the three-inch thick manila folder holding the six-year study of the 1994 Northridge earthquake. "Top Secret" was stamped on it in bold letters. He shook his head contemptuously and turned on the intercom.

"Nancy?"

"Yes, sir."

"Did Dick Emmerson's final summary of the Northridge quake make the rounds up to the head man's office?"

"I believe so. I'll check on it."

"Make sure the report at least got to Mary Morgan." He hung up. "Nasty business," he muttered to himself. "Don't like any of it." He thumped the desk and opened the file. Without looking up, Greg pulled an aspirin bottle out of his bottom desk drawer and swallowed two tablets. For a moment he felt dizzy.

Ten minutes later, Nancy brought in a cup of coffee and left quickly. Greg didn't look up, all the time reading and jotting notes on a pad. Thirty minutes later, he got up to go to the bathroom. As he reached the door, Greg saw a familiar figure hurrying down the corridor.

"That's him!" he muttered to himself. "Can't believe it. I'm reading the file, and Mr. CIA himself runs down the hall under my nose."

He peered out of the door. *Alex Majors is heading for the same rest room. Perfect place for some unofficial chat about official business.*

Greg hurried down the corridor, but paused outside the door and reflected for a moment on exactly what he wanted to say. He knew it should be subtle; he'd wait for some sort of response and then blindside the rat. He strolled into the third floor men's room.

"Morning, Alex."

The short, heavy-set man spun around, surprise written across his pudgy face. Alex Majors blinked several times. "Parker? Greg Parker? Didn't hear you come in."

"How are the big dogs over at the Company?"

Majors glanced around the room and looked at the open space under the stalls. "We stay busy."

"You do. You do, indeed. Surprised to see you on our turf this morning."

"What's that mean?"

"Nothing." Greg smiled broadly. "Only an observation." He waited several seconds. "Based on fact."

Majors's eyes narrowed, and he frowned. He finished drying his hands with a paper towel. "Something on your mind, Parker?"

"Suppose so."

"Yes?"

"I didn't know you boys had gone into the earthquake-creating business," Greg said. "You're quite a bunch of busy beavers."

"I'm not following you." Majors turned his head sideways and watched Parker in the mirror.

Greg spoke to the mirror. "Just completed a fascinating study on the Northridge earthquake. Remember that big one back in '94? Killed at least fifty-one people. Remember?"

"Go away," Majors answered abruptly and turned away. "We play on the same team." He started toward the door.

"Do we?" Greg asked as he frowned. "I'm not sure that's a fact. Every now and then I get this strange feeling, based on research, you understand, that people like you operate from another planet. Then again . . . possibly out of a sewer."

Majors crossed his arms over his chest and set his feet. "I don't like the tone of this conversation. Cut to the chase."

Greg felt the heat rising in his neck. He took a deep breath and tried to relax, but his right fist clenched. "Our boys recently finished an amazing survey of the factors that created the quake. We've come up with some astonishing conclusions, Majors. You remember that investigation on the San Andreas fault our people started a decade ago? The one the front office shut down and turned over to you spooks at the CIA? The latest facts suggest someone manipulated the terrain, using ultrasonic equipment, and triggered the quake."

"Sounds like paranoia," Majors said. "That's crazy talk, Parker, and inappropriate, I might add."

"Really?" Greg stepped forward. "You want the bottom line? I've watched you operate for a long time, you greasy slime. I know you're a lying . . ."

Majors lunged at Parker, grabbing him by the lapel and swinging him against the gray stalls. The small door slammed against the wall behind him. Metal exploded against metal and Greg grabbed for the handle, but Majors shoved him backward into the side of the stall. Greg swung with his left fist but missed. Majors ducked and stepped back. A terrible pain shot through Greg's head, and he gasped for air. Seconds later Majors slung Greg around by his tie toward the opposite wall. Greg's shoulder smashed into the ceramic tile, and his head snapped backward. Everything went black.

CHAPTER 4

Voices floated in like a gentle breeze through a half-opened window. Someone was calling his name, but . . . from some far distant shore. Human sounds seemed to arise from a bottomless abyss overflowing with shapeless dream creatures.

"Dr. Parker?" the gentle voice pleaded. "Oh, Dr. Parker? Wiggle a finger if you can hear me."

Got to answer. Getting into my body is like a child putting on a snowsuit. How do I make my fingers work? Squeeze. Just squeeze.

"Look," the voice said to someone. "The EEG is registering a new response. Hey, the needle jumped. Good sign."

Everything is so black. Why can't I see?

"Yes! Squeeze those fingers again. Good, Dr. Parker," the voice spoke closer to his ear. "That's it. You're coming around."

Must get my eyes open. Why won't the lids open?

"Nurse, page Dr. Jackson." The female voice sounded far away again. "I think we're about to break through. Signs are all there."

I must open my eyes. If I can push hard enough . . .

"Bingo! We've got eye flutter. Our man's coming 'round. Nurse, get Jackson, regardless of what he's doing."

Light flooded Greg's eyes, and he blinked frantically. Everything turned white.

"Dr. Parker? Can you hear me?"

Greg flexed his hands several times and tried to shake his head.

"Wonderful! I'm Dr. Susan Bridwell, your neurologist."

Greg slowly opened his eyes again. A blurry shape hovered just above him. He tried to focus. The fuzzy face took on an edge.

"Welcome back to this world." She patted his hand.

"Where . . . where am I?"

"You've been in the hospital for five days, sir. You're in the intensive care unit at Walter Reed."

"What?" Greg tried to move his head.

"Be careful. You're wired up to an EEG. Got connections and tubes running everywhere. A couple of them are coming out of you."

Greg could see an examination lamp high above him. Out of the corner of his eyes, he recognized banks of monitors with flashing lights. Electronic oscilloscope lines moved in endless undulating patterns against a greenish-phosphorescent background. Something was beeping. Flowers were all over the place.

"You've had a stroke. Apparently an employee found you on the floor in the bathroom in your office building."

"Who?"

"Don't know, but he called an ambulance."

Nothing registered.

"Don't want you to worry. We've got everything under control." A pretty face smiled down at him. "You're going to recover completely. Okay?"

Doubt it. Greg nodded and tried to smile.

"Feeling any pain?"

He shook his head.

"Good." Dr. Bridwell's voice trailed away. "Hey, Jackson. Look here. Our patient's tuned in."

"Excellent. Let me take a look." A young man, fragrant with aftershave, shone a penlight in Greg's eyes. "Good signs!" Jackson's deep voice sounded authoritative.

"No question about it," Dr. Bridwell said. "We've had a significant turnaround."

"Will I be able to walk, talk all right?"

"Should," Dr. Jackson answered. "We think this stroke may be an unusual effect and shouldn't be indicative of your general health. It's like having an accident or being in a car wreck. Strokes occur that way occasionally. You probably had it coming on for some time."

Greg's skin itched because his flesh was coming back to life. Sensation began to return to his feet. His arms seemed to be noodles, but at least he was aware they felt attached.

"We've been doing tests from the moment you came in," Dr. Bridwell said. "We want to continue monitoring the effect of this stroke. Often there are unexpected side effects. We want to study whatever develops."

"Can I sit up?" Greg took a deep breath.

"I don't see why you shouldn't try." Dr. Jackson reached for the control buttons on the side of the bed. "Let's take it slow and easy."

Like a car inching up the ramp on a roller coaster, Greg felt himself rising up until the room came into full view. For a moment, he grew dizzy. Maybe he was about to take a plunge down the other side.

"Can you remember what happened just before you blacked out, Dr. Parker?" the woman probed. "Does anything come to mind?"

Greg shook his head.

"Your symptoms seem almost like you were hit with something," Dr. Jackson mused. "We're not dealing with an ordinary stroke here."

"Don't worry." Dr. Bridwell smiled. "Maybe you'll remember later."

"We've been watching your EEG patterns, Dr. Parker," Dr. Jackson picked up the pace. "Very interesting things going on here. During the last several days, we've noticed some erratic movement. Can you remember any dreams during the time you've been unconscious?"

Greg closed his eyes. Darkness felt strangely more familiar and comfortable. He settled into the vast space. To his surprise, shapes and faces quickly emerged before his inner eye. Trees fell in large holes in the ground. The entire earth seemed to undulate beneath him. Mountains split and prairies buckled. Shapes faded and he flew into the air. His dead wife, Alice, reached toward him and then vanished. Alex Majors flew past. Explosions became deafening, making his heart pound.

"Okay, okay." Dr. Jackson shook him. "Enough. Open your eyes."

Greg inhaled deeply and tried to touch his chest. For the first time, he realized restraints tied him to the bed.

"Oh, sorry about that." Dr. Bridwell immediately untied his arms. "You got restless, and we didn't want you to yank out a needle or pull the sensors loose."

"What were you experiencing just now?" Dr. Jackson pressed.

"Sort of like a dream gone berserk."

Dr. Bridwell loosened the final strap across his legs. "Strokes do strange things to people. At this point, you haven't experienced any permanent physical damage that we can detect; however, your brain waves indicate unusual activity."

"Enough for now." Dr. Jackson pressed the recline button. "Relax and get a little more tuned in. We'll return in several hours."

Greg grabbed the doctor's hand. "Thanks for getting me back."

• • •

During the next three hours, Greg slept intermittently and tried to remember. Nothing came through. When lunch arrived, nothing looked appetizing, so he drifted back to sleep.

"Wake up, sleepy head," a woman insisted.

He opened his eyes but didn't recognize her for a few moments.

"It's Dr. Bridwell," she said. "Dr. Jackson and I are back. We've been studying the EEG results and have a few questions. Are you up to it?"

Greg managed to smile and say, "I think so."

Dr. Jackson sat down on the edge of the bed. "Your brain wave patterns are very fascinating. We'd like to talk with you about being part of a special study. Been having unusual dreams?"

Greg nodded his head.

"Occasionally people develop amazing extrasensory experiences following a stroke," Dr. Jackson added. "Some people develop fascinating psychic abilities."

"Epileptics can develop similar functions," Dr. Bridwell kept working as she explained. "We've even had a few people turn into writers. Big time writers. Their inner experiences during these episodes have become best-sellers."

"Can't tell you who," Dr. Jackson added, "but we have a patient who is a well-known horror writer and does his best work during a frontal lobe seizure."

Greg squinted and frowned. "Just what are you saying? Are we talking about some sort of voodoo? A New Age religious experience, like channeling or an out-of-body experience?"

"No, no, nothing of that sort." Dr. Bridwell shook her head.

"There's nothing esoteric or mystical about this phenomenon. We are talking purely physiological brain responses created by disruption of normal patterns resulting from the stroke."

Greg shook his head. "Sounds wild to me."

"Some years ago Princeton University established The PEAR Program—Princeton Engineering Anomalies Research Program—in their School of Engineering and Applied Science," Dr. Jackson continued. "The purpose was to scientifically investigate the interaction of human consciousness with sensitive physical measuring devices and systems. Some of the results were amazing and made us aware of unconscious mind capacities beyond what anyone dreamed possible."

"Like what?" Greg asked.

"PEAR scientists measured the capacity of the mind to influence mechanical, electronic, and optical devices," Dr. Jackson answered. "They explored the degree to which focusing one's concentration might influence acoustical and fluid measuring devices. Sometimes the subjects were taken thousands of miles from the laboratory, and PEAR was still able to measure the influence of the mind."

Greg opened his eyes in astonishment. "You think some of this stuff is going on with me?"

"Quite possibly," Jackson insisted. "We'd like to observe you carefully and send data to PEAR. They coordinate the International Consciousness Research Laboratories and work with the Academy of Consciousness Studies. These groups explore the role of consciousness in the fields of anthropology, archaeology, psychiatry, and psychology. Your EEG patterns indicate experiences that impinge on their research."

"Sounds a little far out to me." Greg winced. "I'm a rather practical, down-to-earth sort of guy. I deal in hard facts."

"Let me add my perspective," Dr. Bridwell interjected. "For some time I've followed the work of the Stanford Research Institute and the authors of *The Constantine Report*. Ever hear of these folks?"

Greg shook his head.

"This group of scientists is a might more exotic than the Princeton group," she said. "Alex Constantine did some high-powered exploration of electromagnetic mind control. He believes he has concrete evidence that the government and the CIA were involved in trying to develop mind control techniques."

"CIA?" Greg came up out of his bed. "You're serious?"

"Sure. Actually, I'm not so interested in the politics but the possibilities for what they are calling 'remote viewing.' Teams at the Stanford Research Institute worked with projecting words and images directly into the cranium . . ."

"I'm not interested in being involved with anything related to the CIA," Greg objected. "I couldn't consent to such a study without very careful consideration of the consequences."

"Sure." Dr. Jackson puckered his lip and looked contemptuously at Dr. Bridwell out of the corner of his eye. "Actually, the CIA isn't involved any longer in any of this work, to my knowledge. We simply wanted you to know that we expect you to have extraordinary experiences for a period of time, and we would like to monitor their effects."

Greg nodded weakly. "I'll keep the possibility in mind."

"We'll be carefully following your progress," Dr. Jackson concluded

Dr. Jackson left the room, scribbling furiously on his chart. Dr. Bridwell continued to adjust the monitors. Greg turned toward the observation window at the far end of the room. For a moment he thought his daughter was standing there, watching him. He flinched and put his hands to his face, rubbing his eyes vigorously. When he slowly looked between his fingers again, the window was empty.

"Man! The PEAR people are going to love me."

"What?" Dr. Bridwell looked concerned.

"I guess I am having some kind of hallucinatory activity," he said. "I'd better think about your proposal."

"Great." Dr. Bridwell patted him on the arm. "I'm sending you back to your room and hope to have you out of this place as quickly as possible."

Minutes later Greg was in the patients' elevator on his way back to room 547. The orderly said little but quickly whisked him through the fifth floor corridors. "Room's just ahead." The man sounded relieved and disinterested.

Greg was barely back in bed when a nurse entered. "Someone to see you." She stepped back, and a small brunette walked into the room.

"Sharon?" He bolted up in bed and rubbed his eyes. Sharon! "That *was* you in the window downstairs! Where did you come from?"

Giving him a quick, perfunctory kiss on the cheek, Sharon Parker tossed her purse on the cabinet and sat down with a cavalier air of indifference. "It looked like I scared you, so I came back upstairs. Well, how are you?"

Greg blinked several times. "I . . . I haven't heard . . . from you in two years. I didn't . . ."

"Haven't heard from you, either," Sharon cut him off. "So, how are you?"

Greg swallowed. "Getting better. But how did you find out?"

"Your office ran me down. I've been in Israel doing stories on the big bombing. They called and said there wasn't anyone to take care of you. Everyone seemed to think you were in bad shape. Are you?"

Greg lowered himself back on the bed. "I can't believe it. You're *actually* here." He rubbed his eyes again.

"I guess that's what family is for. When you've got no place to go or no one else to help, we all seem to turn into salmon and head upstream again."

"Thank you for coming," Greg muttered. "I think I'm okay. Just not sure yet. Don't think anything's impaired; however, the doctors are concerned that my mind can do weird things now."

"Your mind could *always* do weird things. What's new about that?" Sharon retorted.

Greg bit his lip. "Let's not get off on one of those tangents. You've only been here a couple of minutes. Do you know exactly how I got to the hospital?"

"Actually, I've been here for three days." She raised her eyebrows knowingly. "One of the men on your floor found you in the rest room. Your secretary guessed you might have been in there thirty or forty minutes. They rushed you here in an ambulance."

"I see." Greg sank down into his pillow. "I don't remember anything." He closed his eyes. "I suddenly feel tired. I'm sorry, but I can't seem to stay awake. Mind if I catch a little nap?"

"Of course not," Sharon assured him. "Don't worry, I'll be here. I canceled the assignment I was on in Israel. I'm going to take care of you as long as it is necessary."

"Israel?" He shook his head. "You're kidding."

• • •

A new voice intruded. The imposition annoyed him at first, but slowly the sound became more compelling. Greg strained to come out of his deep sleep, still feeling incredibly tired. His body didn't cooperate, but he wanted to listen. The voice sounded familiar.

"Yes," Sharon was saying, "he's made great leaps forward in the last day. The doctors think we'll be out of here by at least the first of next week."

"Excellent," the other voice answered. "I really need to talk with our boy."

Greg seemed to rise like a diver coming up in a decompression tank. The surface didn't seem too far away.

"Dr. Bridwell assured me there's no permanent physical damage," Sharon told the voice. "He's even walked. I am extremely pleased and encouraged."

With one last burst of effort, Greg opened his eyes. The examination light was off; the room was bathed in soft indirect light. He leaned toward the direction of the sounds.

"I'm supposed to help him get up on his feet today," Sharon confided. "He'll be back in full swing soon."

Greg tried to clear his vision. The voice suddenly had a

face on it. Allan Jones, director of NSA, was standing next to Sharon.

"I don't often get a house call from the big bad boss himself," Greg said as he attempted a smile.

"Well. My, my," Jones chided. "Am I ever glad to see the whites of your red eyes."

"Feeling a little rugged," Greg wheezed.

"You've had us worried silly." Jones offered his hand and then drew it back quickly. "Are you really all right?"

"It's okay. I can shake hands. Got the sap knocked out of me, that's all."

"You're an indispensable man in our organization, Greg. You carry more information around in your head than we've got in the library. Anyone with a Ph.D. in geology is important, but you're the master of earthquakes and investigations. Don't have many of you in existence."

"Not sure much is left up there." Greg pointed to his head.

"Don't kid us," Sharon interrupted. "The doctors assured me that fertile brain is as good as ever."

Greg grinned. "I hoped for a disability retirement."

"Sharon, would you mind if I had a word with your father alone?" The agency director patted her on the shoulder. "It's a security matter."

"Oh, yes. I've lived with those top level secrets my whole life." Sharon started toward the door. "You're like two little boys sharing the password to the clubhouse." She paused at the door and tossed her head nonchalantly. "Call me when you're through."

Allan Jones pushed the chair next to the bed, sat down, and leaned close to Greg. "Don't want to push, you understand?"

"Who are you kidding? They don't call you 'the bulldozer' for nothing."

Jones smiled slyly. "Big, big assignment waiting for you, ole boy. A special commission from the White House. You're the best man for the job."

Greg rolled his eyes and moaned. "I can't wait."

"For years you've been the guy telling everyone we'd better pay attention to the New Madrid fault. Big disaster waiting out there that could affect as many as ten million people and destroy the country financially. Right?" Jones poked his finger at Greg. "Now somebody at the top has the same concern. Your ship has finally come in."

"Earthquake?" Greg blinked several times. "Strange."

Jones frowned. "What do you mean? You've been warning us for years to wake up to the time bomb ticking under our noses."

"Earthquake?" The word vibrated through Greg, setting off strange signals in his memory.

"You following me?" Jones peered into his face. "Sure you're up to talking about this project?"

"I'm still getting tuned in again," Greg forced himself to say. "But you know you can count on me, Allan. As soon as I get out of here, I'll be back on the team."

The agency director stood up. "I'm putting your name on this one. We don't have much time, but we'll wait until you're back behind the desk to start. Sharon says it won't be long."

"Sure." Greg jutted his chin out defiantly. "I'll be back in the saddle before you know it."

Jones waved as he backed away. "You always said that if the New Madrid fault became active, it could release more seismic energy than any quake zone in North America. Here's your chance to prove that a seismic event at the New Madrid would make a San Andreas earthquake look like a bowl of shaking Jell-O." He hurried out of the room.

The word *earthquake* ricocheted around in Greg's mind like a marble in a pinball machine. With disconcerting accuracy, it set off something deep within, making him nervous and disoriented. He sank into the pillow and closed his eyes.

Once again, the images appeared: trees falling in holes, mountains rising and falling like ocean waves. Then a voice said, "I don't like the tone of this conversation. Cut to the chase." The man sounded threatening.

A white room came into view. He could see gray doors. Someone walked toward him, making threatening gestures. "That's crazy talk." Greg strained to see the face and instantly felt as if someone was smothering his face. Out of the darkness, the face of Alex Majors emerged and disappeared.

He squinted, gritted his teeth, and gently shook his head. "Maybe I ought to agree to the study."

CHAPTER 6

The last three days at the hospital had not been easy for Sharon. Her father had been nervous and irritable, and she struggled to avoid fighting with him. As she drove him home from the hospital, he didn't say much. Greg Parker seemed lost in another world, his mind occupied with a hidden agenda.

Sharon eased the '89 Pontiac into the driveway and shut off the engine. She looked up at the brown two-story brick colonial home of her childhood, memories oozing out of every crack and crevice. Sharon blinked several times and turned to her father. "You're home, Dad."

"Nothing's changed," he said. "Just like you *left it* two years ago."

She pursed her lips and squinted, letting the accusatory remark roll around in her head. *Trying to bait me. Don't go there, Dad.*

"I can walk to the door without help." Greg unlocked the car door.

"You don't ever quit playing the blame game, do you?"

Her father looked surprised. "Huh?"

"I'll get the sack with your things out of the trunk." Sharon was out of the car before he could answer. "I've already been here and had the housekeeper tidy things up," she called over her shoulder and bounded up the front steps, pausing only to unlock the front door.

Greg didn't hurry but had no difficulty walking. He shot a quick glance around the living room. "Everything seems in place."

"Of course."

"What'd you mean by that crack about blaming?" He turned slowly toward Sharon. "What were you trying to say?"

"Forget it. Let's get your stuff up to your bedroom."

"No." Greg crossed his arms over his chest. "I'm not going anywhere until I have an explanation."

"Have it your way." Sharon tossed him the sack. "I need to get lunch going."

"I said I want to know what you were implying."

"Look, I'm here," Sharon said as she lowered her chin and met his eyes. "I told you I'd hang around until you were 100 percent again. That ought to be good enough for most *normal* people."

"Normal? See, there you go," her father protested. "The issue isn't blame. You disappeared two years ago like a phantom in the night. Poof! Evaporated into thin air! I still don't have any explanation. *Normal* people expect explanations."

"Mom died. I split. There's nothing more to say."

"You're blaming me for *that*?"

"We'll worry about it tomorrow." Sharon started for the kitchen door.

"I can't believe my eyes," Greg asserted. "My own daughter has grown up and turned into Scarlet O'Hara."

"Yeah, and my old man became the Terminator." She tapped on the rug with the ball of her foot. "I gave up a very important assignment and took a leave of absence to make sure you're okay. I suggest we'll get along nicely if you'll just cool the inquisition and keep things on a simple thank-you-very-much basis."

Greg Parker opened his mouth to speak, but took a deep breath instead. "I appreciate everything you've done, and for being here now."

"Good. Leave it at that." Sharon stormed into the kitchen.

• • •

Greg closed the door to his bedroom and wept. The doctor said he'd have sudden bursts of emotion. He couldn't tell if it was what the doctor said . . . or what Sharon said. "Why do we always get into it?" he asked himself and plopped down on the bed.

Greg dabbed at his eyes. *Sharon always takes everything wrong,* he thought. *Can't say anything without her getting defiant or defensive. At least, this time she didn't accuse me of being interested in nothing but my work. Maybe that's a little progress.*

He looked at his wife's picture on the nightstand, and she smiled back. "Oh, Alice, where are you today? Where are you when I need you so much?"

The picture seemed to reply, "Go easy on the girl, Greg. Trouble is, you're both too much alike, and you love Sharon inordinately. That's your trouble."

Alice must have made that same speech a million times. She started when Sharon first began to walk, and repeated it during grade school, high school, and college. Always the familiar refrain in an ongoing discussion. "Look for the silver lining," she would remind him after her lecture, then smile gently and wink.

"I'm fixing soup," Sharon called up the stairs. "Be ready in one minute."

Greg got up and opened the door. "I'll be right down."

"I'm pouring it in the bowl *right now*," she warned.

"Now *that's* her mother talking," he mumbled to himself and closed the door again.

Greg looked in the mirror. He felt a bit unsteady but looked fine. No blue rings under the eyes. Yes, Sharon did favor him. Same eyes, same mouth. Most folks said so, sooner or later. Yes, they were very much alike.

As he looked at himself, something seemed to happen *in* the mirror. Similar to a mirage, a vision, a picture arose in place of himself. Like an enlarged photograph covering a television screen, he saw a silver ring with a brilliant green stone in the center. His hand went to his mouth. The ring lay in the shadow of a large copper canister marked "flour." He had never seen a ring quite like it. Had to be foreign. Greg shook his head and closed his eyes. The image faded from his mind, and when he looked up again, he only saw himself.

"Dad, I told you I'm waiting." Sharon didn't conceal her impatience.

"Yes, I'm coming." He backed out of the room, still staring in the mirror.

"The tomato soup is hot." Sharon pointed to his chair at the head of the table. "Of course you won't think I'm much of a cook, but it should be easy to digest after that hospital food. I put out some cheese for you too." She scurried about the kitchen, putting two glasses of water on the table. "Just eat what you're up to."

"Sharon?" Greg rubbed his chin.

She gave him a "Don't start" look. "Yes?"

"Do you have a new ring? Or some other piece of jewelry you've purchased recently?"

"Ring?" Sharon looked surprised. "Why, yes. I've misplaced a silver ring that I bought in Israel. Been worrying about it for two days. In fact, I was just looking again. Why?"

"Does it have a green stone?"

"You found it!" Sharon's face brightened.

Greg pointed to a line of canisters on the top of the cabinet. "Look over there next to the sink. Behind that large copper one on the end."

"The flour bin?" Sharon frowned at her father but pushed the copper canisters apart. "My Elliot stone! I must have knocked it back there while I was doing the dishes." Sharon quickly slipped it on her finger. "Wonderful!" She stopped and looked at her father. "But you haven't been in the kitchen since you came home."

"No. No, I haven't."

"How could you possibly have known?"

Greg rubbed the side of his face and pinched his bottom lip. "I was upstairs looking in the mirror. It was like a vision. I suddenly saw the whole thing . . . the ring lying behind the canister," his voice trailed away.

Sharon blinked several times. "You're telling me that you *saw* where my ring was in the mirror in your bedroom?"

"As surely as I'm looking at you right now." He looked down into the bowl of steamy red soup. "That's what I am telling you."

Sharon slipped down at the table and stared. "You had foreknowledge of where the ring was?"

His emotions welled up again, and Greg bit his lip. "That's what happened." He felt tears running down his face. When he looked down, Greg realized his tears were falling into the soup. "I don't know what's happening to me," he choked.

"The doctors said you'd have extreme emotional needs and might experience something like this," she reached over and squeezed his hand. "I'm sure it will be all right . . . somehow."

"Sharon," he said as he struggled to clear his throat, "I just don't know what to say . . . but . . . I need your help."

• • •

Ten hours later, Greg and Sharon sat in the large family den eating popcorn. Greg hung up the phone and hit the remote and turned off the late evening news report. "Looks like the Jews and Arabs are still determined to finish each other off."

"You don't know the half of it," Sharon closed the book she was reading. "I can tell you for a fact that no one in the country seems to know who set off the bomb. Arabs blame Jews; Jews point at Arabs. To find out, you'd need to get close enough to look down their gun barrels."

"And you were right there in the midst of it when the mosque was blown up?"

"If you'd read the byline in the *Post*, you would have seen my name."

"Guess I'll pay more attention next time."

Sharon looked pensively at the telephone. "That call was from Allan Jones, wasn't it?"

Greg rolled his eyes and got a handful of popcorn.

"He wants you back at work?" Sharon persisted.

"Soon as I'm up to it."

Sharon shrugged. "Nothing gets in Uncle Sam's way, including your health and well-being."

"An important project has come up, Sharon."

She got up and put her book back on the shelf. For a moment Sharon stood quietly, looking at the little knickknacks her mother had collected over the years. A thimble from England. Dried flowers from their garden. A picture of five-year-old

Sharon holding Rags, the mutt, long deceased due to a bad habit of running in front of cars. Souvenir spoons from New York City and San Francisco. Her father had not changed or rearranged one item since her mother's death. "That experience this afternoon really frightened you, didn't it?"

Greg kept looking at the blank television screen. "The image in the mirror was so real." He shook his head. "And now, I've started having premonitions. Strange hunches." Greg reached in his pocket and pulled out a crumpled piece of notebook paper. "I've started writing them down to see what comes of it all."

"But you're worried, Dad." Sharon reached in the popcorn bowl and got a handful.

"I think if I go back to work this weird stuff will pass," he mused.

"Work's *always* been the cure for everything anyway." Sharon sounded as accusatory as usual.

Greg looked pained. "I guess that's the way it must appear to you."

Sharon swallowed hard. "Sorry. I didn't mean to make it seem like that. Slip of the tongue."

"Sharon, I'm frightened. Yes, I'll admit it. I don't know whether I'm getting paranoid or just feeling depressed from the stroke or the drugs, but I've developed a deep sense of foreboding about the future, about everything."

Sharon patted him on the shoulder. "If you'd been where I was this last month, I'd call those feelings being in touch with reality."

"The news seems to get worse every day, but this is different. Something way down there in my soul is deeply troubled," Greg admitted. "I hope I'm not coming unglued." He quickly covered his mouth.

"Dad, I called AP while you were sleeping this afternoon. I

am going to work freelance for a while, so I'll be able to work from home."

"But Sharon, what about your career?"

"A change of focus won't hurt me any. I'm going to contact some local religious leaders in the area for backup material on the bombing story. The point is, I'll be here to help you get through this time."

"Sharon," he paused and looked down at the rug. "I really am sorry I sounded so negative this afternoon. I don't mean to play blame games."

"Me neither, Dad." She leaned over and kissed him on the cheek. "Right now, you need to go to bed, because no matter what I or anyone else says, you'll probably be off to work tomorrow . . . or the next day."

"I simply hope I don't prove to be unstable."

Sharon patted him on the shoulder again. "You're the strongest man I've ever met in my life. Whatever is going on with you, you'll find a way to handle it." She walked toward the stairs to the bedroom above. "And if you don't, I'll be here."

Greg tried to smile but looked more bewildered, trapped in consternation. Tears collected in the corners of his eyes.

"The thought alone sort of whacks that old male chauvinist streak in you, doesn't it?" Sharon winked.

"Your mother winked like that," he said and turned out the lamp beside the couch. For a long time he sat in the dark, thinking, trying to sort it out, wishing Alice would come in and tell him she was back from the little trip she started on a couple of years ago.

CHAPTER 7

Greg glanced around his NSA office, and everything looked just as it had for a thousand years. Had he really been gone for two weeks? Nothing was out of place. Pencils and pens were in the holder on the center of his desk. The calendar said September 18. The large green ink blotter pad was still on the top of his worn government-issue gray desk, which had its own unique quality.

He looked around at the pictures he'd seen a thousand times and felt their warmth. The place was exactly as it should be. He thought about his office at home and then the desk and chair he'd had as a boy. Everything felt used, helpful, and good. He suddenly felt emotion coming.

"Welcome back, boss." Nancy, Greg's ever-efficient secretary, abruptly appeared in the office door with a cup of coffee in hand. "You look great! Monday morning, and you're in your place." She offered the coffee. "Your usual straight black, to start the day off with a caffeine punch."

"Thanks for keeping the place running while I was gone the last two weeks. You always do a great job." Greg ran his hand over the desktop. "Not a speck of dust. I even have a clean, orderly room to come back to. No small task, clearing that pile of papers." The old familiar desk felt good.

Nancy set the cup on a coaster in front of him. "Someone

important is already out here waiting to see you. Our boss from upstairs." She stepped aside and called over her shoulder. "Come on in."

"Hey, your demise was greatly exaggerated!" Mary Morgan walked in, smiling from ear to ear. "You still look like the same old Duke to me. Can't see any changes for the worse."

Greg immediately stood. "Mary! Come in. Thanks for the flowers and the card. I guess I was sort of out of it when you visited in the hospital, but I appreciated your coming even if I was on ice." His feelings began to overtake him as he thought about his inadequacy. "Quite a chunk of the last several weeks is still a little fuzzy," he admitted.

Mary sat down across from the desk. "You gave us quite a scare, Greg. Sometimes you don't realize how much someone means to you until something frightening happens to him," Mary said softly.

"Yes. Yes, I understand." Greg looked at the picture on the wall, and Alice's face blotted out his thoughts. He felt weepy and immediately cleared his throat. "Sorry. Sudden emotional pangs appear from out of nowhere," he explained, rolling his eyes and trying to be funny. "Apparently, the problem of over-reaction is par for the course with a stroke."

"Of course." Mary looked at him with big, sincere, blue eyes. "Don't give it a thought. You can always be yourself with me, Greg."

"Thank you." He cleared his throat again and looked away.

"Actually, Allan sent me down to fetch you. He's very pleased you're back and wants to talk with you at your earliest convenience."

"My convenience?" Greg laughed. "That's a nice way to tell me to haul my carcass upstairs at once."

"Not quite, but close," Mary said, laughing. She stood up and started toward the door. "I'll walk with you to his office."

As he got up, Greg glanced around his desk again. "Wait! Wait a minute. I just realized a very important report was here, spread out over my desk; it was a top secret study on the Northridge project. It's not here."

"I have it upstairs," Mary said. "After the ambulance left, I immediately came to your office and closed things down for you. I saw the top secret stamp and knew the material had to be protected. I simply pushed everything back in the folder and put the material in my secure safe upstairs. The file will be back on your desk when you finish talking to Allan."

Greg studied her for a moment. He hadn't really noticed before how caring Mary was. Always there. Always concerned. An exceptional person. "That's very thoughtful, Mary. How can I thank you?"

"Why don't you try coming over for supper at my house this week?"

"I think that's supposed to be my line. I'm the one who owes you a night out." He followed her out the door and, feeling odd, abruptly changed the subject. "Best not to keep Jones waiting. Only makes him more demanding."

"I'm serious, Greg. Why don't you come over and let me put a little meat on your bones!"

"My daughter, Sharon, has been cooking for me. She tries hard enough but, let's just say, writing is her strong suit. I could certainly use a real home-cooked meal."

"Consider it done." Mary pushed the elevator button. "How about tomorrow night?"

"Tomorrow? Well, why not? No problem. I really appreciate the invitation."

"I'll look forward to the evening." She stepped into the elevator, Greg followed, and they waited for the door to close. "I guess it's back-to-work time," Mary continued. "Allan tells me this new project will have an alpha rather than a numeric designation. You don't get higher security classification than that."

Greg watched the elevator rise and the numbers change. He took a deep breath. For the first time since he was a child, Greg cringed at the upward motion of the elevator. "Never takes too long to get to the top," he finally said.

The door opened. "The big enchilada is straight ahead," Mary said and hurried out.

When they walked into the receptionist area, the young secretary immediately pointed toward the hall. "Director Jones said to send you in the moment you arrived. Please go on in."

The door was open. Allan Jones was on his feet at once. "Greg, my man! You didn't let me down. I knew you wouldn't." He was around the desk, extending his hand. Jones had big shoulders, large hands, and big black eyes. When he reached out, his arm looked enormous. He had the eyes and face of a man who had been on television many times. "Wonderful to see you." Jones's wide grin revealed big, thick teeth.

"Watch out, Mary. We're about to be taken for a ride," Greg warned jokingly.

"Nonsense. Sit down." Jones pointed to the large leather-covered couch. "Appreciate your getting Greg for me, Mary. I'll take it from here." He gave her the thanks-but-you-can-disappear-now look. "They don't call him the Duke for nothing. What a man!"

Greg sat down slowly, watching Mary leave the room, realizing she was also more attractive than he'd remembered.

"Call me if you need anything." Mary smiled politely and was gone.

"Yes, sir! You look healthy and ready to take on the world again, Greg," Jones said cheerily.

"No one gets the red-carpet treatment up here unless you want something exceptional—or you're getting ready to do a number on him," Greg commented.

"Greg, Greg, that's cynical." Jones furrowed his brow and smiled warily. He had a rugged handsomeness that made his suit look even more expensive. "Now, you know better."

"No. It's a fact."

Jones belly-laughed. "Trapped by my own history." He picked up a folder from his desk. "You have just been officially appointed head of the top secret study on the New Madrid fault. We've got to have definite information on what might happen if the subterranean plates shift. You've always contended it could break the country in two. Now you have unlimited funds at your disposal to prove your theory. Congratulations."

Greg scratched his chin and pulled at his lip. "Why, Allan? What's created this sudden, burning interest after years of everyone ignoring me?"

"Oh, come on. You get your heart's desire, and the next thing you do is look a gift horse in the mouth."

"The government never spends this kind of money without a significant motive. What's the angle?"

Jones looked blank. "Frankly, I don't have any idea. They just sent the project over from the White House." The director shook his head. "You're the only guy in the world who'd raise that sort of question just as Santa Claus was coming down the chimney."

"I always start with the why, assuming someone's making a bundle either above or below the table."

Jones shrugged. "The important thing is, you've got everything you need to do the job. Our assignment is to get an emergency plan in place for government response in case of a disaster. We want you to put together a team to write up the comprehensive action plan immediately."

"Allan, this project could run into tens of millions of dollars."

"No problem." The director waved his hand nonchalantly. "All bills are paid through the White House. No one's placing restraints on this one."

"I'd feel more comfortable if I knew who and what was behind the whole thing."

"Not ours to ask why." Allan shifted into a lighthearted mode. "Only to do or die."

"How much time do I have?"

"I want your team assembled in forty-eight hours."

"You're kidding!"

Allan winked. "You know I never kid. The red-carpet treatment is over. Slave driving's back in style."

Greg fumed. "Forty-eight hours? You're even worse than I previously thought."

Jones got that smug, self-assured look that Greg dearly hated. "Sure, no question about it. I'm reprehensible."

CHAPTER 8

Always predictably hectic, on this particular Monday morning the CIA headquarters jumped like a needle on a seismograph. Hidden away at the edge of Washington, D.C., "the office," as insiders referred to it, remained a massive complex well hidden from the public. In the conference room of the top secret Office of Civil Affairs, division head Alex Majors sat across the table, speaking frankly with his superior Ian Blackmoor, who was responsible for intelligence connections with the United Kingdom.

"You're sure he's back on the job?" Blackmoor asked frowning.

"My sources watching the NSA called before he even entered the building. Parker's there and probably figured out by now that his research is gone. He'll look in our direction."

"So?"

"All depends on whether he had copies stashed elsewhere. The research looked in a preliminary stage." Majors shrugged. "Doesn't make much difference. He can reconstruct what I took out of his office one way or the other. The point is, Parker is on to what actually happened at Northridge."

Blackmoor's long, narrow English face looked distinctively like the noble lord of some ill-begotten manor. His naturally skinny frame made him appear even taller than six feet, two inches. A stint in the Royal Armed Forces had sent him into military intelligence and initiated contact with the CIA. In time, they hired him, and Ian exchanged life in London for work in Washington. Fiftyish, his light brown hair was thinning, but he still looked wiry and fit.

"I say, old man, Parker worries you?"

Majors grunted. "Sure." He cursed. "For some reason he's on my case, but I'm not sure why. Through this extensive report he cooked up on the California quake, he found my name. Sure I'm concerned."

Blackmoor jutted his chin out and aimed his aquiline nose at Majors like a pointer, zeroing in on a bird in the bush. "I must say, everyone who has seen the report you lifted off his desk is equally troubled." Blackmoor cleared his throat. "I am speaking for the chief. We don't want this clown blowing the lid on our premier secret project."

"How come you're the one leaning on me, Blackmoor?"

The Englishman smiled slyly. "We both know the *real* reason." He shifted his chair. "But from the CIA's point of view, I told the director I'd handle this issue personally to keep from picking up interoffice memos, reviews, and the like. Everyone wants everything kept top secret. Agreed?" Ian winked.

Majors nodded his head knowingly.

"Having said *that*," Blackmoor's voice turned hard and demanding, "I don't need to tell you what's at stake, do I?"

"Of course not!" Majors snapped. Naturally built like a bull, Alex Majors was also overweight. Holding a GM-14 rating, he pulled in $80,000 annually with an unlimited expense account that financed his enormous eating hobby. "Don't worry. I can handle Parker."

"Really?" Ian raised his eyebrows. "I bloody well checked this guy out myself. He has a reputation for winning his battles."

"Not with me." Majors drummed on the desk with his pudgy fingers.

Blackmoor grinned. "Actual-ly," he drawled like a Londoner, "I noticed your report had some blank spaces. My sources tell me Parker ended up in the hospital. Like to share the rest of the story with your old mate?"

"They say Parker had a stroke," Majors conveyed no emotion. "A number of things will cause a stroke. Like getting your head smashed against a concrete wall."

"Why didn't you finish him off?" Blackmoor asked somewhat accusingly.

"Wasn't like that." Majors squinted, his fat eyebrows nearly concealing his eyes, making him look like a gunfighter at high noon. "Parker got confrontational, and I figured he was about to go public with his Northridge material. A scuffle followed, and I turned him into a door-knocker."

Blackmoor frowned again. "You made us look like thugs."

Majors raised an eyebrow questioningly but said nothing.

"Yes, yes. No doubt protecting yourself from attack," Blackmoor rambled along in his distinct English accent. "Let's just keep this story between us, shall we?"

"The point is, we both know these projects operate for the good of the whole," Majors bore down. "Yes, we've caused a few deaths, but look how many lives we've saved from radiation poisoning. Human equations are like that, unfortunately. Win some, lose some."

"And this little problem with Parker fits the equation?" Blackmoor sat back with a smug look on his face.

"Only if he places himself there. If the man comes looking for trouble, he'll get more than he can handle the next time."

"Look, Alex, old chap," the Englishman lowered his voice,

sounding confidential. "Everyone respects your ability to develop new methods and weapons to destroy the economy of countries. You're the King of Chaos. You proved yourself in Africa. We don't want you to get in trouble with some bureaucratic hack over at the NSA. You *do* understand me, don't you?"

"Certainly."

"We'll do *whatever* is necessary to cover you and your tracks," Blackmoor said. "Your ability to set off an earthquake at will is of incredible significance to the office. That knowledge will be protected at all costs."

"Good." Alex pursed his lips for a moment. "The New Madrid seismic study has been passed on to the NSA?"

Blackmoor smiled and nodded. "It's there."

"I'm sure the assignment will go to Parker. He's the earthquake genius."

"Our people in the White House will insist that you end up involved in some way. Whoever is the top dog, whether it's Parker or Jones, we want you to keep your fingers on the pulse of this thing."

"Excellent." Majors pushed back from the table and glanced at his watch. "I need to be on my way. We're helping create a little economic pressure on Israel. Lots of belligerence over there these days. We are about to whip the Jews into shape."

"One more thing." Blackmoor held his long bony fingers in the air. "If you have to deal with Parker, try to keep the earthquakes underground and out of government office building rest rooms."

• • •

Alex Majors immediately returned to his personal office and locked the door behind him. He whirled the combination lock on the briefcase no one ever touched. Inside he found the cellular phone used only for one purpose. He dialed the international number. He could hear several clicks as the encrypted phone line set up.

"*Oui,*" a woman answered the phone.

"The falcon is calling," he answered in perfect French. "I wish to speak to the baron."

"*Oui.*" The phone went on hold.

After two minutes, the phone clicked back on. "I am pleased to hear from you," the man began in Flemish.

"All plans are go," Majors answered in excellent Flemish. "We are proceeding on every front without opposition."

"How soon will we have the data we need for our operation?"

"Your friends will be pleased to know that all due haste has been applied to this project. We can expect research to start accumulating in about a month."

"International developments are moving at a pace faster than anyone thought possible." The baron sounded overbearing and condescending. "We cannot afford delays."

"Of course, you can assure our friends around the big table that I have everything in place and all preliminary matters are completed. You are covered."

"Excellent. You may expect a significant deposit in your Swiss bank account as per our agreement."

"Thank you, sir."

"I will expect to hear from you at least once a week. Understand?"

"Of course."

"Good." The baron hung up.

Alex smiled and clicked the cellular phone off. "I can count on the baron to be a generous man, as long as everything goes his way." He spoke to himself as he put the phone back in the briefcase and locked it. "And I will certainly make sure *everything* does!" He put the briefcase under his desk and flipped on the computer screen. "Now, let's put the squeeze on our Israeli allies."

CHAPTER 9

The initial pages of the projected study gripped Greg's attention so completely that he didn't notice people around him as he returned to his office. He walked out of the elevator in a daze. The scope of the proposal was comprehensive. If done correctly, the country would be well served. Many lives could be saved.

He closed the door to his office and immediately noticed the file stamped Top Secret lying in the center of his desk. "Good!" he exclaimed, putting the new assignment aside for the moment. "Mary doesn't miss a lick. It's the Northridge file."

The portfolio seemed somewhat jumbled, reflecting pages shoved together somewhat at random. Initial sections of the report had already been circulated to select top level personnel in the department, so the muddle didn't matter. The portion that counted was at the end. No one had seen his private conclusions because they were somewhat circumstantial and not entirely substantiated. He'd kept this portion for later distribution. He turned to the back.

"What? Something's wrong?" He started going backward through the file. "Where is it?" He began again.

After a couple of minutes of checking every page, he shut the file. The CIA section had vanished into thin air. Greg felt a terrible sinking feeling and gripped his stomach. Everything that could prove the CIA's role in the Northridge quake was gone. Stolen.

He reached for the phone and hit the automatic dialing button. "Hello, Mary Morgan here."

"Mary," Greg tried not to convey panic, "do you know if anything was taken from the Northridge file?"

"Why, no, Greg. I don't think so. I simply shuffled everything together and took the file upstairs. Been in my office the entire time. Why?"

"Have you looked at the duplicate file I sent you before I, ah, er, got sick?"

"Haven't scrutinized every detail, but I scanned it. Very disturbing material in there."

"You mean the part about the CIA?"

"CIA? I'm afraid I'm not following you."

"I'm talking about the conclusions at the end."

"I can look again, but I don't remember seeing anything on conclusions. I certainly wouldn't have missed mention of the CIA."

"Yes. Certainly. Of course. Just checking." He stared at the cover to the file for a moment. "Oh, I need to tell you one more thing. Jones truly strapped it on me. I've got to work like crazy for the next several days. I'm afraid I'll have to take a rain check on our get-together."

"Oh no, you don't!" Mary groaned.

"Just a postponement. Thanks for your help. I'll be back in touch." He hung up quickly.

Greg rested his head on his hands. *Mary wouldn't have taken the report. No reason for her to do something like that because I would have given it to her anyway. Someone must have rifled through my office between the time I was in the hospital and when Mary retrieved it. The report would have been in plain sight on my desk, but a thief would need access to the building. If only I could remember who I saw in the halls that day!*

Greg swore. "I don't know how they did it," he concluded out loud, "but the CIA is involved in this somehow. I have no alternative but to try and reconstruct everything."

A chill settled over him. Could he remember? What might the stroke have erased? Greg didn't tell Sharon that he couldn't remember where he kept his car keys and had to turn the house upside down to find them. He also couldn't find his old familiar way to DuPont Circle. The streets made no sense. It was as if his memory was a computer with selected files erased. Maybe he wouldn't be able to pick up all those little details that made it clear what actually happened in 1994. Dread turned into anger, and he suddenly slung the file across the office into the wall.

For a moment, Greg stared at the mess on the floor. Pages were scattered everywhere. "Got to get ahold of myself." He clenched his fist. "My emotions are all wacko."

He started to sip the coffee and then put it down. "Caffeine is one thing I don't need." He stood up, crossed his arms over his chest, and hugged himself. "Get a grip, Greg. Get a grip." He started pacing, inhaling, exhaling, trying not to hyperventilate, struggling to maintain a modicum of composure.

The door suddenly opened. "I thought you'd want . . ." Nancy stopped and stared at the pages scattered over the floor for a moment. "Goodness, what happened?" She surveyed the clutter and then stared at Greg with consternation in her eyes. The bent manila folder had hit the wall with considerable force and looked like a truck ran over it. "Let me . . . do you need help? Did you drop . . .?" She stopped, the unsteadiness in her voice revealing her curiosity about venturing into forbidden turf. Nancy looked at Greg with obvious reservations.

"Oh, it's nothing." Greg forced a smile. "Accidentally knocked everything off my desk." He shook his head and feigned casualness. "Won't take a moment to pick it up."

"I've got it." Nancy was on her knees immediately, putting the pages together. "Why don't I take this to my office and get everything sorted out properly." She smiled thinly and backed out of the office, still looking bewildered.

Greg ran his hands nervously through his hair. *Another one of these episodes, and Nancy will be calling the psycho ward. I'm not myself. Shouldn't be here, but I'll tough it out. Just cool the temper.*

Taking another deep breath, Greg looked at the picture of Alice and him with the president. She was vibrant, vital, alive. Simply looking at Alice helped. At least he could sit back down and start over again. After several deep breaths, Greg was ready.

The new project wouldn't allow him time to reconstruct the stolen pages. Possibly, the lost notes could never be reassembled. Obviously, there was no way in the world he could report that the CIA had stolen his research. Even the hint of such an unsubstantiated accusation would fracture his credibility with the powers that be. Such a setback felt worse than the stroke. Then again, another outburst could change his image from the Duke to the Dope. Darkness started to creep into his thoughts like storm clouds gathering on the horizon.

Greg picked up the new assignment. *Can't let myself get emotionally short-circuited. Need a stabilizer. Best just to work and try to allow my feelings to settle. Concentrate on what's at hand. Let the rest float for a bit.*

Carefully analyzing the proposal one line at a time, Greg forced himself to think of nothing but what was on the piece of paper. Slowly the exacting nature of the study closed out intrusive thoughts, and he felt the inner turmoil subside. He turned to the last page and stopped. A special memo concluded the report. Greg blinked several times and read the lines again. He bent closer to the page to make sure he got it right.

"I can't believe this!" He rocked back in his chair and reached for the phone. "This is Parker. Please give me Director Jones."

"Just a minute," the receptionist answered. "He's in a conference and . . ."

"Tell him Greg Parker has an emergency."

"Yes, sir." The phone went on hold for two minutes.

"Parker?" Allan Jones was clearly back to all business.

"I don't think I understand a very important component in this proposal."

"What?" Jones's briskness conveyed his dislike for being pulled out of conferences.

"Two things. First, why is a domestic project classified as top secret? Second, why does the memo at the end say that only the NSA director and I will ever see the finished report?"

"It means what it says."

"Do you realize that caveat implies that some politician in the White House could quash the entire investigation because the material might prove too sensitive?"

"I don't see that as a probable scenario."

"Let me put it another way, Allan. What keeps somebody from developing this study for his or her private purposes? Then, after we've spent millions and countless hours, the whole proposal disappears until it serves that person's ill-conceived designs."

"I think that's on the 'far out' side. The point is to keep this whole project as a classified matter."

"There are lots of ways to achieve that end without taking such drastic measures. Spending endless sums of money on a study that can be instantly suppressed? I smell a rat," Greg insisted.

"That's *your* job, Parker. Keep sniffing and let me know if you see one, but don't slow down the project while you're setting out the cheese." Jones hung up.

Greg's instincts, honed to a fine edge from more than three decades of investigations, screamed at him. One thing he recognized was that the White House knew something about New Madrid that he didn't, and that bothered him. Two strikes in one morning. The CIA got the first one; some nameless politician lurking somewhere around the White House threw the second curve ball. Greg was not a man to strike out, but he didn't even know from which direction the next pitch would come. Not a good place to be.

Greg thought about calling the PEAR people, but he would have to talk with those two doctors at the hospital first. He remembered the last time they talked. After he reported the thoroughly disconcerting incident with Sharon's ring, Dr. Bridwell told him that when such experiences came, he should sit back and settle into silence. "Don't be so uptight," she said. "The former Soviet Union and the United States have spent millions on paranormal research. People everywhere know about these events. Go with the flow."

Easy for her to say. Tough for him.

"Keep a journal," she had said. "It'll help you keep your sanity. Keep track of whatever pops into your head." She had even said the Bible was filled with mystical experience attributed to God. The doctor seemed to feel the sudden visions weren't so abnormal after all. Just unlocking potential that was always there.

Greg didn't like her explanations because what he had read indicated that most of these unusual aberrations couldn't be duplicated under laboratory conditions. Dr. Birdwell's ideas sounded implausible. In fact, at that moment the whole thing was making him nervous, uncomfortable.

Dr. Bridwell had said that when an attack was coming, he should cool it and not fight the images or the feelings. "Try to find a still, quiet place at your center," she had said. "Breathe deeply and don't panic. Don't be afraid. Just let it happen." He closed his eyes.

Something shifted. A very different picture edged its way into the darkness created by closed eyelids. Like a Technicolor dream, Greg could see a massive conference table, with men in expensive suits seated around it, talking. The room filled with smoke, and the executives intensified their discussions. Suddenly the men changed. Rather than businessmen, they abruptly became Dutch Burgers in tall black hats, fluted neck collars, and long coats, looking like the Dutch Masters in a Rembrandt painting. The group turned and looked at him with fierce intensity.

The vision faded, replaced by a terrible headache. Greg reached for an aspirin bottle in his bottom desk drawer.

CHAPTER 10

Sharon glanced down at the September 18 newspaper beside her on the car seat. Faith Community Church shouldn't be far away, maybe two blocks ahead. She had to fight the urge to drive faster. Monday was not a good day to get a ticket.

Sharon's sense of well-being was tested by the thought of not going back to Israel. Although her colleagues at Associated Press were understanding and more than willing to be flexible with her work arrangements, the idea of not returning simply irritated her. Everything about the journalistic foray abroad excited and challenged her.

Sharon pressed the brake to slow down to the speed limit in the southside residential area. *All I need today is a ticket,* she thought. *Dad wouldn't allow me to stay if he knew how I felt, but it's obvious he's got a problem. No one knows exactly how bad the condition is, and a stroke could happen again. Got to stay until I know it won't occur. He's a difficult old geezer!*

She picked up the paper and looked again. The advertisement said that a messianic Jewish rabbi would explain how the recent bombing of the Temple Mount fulfilled biblical expectations. It was a strange angle she had not heard in Israel and, besides, she had no idea what a messianic Jew was and why one would be lecturing in a *church* on a Monday morning. The talk might provide a new slant for a future story, and, at least she would be out of the house and on the beat for a while. The housewife thing didn't sit well with Sharon.

A tall steeple abruptly loomed above the trees, so she slowed down. The big sign out front said she was at the right place. She pulled into the parking lot on the far side and was surprised at the number of cars showing up at 10:00 A.M. Apparently, a good number of people had a similar interest. Just ahead a beat-up '89 Pontiac, looking like her father's car, had an open space next to it. She pulled alongside and stopped.

Sharon turned the ignition off. *Wonder how Dad's doing today? First day back on the job won't be easy. You know, he's actually been easier to get along with than I thought. Even was appreciative . . . some of the time at least.*

She got out of the car, and the breeze caught her long brown hair, tossing it over her shoulder. For a moment, Sharon remembered how the wind had felt in her face as a child. She had loved running up the hill behind their house, letting the gales come down over the top and blow her long brown tresses in every direction, making her feel like she was flying. She had kept her hair long because her father liked it so much.

Dad had staunchly resisted cutting her hair at all costs. The battles went on until Sharon turned seven and her mother intervened. He took the trip to the beauty shop as a personal affront and moped around the house for a week as if the dog had died.

Mom had always been the referee in those father-daughter spats. She'd bide her time and then step in at the strategic moment when things were on the verge of getting out of hand. Always a source of reassurance to Sharon that she wasn't in the ring by herself, Mom knew where Dad's "off" switch was hidden. Occasionally, when the little father-daughter talks started heating up, Mom strolled through humming, "Look for the silver lining," and Mr. Big cooled it.

More than once after storming out of the room, and then listening at the keyhole, she'd heard her mother say, "Go easy on the girl, Greg. Trouble is, you love Sharon too much." Eavesdropping had changed her perspective.

Actually their fierce tugs-of-war had, in some ways, been only love matches. Sharon never doubted that her father loved her. The problem was, his love was so all-consuming. He was always trying to make everything turn out right, in other words, his way. If Sharon hadn't resisted, she would have been engulfed by that love. Without the struggle, there wouldn't have been any Sharon left.

"Oh, Dad!" she said to herself as she walked into the church, "why can't you simply let me in rather trying to make me perfect?"

The sign said "Sanctuary" and pointed down the hall. What looked like a three-hundred-seater had maybe half that number of people scattered around the large room. She picked up a brochure from the back pew. A man was getting up to speak. *Perfect timing.*

"As pastor of our church, I am more than pleased to invite Rabbi Jacov Palenski to our church," the tall, graying minister spoke in pleasant tones. "Many of you may know that his family originally immigrated to the United States at the end of World War II. Unfortunately, his mother and brother were lost in the Holocaust. Reverend Palenski is the rabbi for Beth Yeshua congregation in San Francisco. Please welcome our new friend."

As the audience applauded, a small man with a dark complexion—in his late forties or early fifties—walked to the platform. He wore a small white yarmulke and a black suit. His thick, dark black beard was streaked with strands of gray. He reminded Sharon of many men she'd seen on the streets of Jerusalem.

Jacov Palenski began with a slow, easy description of his work and expressed his pleasure at being there. His voice was certainly pleasant enough, his manner easy and unaffected; the smile didn't fade.

Sharon got out her notepad and jotted down information from the brochure as she listened to Palenski describe his family history. Originally from Krakow, they immigrated by way of Auschwitz to New York City. Jacov grew up in Brooklyn Heights in the midst of the Hasidic world of medieval Judaism; his great-grandfather had been a rabbi, the family kosher, and the boy rebellious. Following a stint as a hippie, Jacov ended up at Berkeley and became a political radical. On the campus of California's most notorious university, he found a group with an even more radical agenda for the world than his. Jesus freaks had brought him into a new world of spiritual reality.

"I didn't feel at home in the Anglo churches," Jacov said as he became more intense. "Too much history of anti-Semitism there. I ended up in the black church because I could identify with their persecution. They taught me another form of radical Christianity and poor Palenski, the family rebel, turned into despicable Jacov, the converted Jew. Those who were left of my kin in Brooklyn Heights warned me not to come back. My own father slammed the door shut."

Sharon put her pen down. *At least Dad never ran me off. In fact, he never would. I can't imagine being shut out because of religion. On the other hand, why would anyone give up his family for a religion?*

"In time I longed to be back in the place I once rejected. The Seder, Rosh Hashana, the kosher cooking, even the Sabbath became important in a new way. Only after I couldn't come home again did I realize how significant each of these experiences was to me." Jacov shook his head. "But how could I give up what I had discovered? As a matter of fact, each of those festivals was now fulfilled in Jesus the Messiah. I could not turn my back on the sacrifice God had made to restore me from my brokenness."

Sharon picked up the notepad again. *Is this guy for real?* she thought. *Either he's a nut, or this is the most amazing thing I've heard yet. Where's all this going?*

"At that point I ran into a group of people starting a synagogue that was designed to be completely faithful to all the old ways and still incorporating the new truth found in the Jewish Messiah. We called him the proper Hebrew name *Yeshua,* so as not to be confused with institutional Christianity. We kept the Sabbath, studied the Torah, and prayed through *Yeshua* to the Holy One of Israel. Little did I know that was a movement of beginning."

Sharon thought about the Jews she worked with at Associated Press. Most of them were ethnically Jewish but didn't put any stock in the old Bible stories. She wondered what they would make of Palenski and his exuberance for this "completed faith," as he called his brand of Judaism. For the next fifteen minutes, Sharon listened to Jacov explain convictions and practices that would surely shake her debonair, sophisticated colleagues to their foundations.

"Now to the reason you've come," Jacov picked up the pace. "You are trying to make biblical sense out of the headlines, yes?" He smiled and wrote a large *1948* on the blackboard behind him. "Obviously, the return of the Jewish people to their homeland in 1948 was the fulfillment of clear Bible prophecy, which no one believed could happen." Jacov stroked his black beard and smiled slyly at the congregation. "The prophet Ezekiel predicted this event immediately after the destruction of Solomon's Temple in 586 B.C., when the armies of Nebuchadnezzar leveled Jerusalem." He raised his eyebrows and waited for the impact to sink in.

"Even in the 1940s, when the British tried to stop the immigration to Palestine, the hand of God was at work, restoring the land to us." Jacov's countenance changed, and he looked hard and demanding. "The prophet said the desolate land would become fruitful, and it has. This resurrection of the 'dry bones' was the first step." His voice became more intense. "Since that moment, the God of Israel has been moving His people into a strategic position for the rest of the biblical prophecies to be completed. Now the former great Dome of the Rock Mosque is nothing but rubble. The area is ready for the new temple to come forth at any moment! Is this not an awesome moment in which we live?" Palenski looked hard at the audience and let the prolonged silence do its work.

"Rather than ramble through material that might be irrelevant, let me respond to your questions." The messianic rabbi suddenly smiled, and warmth exuded over the audience. "We'll develop the rest of our time together. What questions do you have?"

Sharon immediately thought about the Arab Wakf, responsible for controlling the holy site. She could see the soldiers staggering around the bombed Temple Mount, shocked senseless. The bodies of the temple guards were never found. The authorities had said repeatedly that night security was impossible to penetrate. No one could have gotten in without shots being fired, guards killed . . . yet they *obviously* had.

She looked around, wondering if there would be any takers. This Palenski had to be a rather self-assured type to submit himself to random questions. She was struck by the difference in his demeanor and the defensiveness of the Hasidic Jew she had interviewed, Eli Goren. The Jerusalemite seemed to be motivated by fear; Jacov maintained a gentle demeanor with no hint of arrogance toward men or women.

A middle-aged lady near the front stood up. "We're very concerned about the Middle East erupting into full-scale war. The destruction of the Temple Mount seems to have lit the fuse on a powder keg. How do you see the matter?"

Palenski nodded thoughtfully. "Yes, the issues are grave and only turmoil can follow, but such is the plan of God. When the Messiah returns, there must be a place prepared to receive him. The book of Daniel details the prophetic expectation of what must happen in a restored Temple. The removal of the mosque cleared the way for the Temple to be erected."

The pastor of the church raised his hand. "Jacov, I keep hearing rumors that for a long time preparations have been developing for such an event. Any truth to those reports?"

The messianic rabbi nodded his head enthusiastically. "Absolutely. A *yeshiva*, a Jewish school, has existed for years in the old city for the expressed purpose of training the Cohenim, the descendants of the tribe of Levi, to function in the Temple. Special vestments are made, the breastplate with the Urim and Thummin, the utensils for Temple worship are all there. People are already trained to function as soon as the building is erected."

"Truly amazing," the pastor responded. "But is rebuilding the Temple actually an option?"

"For the last few years, conservative Jewish groups have been raising funds for exactly this purpose. While I am not privy to their exact plans, there are significant rumors that sections of the new

Temple are already prefabricated and ready for rapid assembly. As soon as the Temple Mount is cleared and the political issues settled, such a Temple could be in place almost overnight."

Sharon felt as if she were about to get writer's cramp from trying to keep up with every word. She stopped and rubbed her fingers. *Why didn't I bring my tape recorder?* Sharon totally underestimated the significance of this guy for a story. *Don't know whether he's for real or nuts, but is this ever a hot angle. I can see the headline: "Mosque Makes Room for Messiah."*

Sharon glanced at her watch. *This thing is taking longer than I thought, but I don't want to leave. I need to get his conclusions before I split.*

The messianic rabbi finished answering the last person's question. "Now, let me summarize what we've been saying." He cleared his throat. "A recent historic event clearly fulfills what the ancient prophets said would happen centuries ago. While I have no idea who or what group set off the bombs in Jerusalem, they were the inadvertent fulfillment of divine plans. Unfortunately, as the final pieces of history fall into place, the stage is set for the world to turn on Israel. Remember that the book of Revelation predicts, 'Behold, the days are coming when they will surround you, O Jerusalem. Woe to you who stand within her gates in those days.' When that occurs, the final collision of good and evil will follow. It will be as the prophet Jeremiah said, 'Who will have pity on you, O Jerusalem, or will bemoan you?'"

Sharon stuffed the notepad in her purse. *Far out. This guy is the most fascinating of the bunch. Probably three or four good angles here. I bet none of my buddies at AP ever wrote about a messianic Jew!*

CHAPTER 11

An entire day had passed since Allan Jones gave Greg Parker his new assignment. Throughout the evening Greg had stewed and fretted over a number of aspects of the requirements. He knew the task would be the most difficult he'd faced in his career. Nothing about the New Madrid fault was easy.

Greg stared at his office computer, contemplating the overwhelming list of possible agencies. *It's Tuesday afternoon and time is flying. Too many options. No alternative but to call a late afternoon meeting. People will hate me, but that's the only way I'm going to get this thing off the ground in the necessary time restraints.* He glanced at his watch. 4:00 P.M.

"Nancy," he spoke into the intercom. "Go ahead. Call everyone on that list I gave you earlier and confirm that the meeting is on for 5:30 today. Make sure Mary Morgan is coming. She's vital to the discussion."

"I'll be done in twenty minutes."

"Good." He thought for a moment. "Best make this call myself." He punched in his home number.

"Parker residence," Sharon answered.

"Sharon, I'm glad I caught you. Thought you might be out."

"No, earlier in the day I was typing up some notes from a lead I picked up yesterday. Been working on a little, oh, something special for this evening."

"Great. Good. Want you to be happy." He smiled. "Listen. I've got to put together a meeting in a few minutes. Won't be home for supper and may not get there until late."

"What?" she sounded agitated.

"Unfortunately, the front office is putting the pressure on."

"Dad, I already put a roast in the oven. Mom always said you liked roast and mashed potatoes. The potatoes are boiling."

"Let's just eat it tomorrow night?"

"Tomorrow night!"

"Wouldn't that work okay?"

"I stayed home today to fix your favorite meal, and I've been working on it all afternoon."

"Oh, Sharon. I can't believe I'm caught in this bind."

"No problem in my believing it!" She sounded bitter. "Nothing new in this scene. Same old Mr. Big Time, putting his work before everything else. The usual thoughtlessness."

"Now, Sharon that's not fair. Please understand."

"I thought maybe things were different, but did I ever make a mistake! Fix your supper yourself!" She slammed the phone down.

Greg slowly put the phone back in the cradle and thought about why it always happened this way. He shook his head ruefully.

• • •

Mary Morgan entered the conference room last. The other five executives sat solemnly around the table, not looking happy, resentful not to be out there fighting the evening traffic. They glanced at the NSA director's representative but said nothing.

Greg waited until Mary found a seat. "I apologize for calling a meeting this evening. If there'd been anyway to avoid it, please know, I would have done it." He smiled, although no one else did. "We have a deadline imposed on us—from the highest level of government."

The group groaned.

"The White House issued a top-level secret assignment to develop a plan that could well affect more than ten million people. I believe that it is highly possible, and even probable, that the New Madrid fault could shift in the near future. Because this would be an inland event, it would release more seismic energy than any recorded event in North American history. Needless to say, we would be faced with a disaster of unparalleled proportions. Our immediate task is to define what would be required, in the event of such a possibility."

A man at the back of the room raised his hand. "Parker, I'd suggest we simply run in the usual players." Mark Rex's tie dangled loosely around his neck, and he looked bedraggled, bored. "Off the cuff, I can give you a quick list of the cast of characters. The Centers for Disease Control and Prevention always move in to deal with possible cholera or typhus epidemics. I know there must be gas lines down there, so we'll need the National Gas Pipeline Association. Of course, the Department of Transportation naturally comes into play, but I don't see a big deal here."

Mary Morgan looked sternly at the man. "Mark, I don't think you got the full significance of what our chairman just described. A quake of the magnitude we're required to study might well break this country in half. Every aspect of national life would be drastically affected, and the economy could be destroyed. We're not in a 'business as usual' posture on this project. Even the Internal Revenue Service must be included because of the financial consequences that could result from the economic instability of our country."

Rex rolled his eyes but said nothing.

"Obviously, the Federal Emergency Management Agency is at the top of the list," a more amicable man at the other end of the table answered. "FEMA already has extraordinary powers and capacities during national emergencies." He chuckled. "When the axe falls, they virtually control the country."

Greg frowned and scribbled on his pad. Never trusted the top echelons of that organization. Because of Executive Order 12656, they could become more powerful than the president during a disaster. No choice but to put them at the hub of all contingency plans.

"Of course, the U.S. Geological Survey kicks off this sort of thing," someone else said. "Let's quit stalling and get the project done."

Resistance quickly shifted into reluctant cooperation, and the discussion finally took off. Suggestions flew from all directions. Greg hastily scribbled on his notepad. The exchange had a life of its own. He didn't feel the shift in his inner focus, but sounds in the room began fading, and his writing took on a character of its own, almost as if he were free associating through the tip of a pen. He started drawing the outline of an oil well. His mind filled with scenes of men hurrying back and forth between stockpiles of pipes and an oil derrick, their pace feverish and the work urgent. His sketching matched their frantic pace. At the bottom of the drawing, he abruptly wrote, "Four wells are pumping. Time is short." The cold iciness of death gripped his hand.

"Greg?" the voice seemed far off. "Greg!" the voice was in front of him.

He looked up at the table of silent executives staring at him. Mary Morgan was halfway out of her chair speaking to him.

"Greg!" She said with greater urgency.

"Oh." He looked from one astonished face to another. "I'm sorry. I was completely lost in my thoughts. I've been envisioning this project for a long time," he smiled, trying to look casual and hide his embarrassment. "I guess I got lost on a back trail for a moment."

"I have one other organization to add." Rex still sounded uncooperative. "The CIA belongs in the mix."

"Why?" Greg shot back. "The final report isn't a matter of foreign intelligence."

"We need to be prepared for any possibility of opportunism from abroad." Rex returned the volley with intense accuracy.

"We don't need saboteurs," Greg growled and then noticed Mary Morgan looking apprehensive.

"But we need information," Rex continued. "That's their specialty."

"Greg, you've put in a remarkable two days of work, considering you came straight back here from a hospital room," Mary intervened. "I think we now have the basic outline of the initial agencies to be included in the study." She held up a small tape recorder. "I have the complete discussion here. I suggest we adjourn for the day."

"Here, here," Rex exclaimed.

"Good suggestion," Greg answered. "I would like to have your formal responses on my desk by 10:00 tomorrow morning." He forced a smile in the midst of his grim expression. "I know it's an early request, but we don't have much time. Thank you."

The group quickly dispersed.

Mary waited for the room to clear. "You okay, Greg?"

"Sure. I simply got too engrossed in an aspect of the study."

"You've pushed yourself rather hard since you've returned," she sounded concerned.

"You know how Allan gets if projects don't stay on their time schedule." He grimaced and picked up his notes. "Nancy is staying late to get the results of this meeting into gear. By 10:00 tomorrow morning, we'll have the initial agencies notified of their involvement in the study."

"I simply don't want you pushing yourself beyond what's healthy," Mary said firmly.

"Thanks." He felt the little-boy grin breaking out and quickly looked down at the file. "Mary," he paused, "we've always been good friends . . ."

"Of course." She reached for his hand. "What do you need?"

"I'm worried about an aspect of this project." He kept looking at the table.

Mary withdrew her hand. "Yes."

"I need you to find out the reason for the sudden interest in the New Madrid fault. Jones either doesn't know or won't tell me. Think you can get the inside story?"

"You know I'll certainly try."

"See what you can stir up. Something's not quite right, but I can't put my finger on it. A big piece is missing in this puzzle."

CHAPTER 12

Mary Morgan closed her office door and sat down at her desk. The digital clock said 8:10 A.M., Wednesday, September 27. Unquestionably, autumn was in the air. Mary thought about how summer passed so quickly, how quickly everything passed. She never expected a career with the NSA. A Virginia girl by upbringing, she was only supposed to spend a few years in government service, then find the right man, get married, raise kids, do the glass slipper thing, and live happily ever after. Had that been two decades ago? Surely not. But the clock said otherwise.

In a second the two decades flew past again. She remembered her first day as a semi-terrified young woman, sitting behind a big desk and worrying about what she was supposed to do next. Outside, protesters flooded the street, screaming for the Vietnam War to stop. Troops and soldiers were everywhere, and people inside the government buildings were confused, angry, and indignant about being caught in the middle of a riot surging down every street in America. A couple of suggestions came to her about what to do. Mary turned them in. Good things happened. Almost overnight she was on her way upstairs.

A big award plaque on the wall told the rest of the story. She couldn't help being a high achiever. Success came naturally, and her parents had always taught the virtue of hard work. Uncle

Sam said 'thank you' with steady advancements. She kept accumulating graduate hours, attending seminars, working on special projects. And now here she was on the top floor, *alone* on this exhilarating fall day.

The right man simply never came along, until Greg Parker. She'd seen him for the first time about ten years earlier. Their conversations were casual and infrequent, but he always captured her attention. Polite and unassuming but obviously handsome, intelligent, and dynamic, Greg was easy to respect. Not until his wife was killed did Mary see him in any different light. Since that day, he'd been like a lost little boy.

"I've got to help him," she suddenly said aloud. "Yes, we need all the time we can get together. Conversation keeps us in close touch, and he's probably on to something. Greg always is."

She reached for the phone and dialed the director's confidential number. "Allan?" Mary said the second the phone clicked on.

"Why do I know who this is?"

"Yes, yes, you hate me talking before you say hello."

"We've had this conversation before. It makes you sound like a fortune teller—Karnak or someone of that order—particularly at 8:00 in the morning."

"Could you see me for a moment right now?"

"No, the question is, could I keep you from coming over?" Allan Jones chuckled. "How well we get to know one another in our little fish-bowl world. Sure. Come up right now before the circus really gets started."

With a single flourish, Mary hung up the phone, was out of the chair, and on her way to the door. "I'll be across the hall," she explained, rushing past the secretary. "Hold all calls."

She crossed the hall and was in the director's reception area minutes later. His secretary smiled and waved her on. The director's door was already open.

"Good morning, chief." Mary slipped into the chair in front of his desk. "I trust all is well." She smiled professionally.

"I'm being set up," Allan Jones answered without looking up. "I understand that tone of voice." He pushed a file aside. "We both know that in this business nothing is ever 'all is well.' What's on your mind? Another bomb in Jerusalem? Someone find one of those missing portable Russian A-bombs in a car trunk today?"

"You're always so cheerful in the morning." Mary shook her head. "I swear, Allan, you're becoming a cynic in your old age."

The director glared. "I have problems with Congress appropriating enough money for the agency, and then twenty minutes ago the White House orders me to do something that's illegal. No, I'm not a cynic, just a realist."

"Speaking of the White House . . ." Mary jumped on the opening. "I need a little candor."

Allan looked out of the corner of his eye. "Don't push your luck."

"Look. Greg Parker ran all over this place for years, warning everyone about the New Madrid fault, and no one gave him the time of day. Suddenly, money's floating out of the sky for a big study. Why the sudden interest?"

Jones's demeanor changed. "Why do you want to know?" His face became impassive, not an emotion for miles.

"The director comes and goes as American presidents get elected or defeated. I'm number two and will be here probably long after you're gone. Correct?"

Jones grimaced and nodded. "You got that picture right."

"Moreover, I'm on the team evaluating the problem with Parker. I don't like surprises." Mary leaned into his desk. "Since I'm supposed to be your deputy," she let a hint of irony slip in, "I think that makes me a confidential party to privileged information. At least, that's how it was last time I checked my job description."

The director drummed on his desk with his fingers. "I'm not sure I have the information you want."

"If you don't, who does, for heaven's sake?"

"This thing came straight from the White House. What more can I say?"

Mary studied his face. He wasn't being entirely forthright. Lying? Maybe, but Jones wasn't going to say much more.

"You wouldn't kid an old kidder?"

"Look. If Parker's assertions about a giant earthquake have any validity at all, the project is more than worthwhile," Jones replied. "Who knows? Maybe the president woke up one morning and wanted to do something that was more than simply politics as usual."

"We both know that Greg's been the lightning rod more than once," Mary bore down. "I'd hate to find out that the NSA simply made Greg a pawn in a dangerous game no one warned him we were playing."

"You've been watching too many James Bond movies, Mary. I don't know the full scoop or why the project is urgent." He threw his hands up in the air and sounded more forthright. "Who knows? Everyone's edgy right now. The Middle East is a powder keg that could go off any second and blow the world to pieces. Possibly a national security adviser wanted to make sure we don't have any bases left uncovered." Jones took on a distant professional look. "I suggest you take that question back to the committee." He sounded final. "Let them work on it."

"Thank you for your response." Mary got up slowly. "I'll keep our conversation in mind." She smiled politely in a way that meant to say, 'We're not finished with this one yet.'"

"Oh, one last thing."

Mary stopped in place. "Yes?" she raised an eyebrow.

"Just before you called, I got a fax from the CIA, wanting to know if Parker was running the project and strongly urging us to include one of their people on the team. Put that one in your pipe and smoke it." He immediately looked away and picked up the file on his desk.

Mary stared, knowing how devious Jones could be when the political situation demanded and then how he could be suddenly forthright, but he had been anything *but* candid.

• • •

Greg had only been in his office thirty minutes when the phone rang. He glanced at his watch. 8:30. Time for business to start exploding. Team members already had a half hour of work time to process their assignments from yesterday afternoon's meeting. Chaos was now in order.

"Parker," he answered brusquely.

"Greg, I've just come from the director's office." Mary's voice was low but intense. "I've been making the inquiries we discussed last night."

"Mary! Good morning. How are you?"

"Fine but a little concerned."

He pushed the phone closer to his ear. "Concerned?"

"Allan didn't have much more to tell me about why this project is so urgent, but he did drop a little bomb in my lap just before I left. Seems the CIA has been inquiring about your personal role in the New Madrid fault study."

Greg took a deep breath. He felt the muscles in his neck tightening. "Well, well, isn't this a big surprise. My old friends from Spook City." His mouth felt dry.

"Is that what you've been worrying about?"

"Not exactly, but it's one of the possibilities."

"What's going on, Greg?"

"That's what I need you to tell me, Mary. All is not as it seems, and when the CIA shows up, you can bet we've got real old-fashioned problems. I'm going to need more information to make sense out of the puzzle."

"You know I'll do everything I can."

"Mary, you're the only person in this place I trust 100 percent. We've got to stick close together . . . Please continue to keep your ear to the ground." He realized the mere mention of the CIA made him feel edgy.

"You got it. I'll be back in touch."

Greg hung up and settled back in the chair, crossing his arms over his chest. "Now the CIA is sticking its nose into our little project," he said to himself. "That ought to make the hair on the back of our collective necks stand on end." He scratched his head and rubbed his chin. "Yes, we've got big rats in the attic." He felt the blood pounding in his temples. "One can never be too cautious." He lunged forward and grabbed a notepad. "Need to make several memos." He clutched his pencil tightly.

The strange sensation began with a touch of dizziness. His sudden disconnectedness made his thoughts feel jumbled—as if he'd had a tad too much champagne on New Year's Eve. Greg held the pencil even more tightly and hunched over the desk, but the images would not be denied. A swirl of scenes shot through his mind. Greg closed his eyes tightly and pressed his forehead against the palm of his hands.

He was suddenly in the men's room at the end of the hall. Fists flew past his head, each blow calculated to smash his face. A knee caught him in the groin, his balance slipped, he fought to keep from falling into something. The face of the assailant blurred into darkness, but the attack did not stop. Greg felt himself propelled through the air and smashing into the wall. The head-splitting sting of ceramic tile crunched against his skull. Pain was as real as if an assailant had just hit him with a baseball bat. Catching his breath, he ground his teeth and pushed his face into his palms. The apparition slowly faded.

Greg sat upright, his heart still racing. After several deep breaths, he placed his hand on his chest. Only with great effort could he clear his head. The dizziness subsided, and he swallowed hard.

His first cup of coffee was only half gone. Greg finished it off with a single swallow and threw the Styrofoam cup in the trash. He rubbed his temples and tried to think straight.

"The stroke . . ." he mumbled to himself. "A stroke? Or was I attacked?"

CHAPTER 13

Alex Majors checked his computerized electronic organizer to make sure that Wednesday noon was the time to meet Helmut Haussman at the Washington Arms on the banks of the Potomac. The digital readout confirmed he was at the right restaurant, even though the German was ten minutes late. Alex shook his head and glanced toward the front door of the colonial tavern replica. Everywhere exquisite antiques, old farm utensils, and knickknacks added atmosphere and a touch of class. Alex took another long look at the menu. Even when irritated, the mere idea of food soothed his nerves. He rethought what he had already ordered.

"Sorry," a deep rumbling bass voice called out across the small elegant restaurant. "Traffic tied me up."

Majors forced a smile. "I understand," he lied. "Good to see you, Helmut." The CIA agent offered his hand limply.

Haussman gave a firm shake and settled into the chair across the table. He grabbed the menu as if a swift decision could turn back the clock's hands. The Berlin native was tall and big boned with fleshy hands. Too many dumplings and schnitzel had plunged his belly over the belt's edge. The fat face matched a big waist. His receding hairline accentuated a naturally high forehead. Beyond sagging jowls, little distinguished Haussman from any other businessman in a bland gray suit. He would easily be missed in a crowd, a necessity in intelligence and espionage.

"Ah, the Reuben sandwich sounds excellent." Haussman motioned to the waiter, standing only a few feet away. "Give me the Reuben and a large draft of dark beer. You, Alex?"

"I've already ordered," Majors answered dryly.

Helmut Haussman beamed, seemingly oblivious to the hostile undertone in the conversation. "Shall we speak English, German, what?"

"Let's speak Flemish. No one will have a clue."

Haussman nodded. "Brings back those memories of the good times when we both lived in Brugger, that quaint little city in Belgium."

Majors nodded. "Medieval. Wonderful ambiance."

"Still have friends there."

"Speaking of our friends, I talked to the big man in Brussels this week," Majors explained. "He seemed upbeat."

"Should be. Everything's going his way."

"Amazing how all aspects of the global strategy are happening on schedule," Alex added. "We have every reason to believe the master plan will succeed."

Haussman nodded his head back and forth nonchalantly. "Alex, we've come a long way together since we were nothing but small-time spies, only cannon fodder for our mutual governments. Remember those good old days of the Cold War?"

Alex smiled for the first time. "Ah, yes. Good guys and bad guys were so much easier to identify then. Most of the KGB came straight out of a mystery novel. Real bunch of clowns. Electronic surveillance was still limited. Computers were just coming on. We depended far more on what we could see with the naked eye."

Haussman smirked. "No one ever had a hint we were double agents."

Alex cringed. "Don't ever say such a thing out loud . . . even between us. I want to live to a ripe old age."

"A *rich* old age," Haussman quipped cynically. "We both know this caper is going to give us one whale of a retirement fund."

Alex raised an eyebrow. "Like I say, let's not allow such words to slip out of our lips. Too much is at stake."

"You were always cautious, Alex. Maybe you picked that up in your first eight years of life, living in conservative Brussels."

"No, my American father was a very careful entrepreneur. He taught me to keep one eye on where the road is going and the other on where it's coming from."

"Well, dual citizenship gave you the edge. Me? I did well to survive the reconstruction after the war. We nearly starved in Berlin while you dined on steak in America."

Alex snorted. "Poor Helmut. I bet you've got more stashed away in Switzerland than the Arabs do. Didn't you get a hunk of that Jewish gold left in Swiss banks after the Holocaust?"

Haussman stiffened. "Like you say, some things are best *never* mentioned."

"Touché." Alex grinned slyly.

The waiter put Haussman's sandwich in front of him, a large plate of french fries and a big steak before Alex.

"Anything else, gentlemen?"

"No thank you," Alex answered in English.

Haussman waited until the man disappeared back into the kitchen. "How soon will I have the data I need to finish the assignment?" he asked in Flemish.

"Soon. The government has started the study that will give us the exact specifications." Majors pursed his lips thoughtfully. "It will take a while . . . a number of weeks at least, to get what we want for our operation."

Haussman took a big bite of his sandwich. His fat cheeks shook as he chewed viciously and then washed it down with a big gulp of beer. "You will be pleased to know the drilling is going very well. We are certainly on schedule on *our* end of things."

Alex caught the intended jab. "Precision is a German virtue," he grudgingly admitted. "I'm sure you will bring the project in on schedule." He plunged his fork into steak. "What about that farmer who wouldn't lease the site for the last well?"

"Interesting." Haussman answered smugly. "The farmer's house blew up. Killed the old man and his wife." The German rolled his eyes. "Newspaper said it was a propane explosion. The heirs signed the lease."

"Always efficient, Helmut."

"Of course."

• • •

Greg hoped taking Sharon out to supper would make amends for missing her special meal on Tuesday night. He selected the Cheers pub on Constitution Street for many reasons. Sharon had always liked the place, and he was trying to mend fences. A raucous crowded restaurant fit his purposes. Meeting at 8:00 gave him a little extra time at the office with the excuse she'd have to drive in to Washington.

Greg's wristwatch said 8:10. Sharon was making a statement by being late. He fought irritation and looked away at the bill-board by the door. The advertisement promised the Blackbirds played every Tuesday night.

Sharon abruptly appeared out of the shadows. "Been here long?" she asked innocently. "I must have missed you."

She was setting him up. He wanted to take the bait but suppressed the lecture. "Yes. I didn't see you."

"Really?" Sharon sounded cool.

"Sure. Let's go in." Greg opened the door. Cheers was crowded as usual. He slipped a ten to the host. "A table by the band."

"Been expecting you," the man said for the benefit of the people waiting in line. "Your table is waiting."

Sharon seemed unimpressed by the ploy.

The table was only ten feet from the stage. Apparently, the jazz combo was out on a break. Greg sized up the crowd as closer to Sharon's age than his. Typical up-and-coming government career employees. Lawyers. Aides. Secretaries. The latest fashions; the GQ look.

Sharon studied the menu, avoiding small talk.

"Want a buffalo wing starter?" Greg offered.

"Maybe not." She didn't look up.

"Think I'll try a cup of clam chowder."

A waiter showed up with pad in hand. "What'll it be?"

"I'll go with the steamed vegetables," Sharon answered. "And a Diet Coke."

"Make it a bowl of chowder and the Caesar salad." He waited until the waiter left. "Now there was a real piece of work."

Sharon said nothing.

"Place is really jumping."

"Always is." Sharon looked away.

Greg rolled his tongue around the inside of his mouth and struggled to be civil. "Sharon," he began haltingly, "I want to apologize again about last Tuesday night. I *am* sorry I ruined your special meal."

She looked down and seemed to be waiting for an excuse.

"It's my fault for not calling you sooner." Now, he'd wait. The ball was completely in her court.

Sharon looked around the room. Finally she pursed her lips. "I shouldn't have assumed anything."

"I think we often miss each other out of the best intentions." Greg presented his final offering. "Simple lack of communication."

"Sure."

He reached for Sharon's hand. "I can't tell you how much I appreciate what you've done." She didn't turn away.

"I shouldn't have gotten mad and thrown everything out."

"You did what?" Greg's voice went up an octave.

Sharon shrugged. "Dad, I didn't get angry just because I'd put in a little extra work. You needed to be home resting, not killing yourself down there at that cursed government office building. If you don't rest . . ."

"I need to tell you something important," Greg broke in. "I don't think my health is the big issue right now."

"Really?" Sharon raised her eyebrows in mock consternation.

"I want you to listen carefully." Greg looked around. The jazz band was assembling again. "Sure, we discovered I had a weak blood vessel, but I have reason to think that the stroke followed my head being banged against the wall."

Sharon's eyes widened. "What?"

"I believe someone was trying to kill me."

She leaned over the table, looking perplexed. The guitarist plunked a few notes, and the bass player tuned his instrument to the keyboard. The drummer took a couple of rim shots.

"I'm not sure I heard you right." Sharon frowned at the combo. "It's going to be hard to hear."

"Exactly. That's why I slipped the maître d' a little extra change to get us here."

Sharon leaned farther over the table. "Dad, what is going on?"

"I am sorry for our misunderstanding, Sharon. And I want you to know how much I appreciate your staying with me, but I also needed to be in a place where electronic eavesdropping would be difficult. Unfortunately, our house may already be bugged."

Sharon's jaw dropped. "You're kidding!"

The Blackbirds launched into a version of "Lullaby of Bird Land," their theme. The guitar player picked up a cornet and blasted out the melody line.

Greg leaned closer. "Remember when you were a freshman in high school and we underwent a government protection program? FBI agents watched our house from cars parked up and down the street. Remember?"

"How could I forget? Nearly scared me to death."

"I had discovered an industrialist bilked the government out of millions of dollars. When I blew the whistle, things got hot."

"Yeah, was Mother ever upset."

"The FBI secretly recorded a conversation indicating the industrialist was hiring a man to shoot me."

Sharon caught her breath. "No one ever told me that part of the story!"

"Cutting off the money faucet on the big boys is very dangerous business." Greg smiled weakly. "Comes with the territory. We call those interventions touching the tail of the dragon."

Sharon looked around the room. "They're in here?"

"Could be. Apparently I've unwittingly entered the dragon's den. This time the bad guys are in our own government."

The Blackbirds shifted into high gear, and the drummer exploded like a machine gun gone crazy. Sharon shivered.

Greg put his hand over his daughter's. "Dear, our house could be bugged. I'll have it checked out, but in the meantime you must assume our conversations might be tapped. These people have incredible intrusive powers."

Sharon's expression changed from consternation to fear. "I have no idea of even what to say."

"Look. You've been a wonderful nurse." Greg swallowed hard. "I can't possibly tell you what it meant to wake up in the hospital and see your face." He felt tears welling up. "Having you in the house has been like a burst of new life." He struggled to go on.

"Thank you, Dad." Sharon said over the blur of the band. "Thank you very much."

"But maybe now is the right time for you to get back full time to your career. Maybe you could get another assignment out of the country. Not back to Israel, but possibly . . ."

"Are you kidding?" Sharon cut him off. "Leave you at a time like this? Not on your life!"

"But Sharon . . ."

"Don't 'but' me. You need me now more than ever."

"I don't think you understand. I'm talking about evil people. I believe one of them slammed me into a wall and put me in the hospital."

"And you want me to get out of Dodge? Not on your life!"

The Blackbirds slid into a blasting finish, and the room broke into applause.

"Dad, there's just the two of us left. We're all we've got now. We must stick together."

Greg fought to keep the tears back. "I was afraid you'd say that." He reached for a handkerchief.

"Hot stuff." The waiter appeared with a large circular tray balanced over his head. "Chowder for the gentleman. Veggies for the sweet young thing." He winked at Greg and quickly put the food on the table. "Enjoy." He was gone.

Sharon said little while the band played full tilt. She seemed completely absorbed in what she had heard. The Blackbirds finally eased into a few pieces on the more sedate side. "Can you tell me what this new threat is really all about?"

Greg finished the last of his chowder. "Sharon, I can't talk about the details, and you're better off not knowing." He set the bowl aside and reached in his pocket. "But I can tell you more about what's been going on inside me." He pulled out a folded piece of paper and spread it out on the table. "I keep having these strange flashes of insight. Images fill my mind. I get completely absorbed in bizarre thoughts."

"The doctors said something like this might happen. Didn't they want to study you? Have you talked with the researchers at the PEAR place?"

Greg nodded. "I don't want to get entangled with anyone else having access to our private world. Too much is at stake."

"But you are having the experiences they predicted." Sharon looked deeply into his eyes. "And I can tell they bother you."

Greg looked down at the piece of paper in front of him. "Just before I left the office I suddenly had an impulse to write something. Sharon, I never talk like this stuff sounds." He handed her the paper.

Sharon looked at the scribbling for a moment. "Hard to make out your handwriting, but I'll try." She blinked several times. "You wrote this?"

He nodded his head.

"Who will pity you, O Jerusalem," Sharon read aloud. "Or who will bemoan you?"

"Sharon, I never talk like *that*. Sounds like the Bible, and we both know that I'm way behind on reading what's in that book. See what I mean? You really don't want to know anymore about what's going on."

"Dad!" Sharon stopped and swallowed hard. "Last week I heard almost exactly those same words at the Messianic Conference in a church. They were from the book of Revelation!"

CHAPTER 14

Thursday morning felt better than Wednesday night. At least Sharon wasn't miffed anymore. Even better, a new degree of understanding had emerged. Greg came into his office in a good mood. October was just a couple of days away.

Nancy had his long expected cup of coffee waiting in the center of the desk with the unopened mail. Things were looking good. Greg hung his coat in the side closet and prepared to dig in. Sometime during the morning he had to get a crew out to the house to make sure nothing was bugged. Explaining that effort would prove interesting.

"Sorry to interrupt you." Nancy appeared in the doorway.

"Interrupt? Hey, anyone whose coffee beats Starbucks can't be an interruption."

"You're not going to be a happy camper." Nancy sat down opposite Greg. "You ordered acquisition of all previous studies on the New Madrid fault two days ago. Right?"

"Right."

"The most comprehensive information is with the Alcohol, Tobacco, and Firearms people.

"Sure."

"Moments ago a memo was faxed from Joe Hatch, their agency head. After you cut through the *if*s and *and*s, the bottom line is they're not releasing anything to us."

Greg felt his chest sag. "I knew everything was going too well this morning."

"The guy sounds like a jerk."

"Probably is." Greg sipped the coffee. "The point is that he wants one of his people in on the study. If I say, 'Come on over,' the material will mysteriously arrive with their representative. That's how the game is played."

"What should I do?"

"Let me think about it for a while." He nodded toward the door. "Thanks for letting me know at once."

Nancy smiled politely and left quickly.

Greg pounded the desk. *Just what I need. The more people we get in on this thing, the greater the chances are for the study to be compromised.* He shook his head and leaned back in the chair.

"Probably no way around it," he muttered to himself. "Call ATF and invite them to the party."

The phone rang. "Yes."

"Sorry to bother you again so soon," Nancy said. "Allan Jones just rang for you to come up right now."

"Oh, great!" Greg thumped the top of his desk again. "Once things start downhill, it's a slide. Tell Jones I'm on my way upstairs." He hung up and reached for his coat.

Five minutes later Greg walked into the NSA director's office. A tall heavyset man sat across from Jones, talking and poking at him with his index finger. His receding hairline and high forehead gave him an aristocratic European appearance. Sagging jowls and a large stomach added to his portly dimension. Greg nodded pleasantly and waited for Jones to acknowledge him.

"Greg! Thanks for coming at once." Jones stood up. "I have someone I want you to meet." He pointed to the man in the chair. "This is Helmut Haussman, special assistant to the president."

Haussman stood and offered a large fleshy hand. "Glad to meet you, Mr. Parker," he said with a slight accent. "My pleasure."

Greg shook his hand warmly. "Nice to meet you."

"I inquired about *your* questions concerning the initiation of the New Madrid fault study, and Mr. Haussman was sent over."

Haussman smiled at Greg but with a condescending smirk.

"Helmut's specialty has been foreign affairs," Jones rambled. "He is originally from Germany and an expert on the internal affairs of our German friends. However, he is our contact man on this assignment."

"Not quite," Haussman corrected the director. "I am *in charge*," he dictated. Rising to his full height, he took on a commanding presence. "This matter is to be discussed with no one, and all inquiries must come through me. I am here today because you are already asking more than is necessary for you to know."

Greg looked at Allan. The director's mouth was slightly ajar.

"Yes, I am the president's liaison, but you are to consider me his eyes and ears." Haussman put his hands behind his back and leaned forward like a teacher addressing pupils. "You are not to acknowledge your relationship with me to anyone. Understood?"

Allan Jones's eyes narrowed. "Isn't it a bit unusual to evoke such a restricted context this early in a projected study?"

"The proposal is unusual," Haussman shot back. "Top secret projects require the highest level of clearance. You know that."

"I'm not sure I understand," Jones puzzled.

"I have total and direct oversight on this project," Haussman bore down. "All appointees to the investigatory team will require my direct approval. I have complete control and will reject anyone who does not meet our specifications."

Greg stared in disbelief.

"You are superseding my office?" Jones sounded incredulous.

"Absolutely," Haussman answered defiantly. "The president has given me total authority. I expect you to follow my directives without question."

Greg watched the director's face. No one ever talked to Jones like Haussman had. Behind Jones's frozen countenance, Greg could see anger, controlled but seething rage. Jones clenched his right fist and turned away.

"Any other questions, gentlemen?" Haussman looked back and forth between the two NSA employees.

Greg shook his head. Jones didn't move.

"Thank you." Haussman smiled disdainfully and jutted his chin out. He hoisted his large frame out of the chair, turned on his heel, and marched out of the room.

Allan shut the door behind Hausmann and returned to his desk. He sat down, placed his hands on the top, and silently stared into space. Greg sat down across from him and waited.

After several minutes, Jones spoke. "I presume we have heard a directive from the White House and have no choice but to comply fully. My offices have been preempted, but I would request a memo on all communications with Mr. Haussman." He looked away.

"Allan," Greg began quietly, "I don't know what's going on, but we've always leveled with each other. What in the world is happening?"

Jones looked up slowly. "I think we have no choice but to keep all conversations on a professional level. Thank you for your sensitivity."

Greg stared in consternation. After a few moments, he shook his head and answered. "Look, I wouldn't have gotten into this thing without your urging. Your friendship goes with the deal. I don't want to be sent down the river in a boat by myself."

"I can say no more," Jones sounded uncharacteristically distant. "Thank you for coming." He stood and gestured toward the door.

Greg backed out, watching Allan's face. The director would not make eye contact. "I'll be in touch."

For several moments, Greg stood outside the director's office. Then he started a long, slow walk back to his office. Greg said nothing when he walked past Nancy. He closed his door and leaned against it. "What is going on, and *who* in the world is this Haussman?"

• • •

Once again the NSA roller coaster careened down the tracks. What had begun as a morning of promise had become another day of chaos. Mary Morgan wasn't in her office, so there was no guidance from the only front that might be of significant help. Haussman's dictatorial attitude made it dangerous to push beyond Mary. Things were not good.

By mid-morning, Greg had talked with Hatch in the ATF offices. The promise of inclusion brought the hint that the ATF's comprehensive information on the New Madrid fault might yet be available after some searching. Greg knew it would be.

No matter what he did, Greg returned again and again to the abrasive confrontation with Helmut Haussman. He had not seen such a difficult exercise of authority in years. Maybe the man was somebody big with a nefarious purpose, or maybe the guy was nothing but a small-time power broker with a king-size ego over-inflated from too much contact with the White House. Hard to think clearly about politicians. Apart from the issues, Haussman had the sensitivity of a gorilla.

Greg leaned back in his chair and thought long and hard on his dilemma of how to proceed with this stern German at the helm. His eyes settled on Sharon's picture, staring up at him with those big brown eyes, searching his face, wanting something he couldn't quite define. The picture seemed to pose a question he couldn't understand.

He picked up the picture and looked at his daughter, always striking, lovely with a hint of defiance lurking just below the surface. Why had she always been so headstrong?

His wife always had the answer. Alice would say, "Go easy on the girl, Greg. Trouble is, you're both too much alike. What do *you* do when people push you?"

Alice's old familiar question echoed around the room like a voice in a canyon. *What do you do when people push you?* Sure. Just as this Haussman character leaned too hard, his own endless demands had molded and shaped his daughter's personality.

Insights bubbled up. One of the reasons Sharon probably had not married was her resistance to any man leaning on her. He remembered how difficult she would quickly become when he had tried to help her with piano lessons. The things he said seemed obvious enough and didn't leave cause for belligerence, but they always incited anger in Sharon. Greg shuddered. Maybe his best intentions ended in disaster so often because of a similarly high-handed approach. Had he been nothing more than a Haussman strutting around like Mussolini in his own family? Although Alice was always kind about what she said, maybe, just maybe, that was her message when she asked ever so gently, "What do you do when people lean on you, Greg?"

CHAPTER 15

October in Houston, Texas, still felt hot, humid, and sticky. Business at NASA headquarters hummed along at a fever pitch, anticipating the launching of a new satellite from Cape Kennedy in two days. Greg Parker's NSA fax was picked up in the director's office and forwarded on to Dr. Jack Forbes, NASA scientist in charge of global mapping. Forbes knew Parker's name and work but had never met him. Forbes's Ph.D. dissertation on the continental drift theory established his own reputation, even though he was still a young man and many of his ideas were controversial. After a quick scan of the NSA request, Forbes tossed the memo in the pile he referenced only when he had time on his hands. Yesterday's urgent request for an 8:30 A.M. conference with Malcolm Cable was far more pressing.

Ten minutes later Forbes entered the conference room on the fourth floor. Two officials were present. Charts cluttered the long walnut tabletop. The scientists' intense conversation kept them from noticing his arrival.

"Ahem," Forbes cleared his voice.

"Jack!" Malcolm Cable looked up. "Thanks for coming over." The white-haired expert gestured for him to come closer. "I think you've heard of Dr. Randolph Worthington, Oxford scholar in residence with us. He's England's best."

"My pleasure." Forbes offered his hand. Even though he was a good thirty years younger than both scientists, Jack Forbes had already earned his stripes at NASA. "I am honored to be working with you, sir."

Randolph Worthington smiled politely. "I say, old man, I think we have a discovery here to give you something new to think about." He pointed at the maps. "Your colleague Cable is quite a clever man."

"Jack, you're going to be very encouraged by what I've found." The older man straightened up and rubbed his back. "A lot of people scoffed at one of those ideas you put forth in your dissertation, but I always thought you were on to something significant. Just didn't say much about it to you."

Forbes frowned. "I don't think I'm following you guys."

"I'm talking about global warming and the subsequent effect on continental stability." Cable winked. "We've still got people around here who think you're nuts."

Jack blushed. "The whole thing's been the source of quite a bit of embarrassment. I picked up the name 'The Alarmist' over this idea."

"Ah, but not to us, mate." Worthington slapped him on the back. "People at Oxford took note, Forbes. We've been paying attention to your theory."

Forbes ran his hands nervously through his hair. "The whole theory turned out to be too controversial. I didn't have any idea that anybody anywhere really paid serious attention to me."

Malcolm Cable tossed a file filled with computer data toward Forbes. "That's the last batch of material the satellite sent in. We've confirmed that the polar ice caps are now melting at an uneven rate. Global warming is already affecting the normal winter cycles. Everyone can tell that the seasons have shifted."

"Yes?"

"We've just started understanding the implications of what is going on," Worthington explained. "But we can prove that the

North Pole is losing ice while the South Pole is gaining mass at an alarming rate."

"You're kidding!" Jack's mouth dropped. "That's exactly what I postulated could happen as a result of global warming. It can be demonstrated?" His eyes widened. "I knew it." He stopped, swallowed hard, and added, "Unfortunately."

"Now, old man," Worthington continued, "here's the new twist that we've discovered in the past few months and confirmed in the last few days. These changes in ice mass are beginning to affect the earth's wobble. Cable and his people have fairly well nailed this one down."

Malcom Cable shook his head. "Jack, my staff believes the wobble has increased as much as seven to ten degrees. What do you think of them apples?"

Dr. Forbes eased down into the chair at the end of the table. "Are you sure?"

Both men nodded.

"You both know what I'm about to say." Forbes looked back and forth between the two men. "The implications point to major instability in the earth's geological system. The continental bedrock plates cannot help but be affected. We're looking at increased frequency of earthquakes."

"We thought you'd say that," Cable answered. "I guess our big question is, what can we expect and when? Just how wild could things get?"

"I think we're already there and don't realize it." Forbes reached into his briefcase. "I just received a copy of a report from the National Oceanic and Atmospheric Administration in the U.S. Department of Commerce." He thumbed through the thick document. "You'll find their recent summary of earthquake database statistics very interesting."

"What does it say?" Worthington peered over the table.

"The study is divided into nineteen periods. You'll note that from 1929 to 1948, the world averaged ninety-two quakes per year." Jack pulled a bar graph out of the pages and laid it before the other two men. "In the next two decades ending in 1967, there were 1,726 quakes each year. Gives you something to think about."

"Let me see that," Cable inched forward.

"Then, look at how things had progressed to 1986," Forbes continued. "The average had gone up to 6,579 a year. In the short period ending in 1994, the rate increased to 15,539 earthquakes a year. Their projections into the year 2005 keep climbing. Look at this figure. The impact of the Industrial Age on the climate is overwhelming. By 2205, they anticipate 124,311,000 quakes a year!"

For a moment Forbes stared at the projections and thought about the ever-increasing number of people who would be caught unaware and crushed. He could see faces of women and children disappearing into the earth and shuddered.

"Staggering!" Worthington gasped. "Alarming!"

"As always, Jack, you're ahead of us," Cable said. "How do you collate the earthquake data with our findings on earth wobble?"

Forbes's thoughts were still locked on the vast numbers who would die in the earthquakes. He silently shook his head.

"Jack, you hear me?"

Forbes continued to shake his head. "You've probably explained why earthquakes are on the increase. Look, if your observations are accurate, we are really in big trouble. Not only can I *not* predict earthquake frequency; all current geological data becomes suspect. All our charts and projections are skewed by these findings."

"You're the expert," Cable replied. "If you don't have the answer, no one does. Doesn't lack of certainty put us in considerable jeopardy?"

"No question about it," Forbes explained. "We'd best start a new round of satellite inquiries. The fate of the United States may well depend on our accuracy."

The Englishman laughed. "I told you Cable, old boy. Forbes just said exactly what I predicted. We're onto something very big."

Malcolm Cable rubbed his chin and pursed his lips. "But we really can't tell anyone." He slipped down into the chair. "The politicians would never allow us to let this cat out of the bag. People would panic. No telling what sort of chaos might follow."

"We can't simply sit on the possibilities!" Worthington protested. "After all, we do have responsibilities!"

"He's right," Forbes joined in. "This data can't be allowed to disappear in some filing cabinet until a disaster strikes."

"I know, I know." Cable sounded as if he were brushing the objections aside. "But everything we do is classified until the boys upstairs release it. That's the bind we're always in."

"Obviously we can't hold a press conference and start a riot over a theory," Forbes countered. "Nevertheless, we must make sure the results of your findings end up in responsible hands. Personally, I want confirmation from other sources that my ideas are valid."

"Got to be cautious." Cable shook his head. "Our people don't want to get crossways with Congress or the opinion polls. Let me think about it."

"Okay," Forbes countered, "but I need a complete picture of what you've found. How soon can you put the results into a study?"

"Probably take us a couple of days," Worthington interjected.

"I can guarantee that your conclusions will get my immediate attention," Forbes said. "We're talking dramatic implications."

"Thanks, Jack," Cable said. "We'll get right on the project immediately."

"Glad to have met you, Dr. Worthington." Forbes and the Englishman shook hands.

"Oh, but the pleasure is all mine." Worthington returned the compliment.

Quickly returning to his office, Forbes stopped by the water fountain and took a long drink. *Cable is right. Our PR office and the politicos will shut this thing down. Years could pass before they release the data. I can't let it happen. Too much is at stake.*

He hurried upstairs lost in thought. Just as he approached his office, one of the staff stopped him.

"Hey, Jack. I got a copy of this request from Parker at NSA for an update on the possibilities of movement in the bedrock plates affecting the northern hemisphere. What do you want me to send?"

"What?" Forbes looked blankly at the man. "What did you say?"

"Didn't you see this thing?" The young man held up a copy. "I thought it came to your office first thing this morning."

Forbes read the fax quickly. "Yes. Yes, this request did come through . . ."

"What do we send?"

"Nothing . . . for the moment." He started walking backward. "Let me give it some thought. I'll be back with you by the end of the day. Thanks."

The staffer shrugged and walked away. "Whatever you say."

Forbes shut the door behind him. *Exactly what we need. I can ask the help of the U. S. Geological Survey and these people at the NSA without getting into NASA's red tape. Perfect solution.*

He sat down at his desk and picked up the small Dictaphone to start a memo, then paused. "I suppose I ought to alert the

Nothing was more welcome in Washington than the end of the week, even though the NSA virtually never shut down. Greg Parker considered Friday a prelude to working at home on the weekends. A pile of responses to his initial memorandums stared up at him from his desk. He stared at the NASA response. Jack Forbes's answer jarred Greg and left him feeling unsettled.

Suspicion and contention hung in the office like fog over an airport. The night before Greg hadn't slept well, tossing, turning, and worrying about the conversation in the director's office with Helmut Haussman, on loan from the Gestapo. Greg was certain that he should not try to talk with Allan again. Could be crossing boundaries. Nothing fit. Greg didn't like the atmosphere the new project was creating. Mary Morgan was his only hopeful link.

More in resignation than enthusiasm, Greg reached for the carefully stacked pile, waiting as always on the left-hand side of his desk. Nancy, the ever-efficient secretary, had the knack for making paper-shuffling look like an art. Thumbing through the stack, he recognized that many government agencies had responded affirmatively to his requests. The team was quickly taking shape, unless this Haussman character didn't approve.

Greg's personal fax abruptly growled like an inanimate beast coming to life behind him. Generally no one used this number unless the information was only for his eyes. Greg turned in his chair and looked at the sputtering machine on the credenza. Mary Morgan was advising him that a top-secret communiqué was to follow her memo.

Pushing the papers aside, Greg swung around in his chair and watched Mary's fax climb out of the machine. The Department of Energy report described twelve major pipelines converging in the New Madrid area. Their loss would result in the disappearance of 92 percent of all natural gas in every state east of the Mississippi River. The long-term economic impact on the nation would be catastrophic. As well as factories shutting down, homes and hospitals would be without heat. Mary wanted him to understand why the pipeline people were very concerned with his discovery of what an earthquake would do.

Shaking his head, Greg read the next impact statement from the Department of Transportation. The loss of rail and motor vehicle bridges from St. Louis to Vicksburg, Mississippi, would have disastrous results on the movement of necessary goods across the country. At least seven thousand tractor-trailer trucks loaded with food cross the Memphis Bridge every day to keep a two-day supply of food in American grocery stores. Within seventy-two hours of an earthquake, major American cities would experience food shortages. In fourteen days, businesses would start to fail.

Greg took a deep breath as he read on. Since the major insurance companies in America had overinsured homes in the New Madrid area, an earthquake in this area would cause the insurance companies to sell off large blocks of stocks to meet their financial obligations. The sell-off, in turn, would have dramatic effects on the stock market. Furthermore, the insurance companies would not have the necessary assets to insure new homes or automobiles. The housing and automotive industries would collapse.

Greg looked out of the window at the cars filling the streets, bunching up at the stoplights. Masses of people hurried across when the lights changed. Everything appeared orderly, planned, deceptively predictable. The lights turned green. Cars sped away. But what if all those people were so frightened that they ignored the rules?

He read the rest of the letter. It said that within ninety days, the United States would be in chaos because the government would quickly become bankrupt. Nodding his head slowly, Greg looked at the communiqué again. "Yep, you got the picture. We're talking real disaster."

Placing the fax on the right side of his desk, he returned to the rest of the memos. Each one added a comment or a directive for the project. The reading was slow and boring.

Thirty minutes later his phone rang. "Yes," he answered in his usual brusque manner. "Greg," Mary Morgan began softly, "did you get my fax?"

"Indeed! Highly disturbing. Sounds like a replay of Argentina, but on a much larger scale."

"How could the entire government wait so long to pay attention to what you've been trying to tell us forever?" her voice sounded urgent but pleasing. "This thing is taking on an avalanche effect. The longer we look at the data, the worse the picture gets!"

"Not a pretty scene." He paused, searching for the right words. "I don't want to put you in the middle of anything, but let me just tell you that if the American government goes bankrupt, seventy million baby boomers will lose their retirement savings and end up homeless. We're looking at a problem of incredible magnitude."

"Greg, I'm here for you. You know that's a fact, so simply shoot straight."

"Allan Jones has become quite distant." He rolled his tongue around inside his mouth. "I've never seen him act like this before. Know what I mean?"

For several moments Mary didn't answer. "Yes," she said slowly, "I've noticed this project is being approached differently." Her usual politically correct way of responding.

"Ever hear of a politico named Helmut Haussman? Has Jones spoken of him?"

"No. No, the name doesn't ring a bell."

"I see," Greg answered in his politically correct voice.

"Why?"

"Just checking. I'm not sure yet, myself. Now about this report you just faxed . . ."

"Oh, I've got more information for you," Mary said. "I've been working on this angle all week and turned up an important young man who could be of significant help. Have you heard of Al Smith, a recent acquisition the USGS hired from the Colorado School of Mines?"

"So many personnel come and go that I only keep up with the people near the top. The name doesn't ring a bell."

"I had an aide working on your project, and he turned up Smith. I'd like to have him bring his research up to our conference room and have you listen to his story. Can you make it in, say, fifteen minutes?"

"I'll be there. Thanks for all your efforts."

"Wouldn't do a fraction less."

Greg picked up the National Gas Pipeline letter and read it again. The loss of 92 percent of the natural gas east of the Mississippi would be economically disastrous. These facts ought to give Herr Haussman something to chew on. He put the letter back on the right side of his desk.

• • •

When Greg entered the conference room, Mary was looking over the shoulder of a young man sitting before a pile of maps and charts. With close-cropped hair and thin horn-rimmed glasses, Smith looked more like a sophomore in college than a professional geologist.

"Greg." She brightened. "Glad you're here." She extended her palm. Instead of a shake she squeezed his hand. "You okay this morning?"

"In this business, every day's a new one. Never know when the surprise of the day is going to hit you." He forced a smile.

"You look a little tired. Not pushing yourself too hard again?"

He winked. "Me? *Moi*? Of course not."

"Be careful." Mary frowned and turned toward the young man. "I want you to meet Al Smith. He came to the USGS about nine months ago."

"Dr. Parker!" Smith leaped to his feet. "I've heard so much about you. Didn't expect to ever meet you in person." He offered his hand. The V-neck sweater and open neck shirt added to the youthful appearance.

"Thank you." Greg smiled thinly and shook hands.

"The Colorado School of Mines used your studies on earthquakes as one of our textbooks. In fact, a set of your projections started me working on the history of the New Madrid fault. I wrote a couple of papers that got published in my senior year."

"That's how we found out about Al's work," Mary added. "My aide read his report."

"Well, good. What do you have?" Greg cut to the chase.

"I was fascinated by your work on the 1811 quake along the New Madrid fault. When I read that the terrain was so violently affected that the Mississippi River moved more than an entire mile, I was absolutely fascinated. The part about the Mississippi flowing north for a while amazed me. I wanted to know everything I could about what happened."

Greg broke into a broad grin. "That's exactly how the whole episode hit me the first time I looked at the evidence. Extraordinary story."

"I worked on various dimensions of the geologic features of the area for some time." Smith pointed to the maps in front of him. "Eventually I wrote the journal report that Ms. Morgan called me about yesterday." He held up a copy.

"What caught our attention was one of the facts Al has in his study," Mary added. "He found that the area stayed active for more than a year with nearly two hundred moderate quakes following the initial event."

"The whole area must have turned into a bowl of Jell-O," Smith beamed. "I bet any of the settlers left in the area were running for their lives."

"More than two hundred quakes?" Greg asked again.

"Yeah!" Al shook his head. "Then I made some projections. If this thing ever hit again, I believe the same effect would follow but be much worse this time. It'd be impossible to repair the damage done to the infrastructure." He pulled the top map forward and ran his finger down the Mississippi basin. "Of course, no one could predict such a thing with absolute certainty. As a matter of fact, the uncertainty would be the real issue." The young man peered down at the maps. "Only thing that's for sure is that the middle of the United States would be as unstable as a bunch of politicians running for reelection." He sounded like a college boy making the fall football projections. "Yes, sir! It would be shake-and-bake time."

Greg and Mary looked at each other.

"The United States as we know it would be gone forever. The entire country would be paralyzed," Mary concluded, "for a long time. Executive Order 12656 might be invoked, and the Constitution could become null and void. We would go from being the greatest democracy the world has ever known to a police state almost overnight."

· · ·

The streetlights had been on for several hours when Greg pulled into the driveway. One glance at the clock on the dashboard reminded him Sharon would not be a happy camper. The porch light wasn't on, and that wasn't a good sign. He braced himself for the inevitable lecture about coming home at 8:00 at night and punched the clicker on the garage door.

Greg opened the back door and walked into the landing between the garage and the kitchen. The washing machine and dryer were cold. No one was in the kitchen. Things were far too quiet.

"Sharon?" he called. Nothing. "Sharon!" Greg shouted.

"In here," a quiet soft voice called from the living room.

Greg hurried down the hall. A light from the top of the stairs threw shadows across the dark room. A small shape huddled near the front window, peering out behind the drapes.

"Sharon?" Greg inched forward. "What's going on?"

"Stay there," Sharon warned. "Don't get near the window where you can be seen."

Greg rubbed his mouth nervously. "Are you okay?"

"Yes," Sharon sounded tentative. "I'm not hurt or anything."

"Then what in heaven's name are you doing on the floor in the dark peeking out the window?"

"There's a car half a block down the street; it's been there for hours." She closed the curtain and turned around. "Dad, our house is under surveillance."

CHAPTER 17

Greg glanced at the clock beside his bed. Friday night.
Shouldn't stay up late. 11:30. The doctors said don't push your
luck. Get plenty of sleep. Watching a TV movie would run past
1:00. He reached for the light switch.

• • •

At that moment lights were going on in the high-rise glass
tower in the center of Belgium's financial district. Functionaries of
the Gent Institute were already arriving at their offices in Brussels'
banking center to start preparations for an important executive
meeting beginning in a few hours. Founded by the European
magnet and industrial developer Sandor Trento, the Institute regularly produced position papers on economic and political issues
facing Europe. The public and the press had no access to these
highly detailed and carefully researched studies.

Over the years, the Institute's directors had been carefully cul-
tivated and selected from European heads of state, wealthy aristocratic families, corporate CEOs, and international power brokers.
Some of the most opulent men in Europe secretly maintained
seats on the board. Jews or any representatives of the state of Israel
were forbidden entry. Yvonne Galla, the exception to the male
club, remained the largest stockholder and the brains behind one
of France's major banks.

Even though the Gent Institute kept a low profile, it regularly contributed ideas and suggestions to the United Nations, NATO, and meetings of the European Union executives. When lobbying their interests, the Institute used other entities as screens, such as The European Center for Economic Studies and the International Economic Cartel, their most commonly used covers.

Although few people in the United States would ever hear of Gent, the Institute's positions usually became the national policy of the world's leading economic powers. *No* was an unacceptable word in the thickly carpeted halls of Brussels' most luxurious commercial center.

A small, thin secretary hurried passed the fashionable shops on Brussels' main boulevard and quickly entered the ultramodern chrome and glass skyscraper through the bronze front doors. Gent Institute demanded absolute security verification, so she was required to give a thumbprint as well as present a coded ID to the guards.

Once inside and on the third floor, the secretary greeted several other secretaries, then hurried to get graphs, papers, and charts to take to the large executive conference room on the fifteenth floor, which she was not allowed to enter. Other employees with higher security clearance would set the order of business and the reports on the long walnut table surrounded by gigantic glass windows overlooking the whole city.

Limousines began arriving around 8:45, depositing the executives at a special entrance under the building where the elevators whisked them up to the fifteenth floor. No one would see them come or go. Employees had no idea of their identity. Wearing Italian silk, the finest Scottish wool, or French suits and Bruno Magli quality shoes, the powerful greeted each other like old cronies on a golf course. Members of the board of directors had the steely cold look of executives expecting to win every throw of the dice. The elite often referred to themselves as "the Dutch Masters" and considered their organization to be the true heir to the former days of European greatness when the Low Countries controlled the economy of the world.

"Whatever happened on *der* ocean front strip you were negotiating in downtown Hong Kong?" a heavyset German asked the Frenchman sitting next to him at the long table.

The Frenchman laughed. "Like you didn't know, *monsieur.* Of course, we had to pay off the Chinese Communists under the table to close the deal."

"And how much did they clip you for?" The German raised his bushy eyebrows and pursed his fat lips.

"Cost us an additional five million."

The German cursed. "*Nein!* If it cost you a penny, it cost you twice that much. You don't fool me."

"But look what we control in Hong Kong."

"*Ja. Ja.*" The German shrugged. "And look at the hooks you've got in the Chinese government. Closing such a deal is worth dancing to the tune of the boys in Beijing."

"All in a day's work," the Frenchman answered noncommittally.

Yvonne Galla walked in carrying an eel-skin briefcase and wearing a white cashmere, single-breasted jacket with a shawl collar and cutaway front fastened at the waist with a single matte silver-toned metal button. With sunglasses and a wrap-around silk head scarf, her appearance was crisp, cool, and yet professional. She nodded perfunctorily at the men around her, anticipating they would follow her stunning figure across the room. After all, she had the best body money could buy. The directors parted in front of her as if she were Moses crossing the Red Sea. She smiled and took her place at the table with a commanding presence.

On the other side of the table, an Italian talked with the Englishman seated next to him. "Will you join the European Union?" he asked bluntly. "The coalition needs England."

"We're putting a considerable amount of pressure on Parliament," the Brit answered with no show of emotion. "The problem is with the people. The blokes want England to stand alone. Currently, the polls are against us."

"Then what will you do?" The Italian crossed his arms over his chest. "You going to leave it to the locals to decide the future?"

"We're close to owning the Tories," he answered. "When the right moment arrives, we'll be ready to strike."

"Hmm," the Italian grunted. "I'll be watching. In the meantime, I want to talk with you privately about getting into the action on this Canary Walk operation that's still open. You know, the one the Prince of Wales is pushing."

The Englishman nodded his head slowly and raised an eyebrow.

Within a few minutes a dozen more directors came through the doors, carrying materials offered at the door by men in tuxedos. Similarly dressed butlers moved among the men, offering champagne and premium cigars. Cordiality seemed to be the order of the day.

Yvonne Galla snapped her fingers, and one of the butlers offered her the tray. Shunning the champagne, she picked up a cigar. The servant immediately offered her a light. She blew a billowy cloud of smoke across the table and smiled at the stoic waiter.

At precisely 9:00 A.M., the plain unmarked door at the far end of the room opened, and the impeccably dressed Baron Wilhelm Leestma walked briskly into the room, taking his position at the head of the table. He wore a dark blue Armani suit. The handkerchief in the breast pocket matched his silk tie, adding a final touch of elegance. Although he said nothing, the remaining directors quickly took their seats, and the small talk faded away.

"Good morning, my friends," the baron began in English. "I appreciate your coming at this early hour. Unfortunately, we have many things to cover today and need the extra time. Let us turn immediately to our order of business."

The baron ran down the printed agenda, commenting on various items, explaining the importance of each issue, clearly taking control of the meeting. Tall and thin, with brilliant white hair, Wilhelm Leestma might have stepped out of a Rembrandt painting of Dutch Burgers, the sixteenth-century masters of commerce and shipping. High cheekbones and a narrow thin nose gave his face the sculptured look of an aristocrat. Bushy white eyebrows made his sky-blue eyes seem particularly piercing. His air of regal demeanor made him appear more condescending than noble. Leestma spoke with the inflection of one schooled in the finest European academic institutions, often switching back and forth between English, German, and French with some explanations in Dutch. Yet, his tone was cold, hard, and precise like the edge of a carving knife.

"The first item of business is to examine some aspects of our quest to return Europe to world dominance and gain control of global oil resources," the baron spoke with deliberate precision. "Each of us is well aware of the location of international oil reserves." He pushed a button and a wall panel opened, exposing a large white screen. A moment later a multicolored picture of the world indicating major oil reserves rolled up on the white shield. "Each of us has thoroughly digested these facts. The pressing question is how to establish our capacity to gain complete control of the majority of these fields. Let us receive the report of our representative in the Middle East, Mr. Asim Abu Bakr."

A short dark Arab with a pencil-thin moustache stood at the opposite end of the table. "Good morning, gentlemen," he spoke with a distinct Oxford accent. "I am pleased to report that matters are progressing nicely. As you are aware, no one has uncovered any clues indicating responsibility for the bombing of Haram es-Sharif. Even though over forty-five days have passed, experts from across the world have not been able to find one significant lead on the source of the detonation that destroyed the area. The name of the Gent Institute was not even raised." He paused and looked around the room with a self-satisfied smile. "As the controversy rages, each day of turmoil moves us closer to our objective of manipulating the entire flow of Arab oil into our hands. As the potential for a stable Arab Union grows, we are increasingly positioned to direct the political interest of this possible federation toward Europe. As always, no one has the slightest idea that the Gent Institute is the dominant force." Abu Bakr sat down.

"Our friend has done well," the baron commented. "His work in developing and executing the bombing plot is outstanding." Leestma clapped and the directors followed suit. "And what has become of our terrorist friends?"

"They seem to have disappeared off the face of the earth." Abu Bakr's eyes widened in mock consternation, and he sounded as if he had no idea what had occurred. Several directors laughed.

"As you know, our primary target of concern remains the destruction of the economic capacity of the United States of America," the baron continued. "Our only hope for total and final success in Europe is their demise. This morning Dr. Hans Gerhard is presenting an analysis, speaking on behalf of the

Bonn government." He pointed to the middle of the table. "Dr. Gerhard."

The thick, heavyset German arose slowly from his seat and opened a thick file. Considerably younger than most of the men around the table, Hans Gerhard's heavy sagging jowls gave him a deceptively older appearance than his forty-five years.

Gerhard began with a lengthy description of how the current American scene had developed. Abruptly, the German changed course. "Our most recent analysis of all significant economic data now indicates that the Americans are completely vulnerable because their politicians and government bureaucrats steadfastly refuse to recognize their own economic realities. Let me demonstrate." Gerhard pushed a button on the table and a new set of graphs appeared on the wall screen.

The German picked up a laser pointer and highlighted his own data. "You will observe that in the early 1960s the United States controlled 65 percent of global wealth with only 5 percent of the world's population. An enviable figure."

A murmur of appreciation rippled around the table.

"By 1990, the country was borrowing 65 percent of the world's available moneys but still had only 5 percent of global population," Gerhard continued. "I could give you many facts and statistics, but the bottom line is simple. America has become a service nation with total dependence on foreign imports and funds." He cleared his throat and waited a moment. "We believe they no longer have the means or the will power to overcome the effects of a devastating depression. The time to strike is now!" He allowed the dramatic impact to settle, then he sat down.

"And what are we going to do?" Yvonne Galla interjected, tapping her cigar against the crystal ashtray in front of her.

"Herr Gerhardt has just told you that now is the time to strike," the baron answered, "and we are positioned to do so in the immediate future."

One of the board of directors at the back clapped. Another followed. The room quickly filled with a roar of enthusiastic applause.

"How?" Galla pursued the baron defiantly.

"That, my friend," the baron paused and smiled condescendingly at the woman, "is such a sensitive secret, it is not shared *even* around this table."

CHAPTER 18

Sharon's weekend hadn't been great. She had watched her father work through most of Saturday and stare at football games all day Sunday. Not that he hadn't tried hard to please her; still, Dad lived mostly in his own world. Hard to touch, difficult to open up, like a firmly sealed clam clamped on the bottom of the ocean.

On a whim, Sharon went to services at Faith Community Church where she had heard Rabbi Palenski, the messianic Jew, speak. Seemed like a good way to spend the morning and pick up a few details for the story she was still working on. The experience proved unexpectedly pleasant and thought provoking. The minister talked about finding peace in the midst of the storm and explored the implications of the story of the twelve apostles getting caught in a sudden tempest on the Lake of Galilee. His thoughts proved startlingly appropriate.

Not far from the church, a park with a large lake seemed like a good place to stop. Strolling past rose bushes that hovered on the edge of fall, Sharon sat down at a stone picnic table and thought about the years behind her. The family had always gone to church and prayed at meals. No one could have doubted they were Christians.

When she was eight years old, her all-time favorite cat, Buffy, got hit by a car and died in her arms. Sharon had thought she might die too. Dad and Mom dug a special place in the flower bed and even had a little funeral for Buffy. She cried, prayed, and put flowers on Buffy's grave every day for at least a week. And then life went on.

But her mother's death killed something that had always tied the family together. The pain had been so great that they couldn't touch the emotional side of their lives after she was gone. Prayers, Bible reading, and going to church just slipped away. And then Sharon couldn't stand to be around the house anymore, so she just left.

She had needed to be mad at someone, angry enough to run away. Her father had made a perfect target. She decided to just leave and not say where she was going. Suddenly Sharon started crying. She didn't want to think about the past anymore and hurried back to her car.

After lunch alone, Sharon called an old girlfriend. By the time she got home, Greg was already asleep in his chair. Of course, come Monday morning, good ole "go get 'em Greg" was gone before she awoke. The day quickly filled with contacts for several other freelance stories and some research at the library. She returned home on Monday afternoon around 4:30 and walked into an empty house.

Depressing.

Several years earlier Sharon had started reading her stories aloud to hear how they sounded as well as looked on paper. As a result, she developed the habit of talking to herself when trying to work through a problem. The monologues could go on for hours. The empty house flipped her switch.

"Wonder if the bad guys are out today?" She crept across the living room to peek out.

Sharon pulled the curtain back, looking up and down the

street. *No strange cars in sight, but who knows. Dad said his people went over the house with a fine-tooth electronic comb to make sure nothing was bugged.*

"Woo hoo!" She made whirling motions with her index finger high over her head. "Have to make sure my own bedroom isn't being monitored by some creep down at the State Department!"

She wandered across the room and into her father's study. Always packed with volumes, filling floor-to-ceiling bookcases, the small room contained an ornate French Provincial desk that Mother bought and Father hated, a matching chair, and a computer screen in the middle of the desk. The usual messy pile of files sat on the edge of the desk. Everything looked untidy, used, and maddeningly busy. Sort of like Dad.

Sharon eased down in his chair, beginning to feel angry. This seemed to be the only room in the house where he actually lived. Did Greg Parker work to live or live to work? Did it make any difference? Sharon wondered and shook her head.

She'd never thought of her father being involved with any other women but her mother. If he had a mistress, her name would have to be Ms. Work.

"He's never *here*," she said to herself. "Always in gear, he only knows one position . . . drive!" She picked up a pencil and bounced it on the leather-inlaid top of the desk. "The man doesn't even know there is a neutral."

She glanced out of the small office window and noticed a man in a topcoat walking down the street. The stranger seemed to linger, dawdle a bit in front of their house. He looked shabby. Immediately Sharon pushed closer to the window and watched until the man disappeared around the corner. She closed the blinds.

"Great! I'm starting to think street people are spies. Can't even relax in my own home!" She tossed the pencil at the bookcases. "Thanks, Dad! Thanks for the memories."

A photo album stuck out of the middle shelf. Old and dog-eared, the worn green cover had warped with time. "My gosh, I haven't seen that thing in ten years." Sharon immediately reached for it and opened the scrapbook on the desk, thumbing quickly through the pages. "Mom kept this collection up for years. Look at this! My baby pictures, graduations, vacations."

She started at the front, slowly turning the pages, watching herself evolve from a baby into a schoolgirl, then a young woman, remembering a hundred wonderful moments that had slipped from memory. Sharon grinned, giggled, and laughed.

"Oh, wow! Christmas 1973." She bent closer to scrutinize the little girl under the Christmas tree surrounded by a pile of tissue paper and empty boxes.

The joy of little experiences and great times bubbled up, leaped off the page, and captivated her. She studied the pictures of her development carefully. The moment felt almost like she'd dropped into a hole and come out of a time tunnel, emptying into yesterday-land.

Once through the journey of her past, Sharon started again, looking only at her mother's pictures, studying the face, the stance, the eyes, the always happy mother and wife. No matter which picture Sharon turned to, always the smile. Alice Parker, wife and mother, faithful mate, true friend, consummate mother, never looked perplexed or perturbed.

Here they were in the Catskills, up the Hudson River Valley, the place comedians called the Borscht Circuit. All the trees turning red, gold, crimson, a hundred shades of fall. Someone must have taken the picture of the three of them. Mother, father, five-year-old daughter. And then the trip came back into focus. For a reason she'd never known, their family had gone to this quaint little resort that had wonderful cats everywhere. All the flowers in the window boxes were still blooming, the frost not yet devouring them.

Sharon remembered the gray kitten she wanted to take home and couldn't. Her father had carried her piggyback up and down the steep hills when she got tired during their long walks. He helped her catch a fish, a little wiggly bluegill. They cooked it for supper. It was hardly two bites, but she ate it all. Dad could do anything.

Christmas 1977. A picture of her standing next to a shiny new red bike. *Oh, that wonderful bike; it's still stored out in a corner of the garage somewhere.* Dad holding her and the bike up in the snow. Waving. Smiling. Mother had to be taking the picture. That was the year he surprised Mom with the only mink coat she had in her life. She was so happy she cried, and Dad thought he'd done something wrong until Mom buried her face in the dark brown fur and laughed through the tears. On Christmas night she sat by the fireplace with the coat on her lap until the embers burned out. Mom said it was the best Christmas in her entire life.

Easter 1980. Daffodils poking through the snow. Shiny new black shoes. Mom in a new dress. Yes, they *had* gone to church as a family. In fact, they'd gone more often than she really remembered. Church was important to Mother. In her own quiet, unassuming way, she'd always held onto what was really important. Always in the background like the unseen beam that holds up the entire building.

And when she was gone . . . Sharon abruptly closed the photo album and hugged it close to her chest. She pulled her knees up under her chin and made herself into a tight little ball. The memories had turned bittersweet.

And when she was gone . . . Sharon caught her breath . . . the world of vacations, wonderful Christmases and Easters disappeared. Sharon always assumed those days would last forever and then, in a split second, everything vanished. Conversations were over. Sound became silence. Joy changed into pain. No grand finale, only an unfinished symphony.

Like a videotape on fast forward, Sharon experienced in the space of a few moments that awful metamorphosis of innocent childhood trust to adult skepticism and disillusionment. She felt the sensation of years rushing past in a blur and the stark realization of where everything was *really* going.

Sharon could no longer remember what her mother's voice sounded like. Occasionally, she'd find a perfume, discover a certain cosmetic, or locate a skin moisturizer and the smell would come back, the wonderful fragrance of her mother that once lingered on pillows, dresses, handkerchiefs; the voice, though, had been silenced for a long time.

A tear edged down her cheek. Her vision blurred, and tears dampened the edges of the album pages. Sharon fumbled for a tissue and tried not to give ground again to her grief, but she couldn't stop crying.

Somewhere in the following five minutes, her grief shifted, changed, and turned into anger. Why hadn't he stopped her from dying? Dad was supposed to be able to do anything. Was it too much to ask that he take care of the one thing in the whole world that truly mattered? Why had he failed everyone in such a critical task?

But Dad's favorite picture of Mom was staring back at her from the center of the bookcase, the portrait made as a gift for their wedding anniversary, a month before the car wreck. Smile and all, she seemed to look Sharon straight in the eye as if to say one more time, "Child, why in creation do you get yourself so worked up over so little? Leave the man be. He didn't make the world like it is. Don't ya know?"

How many times had she said, "Leave the man be?" The expression was her way of saying, "Get off your father's back. Be nice to the man." Always the referee, Mom had demanded daily reconciliation before the sun went down. Like a seamstress piecing the frayed ends of a torn garment together, Alice had minimized the major disagreements and helped the bickering parties bury the trivial ones.

"Leave the man be" was her way of saying "Don't sweat the small stuff—and it's all small stuff."

Suddenly a new thought slipped in out of nowhere. It had never occurred to Sharon that her mother's death was something over which her father had no control. Of course, he didn't. How could it be otherwise? Yet, like catching fish and climbing steep hills, she had expected him to fix everything . . . always.

And she had been angry for the last two years because he had failed.

"Oh, Dad!" Sharon wailed. "Why couldn't I just 'let you be'? I was so absorbed in my pain that I couldn't see anything beyond my own anguish. And what did you do? You took the only pain pill that's ever helped you, the one labeled 'work.' If you could just go full tilt twenty hours a day, you wouldn't mind those other four empty ones."

The knot welled up in her throat and the tears returned. "Oh, God," she pleaded, "how we miss that woman! How we *all* miss her," she sobbed.

Sharon looked at the picture again. Her mother had never

griped about how hard her father worked. Didn't complain. Their partnership superseded the impositions of late hours and working weekends. Why couldn't *she* be like that? Why hadn't she been more gentle, easygoing, and accepting like her mother?

The face in the picture seemed to say, "Because you are always like your father."

Suddenly Mom's voice was there again. Sharon could hear it. The soft, alto sound was back in her ears. She was speaking just as she had sounded five years ago. Sharon could hear it, remember it. And Alice said gently, "Because you *will always* be like your father."

For a long time Sharon sat in the chair, staring at her mother's picture. Finally, she put the photo album back on the shelf and placed the chair behind the desk. The room looked the same, but the atmosphere had changed. "Let the man be," her mother had said so often. A little late in the game, but perhaps it was time to pay attention.

CHAPTER 19

Before he left for work, Greg watched his daughter sleeping and started to wake her. For a moment, the urge to tell her how much he loved her was almost overpowering, but he didn't. He left Sharon dozing soundly and peacefully. Driving into the capital, he thought about her, how attractive she always was, her way with people, wondering what would be best for her future. Before he knew it, the subway station was just ahead. He parked and started toward the entrance with dogged determination. Another day was beginning.

As Parker hurried up the steps, he thought again about the report that Dr. Jack Forbes from NASA had faxed from Houston. The ever-increasing rate of earthquakes worried Greg. Moreover, Forbes indicated that the earth was increasingly unstable. Maybe no one could predict when a truly big quake would hit.

Greg spent Monday morning, October 2, getting ready for the first complete meeting of the research team. Preparations spilled over into the lunch hour, and his secretary, Nancy, brought in a chef salad. Mary happened to show up about the time Nancy returned and shared what was left of the noon period with Greg. She stayed in the office through the early part of the afternoon, assisting in making sure all the pieces were in place for the team to assemble in the late afternoon.

Greg convened the group in a small auditorium on the first floor of the NSA building. Although he wasn't happy about the large size of the group, he had no other option.

"My secretary brought down a memo that just came in from the White House, affirming your selection of personnel to date." Mary handed the memo to Greg while they both stood outside the auditorium, watching government agents file in. "It's signed by this Haussman character."

Greg took a quick disdainful look. "I'm glad the Gestapo approves of what we're doing." He stuck the note in a file.

"Greg?" Mary gently touched his hand. "I know the pressure you're under, but you're doing well. Call on me if I can help." She squeezed his hand and winked at him.

Greg did a double take. The wink had a strangely meaningful quality. "You've really helped today," he said appreciatively as they walked into the auditorium.

For a moment he surveyed the twenty people sitting near the front. Many old friends. A good number of strangers. Each person an expert. They could be counted on to do an outstanding job. When he walked forward, several people made small gestures of recognition or acknowledgment. He felt more at ease. Mary took a seat on the front row, signaling time to begin. He hurried up the steps and onto the stage.

"I want to begin by expressing my appreciation for each one of you being here this afternoon," Greg began. "We have an important job to accomplish, and you can make it happen."

The group looked attentive. He watched their faces while speaking from his notes, laying out the details of the assignment. One or two looked only mildly interested, but most took notes or listened intently.

"I don't need to tell you what top security clearance means,"

Greg bore down. "We are not about business as usual. The classified nature of this project will become even more obvious as we assemble all the data in the final report. A great deal is at stake."

A number of people nodded their heads solemnly. Enough preliminary work had been done to reveal the seriousness of the problem. He saw a couple of agents reach for files. No question about it. The project was well under way.

"You've already reviewed the initial geologic studies and know the nature of the problem of a major earthquake in mid-America," Greg continued. "This afternoon I want to shift the focus of our inquiry toward economic consequences. Our final report must present a plan the country can follow in order to reestablish national financial security. I asked three members of the team to present short overviews of concern. Would each of you please come to the platform?"

A woman and two men quickly joined him on stage. Greg pushed three chairs together and nodded to the woman to be first as she came up the steps.

"I am Dolores Abrams with the Brookings Institution," the middle-aged woman began, "and I work on economic impact statements." The straight simple lines of her business suit gave her a no-nonsense look. She didn't wear jewelry, and her hair was pulled back in a severe bun on the back of her head. "Following the initial request from the NSA, I began running a survey on how insurance companies would respond to an earthquake of the magnitude presented in the study. I targeted the eight major insurance carriers in the region under consideration. I asked for data on fire, automobiles, property destruction, and their projections on potential loss of income in the region. The survey included both business and home owner losses."

Abrams took off her glasses and glanced at Greg. "Mr.

Chairman, let me assure you that no one in the insurance industry is prepared to face the consequences of such a catastrophic earthquake. The companies were unanimous in their conclusion that they would be forced to sell enormous amounts of their investments and then probably wouldn't be able to maintain solvency. Our projections indicate that such a sell-off would destroy both the bond and stock markets." She paused and looked out over the group. "The domino effect would subsequently dry up insurance on homes and kill the new housing market. In turn, the automobile industry would be in jeopardy because insurance companies would not have the necessary assets to insure new cars. Thank you." She sat down in the chair behind her.

The next two men looked at each other for a moment, and then the one closest to the microphone got up. "Treasury Agent Mark Fowler here." The middle-aged bureaucrat with a crew cut clipped his words with a New England accent. "I was asked to gather projections on the foreign impact of such a catastrophic national disaster." His pinstriped suit countered the casualness of the crew cut and made him look like an executive. "Always glad to be working with the Duke." He turned and saluted Greg.

The audience laughed.

"We are still working on the long-range international consequences but quickly recognized the same severe problems that surfaced in the insurance industry study," Fowler reported. "Foreign markets, drained by American financial losses, would quickly dry up. Europe would be thrown into chaos, and international stability would be in peril." He nodded his head emphatically and looked over the top of his half-rimmed glasses. "We're talking big-time political instabilities here."

Fowler scratched his head and thumbed through his papers. "I believe our study must concentrate on the ripple effect in the Middle East. Many Islamic nations perceive the United States as the enemy, the Great Satan. Weakness in this country would not only be applauded but exploited. If Arab oil-producing nations closed their markets, we would suffer dire consequences." He held up a regional map of the Middle East. "As we are all aware, a United Arab Federation seems to be emerging from the recent bombing in Israel. American weakness would release the Arab block to turn on the state of Israel. However, no one can predict what shape economic warfare might take if aimed at America." Fowler cleared his throat and scratched his head again. "If we weren't involved in this current study, in light of what I've seen in the last week, I'd demand an immediate investigation of how vulnerable we are to an international assault through economic manipulation." He closed the file. "Folks, this thing is terrifying." Fowler sat down.

The last man stood up. Tall and lanky, his light-brown cashmere sport coat gave him a more casual look than the other two representatives. "Ed Adams," he began, "special research agent with Alcohol, Tobacco, and Firearms. ATF does more than chase militia nuts hiding in the woods." He rolled his eyes, signaling a joke. No one laughed.

"Well, ole Ed Adams isn't big on these dire international predictions." He shrugged. "I'd suggest we best pay attention to what can happen within our own borders."

Greg noticed the receptionist from Allan Jones's office enter the back door. She looked around the auditorium as she inched toward the front. The receptionist walked to the front row and whispered in Mary's ear. She immediately got up and followed the woman. Mary paused at the back door, looked at Greg, winked, and then was gone.

Greg could hear Ed Adams hammering away on the possibilities of street violence should food shortages occur, but his mind was on Mary. Something about her was different. A quality he'd not noticed before. The wink did it. He'd always assumed her attentiveness was because she was a hard-working employee, but for the first time he recognized her interest was far more personal. Although he couldn't put his finger on it, she had connected with him in a different way.

"I must predict that rioting will result in gangs controlling the city streets," Adams preached. "Chinese SKS rifles are already flooding this country, and you can bet responsible citizens aren't hiding them in their closets." The ATF agent caught his breath and started in again. "From the preliminary studies I've seen on this earthquake problem, I'd have to say that food and fuel shortages would lead to the breakdown of civil authority. Quite possibly, local police simply couldn't keep law and order."

Adams obviously loved center stage. Greg thought the ATF agent sounded on the verge of spinning out of control. He tried to give Adams his full attention, but he kept thinking about Mary. *Why did she leave?* The director must have called her out. Maybe it had nothing to do with the project. Maybe it had everything to do with it.

"In conclusion," Adams paused and closed his file, "the Watts riots would be a picnic in the park compared to what would immediately follow if this New Madrid thing rips loose." He pursed his lips and nodded his head emphatically. "Thank you." Adams sat down.

Greg watched the faces of the audience. Most of the people sat there with mouths open. Whatever his intent, Adams had rocked them. At least the team would take their assignments more seriously.

"I'd like to respond," Treasury Agent Fowler spoke and held up his hand.

"Sure." Greg offered the podium.

"I'm not comfortable with Mr. Adams minimizing the foreign situation," Fowler began. "The Treasury Department is keenly aware of the impact of international politics on our national currency. If the global setting is not carefully managed, we can reap the whirlwind before anyone grasps the gravity of the situation." He turned slowly toward the ATF agent. "At the same time, I must underscore the potential seriousness of what an economic breakdown could do to the average American city. We are not prepared for disruption on such a massive scale." He turned to Greg. "Am I correct that the epicenter of a New Madrid seismic event could well be around Paducah, Kentucky?"

Greg nodded.

"One doesn't have to draw too many large concentric circles outward from that point to get the picture," Fowler continued. "Even people living in the mountains might well turn to criminal activity to survive." He sat down next to the ATF agent, who looked straight ahead.

Greg returned to the podium. "I want to make sure we are all acquainted with each other. Please take a few moments at the conclusion of this session and meet the people around you. I deeply appreciate your speedy response to requests for reports. Later in the week we will compile what we have garnered to this point and make an initial report to the White House. Keep up the good work. You are dismissed."

Greg shook hands with the three people still on the stage and thanked them for their timely reports. Fowler found himself quickly embroiled in an argument with Adams. Greg hurried to the back, looking for Mary.

Just as he left the auditorium, the elevator door on the other side of the foyer opened, and Mary walked out.

"Hey, what happened to you?" Greg asked.

Mary glanced around the foyer. "Thank you for including me in the meeting." Her professional, no-nonsense voice. "I'll be in touch as the reports come in."

Greg studied her face. No sign of warmth or emotion. She might have been a cafeteria worker dishing up spaghetti. "Something's going on here."

"I need to be on my way home," Mary smiled politely. "However, I am going to walk by the Vietnam Memorial for a bit of exercise. Maybe sit and watch tourists for a while. Have a good evening."

"Yes," Greg returned the detached tone. "A nice idea. I would probably profit from some exercise myself." He started backing away. "See you in the morning."

"Hopefully before then," Mary said quietly and hurried out the front door.

CHAPTER 20

Once the team members left the auditorium, Greg hurried back to his office. Because he stayed late so often, no one paid attention to his hours, but tonight he didn't want to be observed. And yet, he wasn't sure that was possible. Something strange was going on, and Mary was caught up in it. If he was under surveillance, shaking the government's all-seeing eye would be difficult, if not impossible, but Greg had to try. Rather than following his usual route out the front door, he took the stairwell and a back door exit. The Vietnam Memorial wasn't close, and he would have to hurry to catch up with Mary.

He pulled up the collar on his trench coat and abruptly cut across the traffic. Hard to tail someone who was erratic and unpredictable. Greg doubled his pace and cut through an alley. At the other end, he stopped to see if anyone had followed him through the narrow causeway. No one showed. He started again at a slower gait, still cutting across streets and taking short cuts.

The days were getting shorter, and the trees cast long shadows across the sidewalks. He watched couples hurry past, holding hands, huddling together as if the evening was much colder than it really was, lovers glowing against the setting sun and then merging back into the shadows. How lonely they made him feel.

He walked two blocks through falling leaves. The air smelled damp and chilly yet invigorating. Alice had loved this time of the year and had often hummed a song that came with the season. Lyrics of "Autumn Leaves" came back to mind. "The days grow shorter, dwindling down to a precious few. September, October; we have these days together." He stopped and watched a yellow leaf settle on the grass. A puff of wind picked it up and sent the golden remnant of summer sliding over the concrete and into the gutter. "We *had* those days together," he said aloud and watched the leaf disappear down the drain.

For the first time Greg realized that he had not allowed himself to face the changing seasons in his own life. He never had recognized change. Everything had frozen in place on that day the policeman came to his office, requesting verification of identity, insisting his wife was dead, telling him the outrageous lie that twenty-three years of bliss were over. He refused to believe the officer, steadfastly resisting the finality of it all. Leaves were supposed to stay on the trees forever.

But they didn't. Seasons changed. And, maybe, the time had come to let autumn leaves be autumn leaves, to let them turn, to let them die. He rounded the corner and set his face into the wind. He walked faster.

Before Greg reached the Vietnam Memorial, he saw Mary sitting on a park bench near the edge of the long black stone cenotaph with the seemingly endless roster of the dead. For a moment, Greg reflected on the countless numbers of people who had anguished over the fate of those names, mourned them, and then rebuilt their lives without the names which had been the center of all of their dreams and tomorrows. Time had forced that marching army of mourners to go on with their lives. He needed to join them.

For a moment Greg studied the area and the memorial. He

didn't see anything or anyone who looked suspicious. Mary couldn't see him from the side. She sat there clutching her purse with a fierce resolution, looking straight ahead, wind blowing through her hair. She was obviously waiting for him to come. He started walking again.

"Hello." Greg walked closer to her right side.

Mary jumped. "I was afraid you wouldn't come," she spoke rapidly, "that you wouldn't understand."

"Obviously something happened between your leaving the auditorium and getting off the elevator. You sounded like two different people. I concluded you'd been in the director's office."

"Are you sure you weren't followed?"

Greg looked around again. "Reasonably sure."

"Sit down." Mary patted the seat next to her. "We need to talk."

Greg eased down on the bench, leaned back, and stretched out. He kept his hands in his pockets. "You know, it could get cold out here quickly."

"Yes." Mary turned up the collar on her coat. "Winter can't be too far away." She sounded tense, strained. "Greg, we've got problems." She set her purse down.

"I guess so," he observed sardonically. "At the elevator you acted like I'd developed a case of terminal halitosis."

"I had no idea who was watching, and the director had just scared the bejeebers out of me. I've never seen Allan Jones like he was this afternoon. You would have thought someone accused me of stealing Fort Knox." Mary shook her head. "I've always had something of a buddy-buddy relationship with Allan. No more! He was like a cop interrogating a criminal, the principal lecturing a naughty school girl."

"What's the big problem?" Greg kept looking around the park. "What pushed his button?"

"I've been making inquiries for you, trying to get some insight into what and who is behind the sudden interest in the New Madrid fault. A couple of days ago, I decided to focus my investigation on Helmut Haussman. I put out feelers."

"So?"

"The inquiry boomeranged. The word got back to the director, and Jones was livid. Apparently Haussman found out and came down on him." Mary looked down at the ground and exhaled forcefully. "Allan implied that if I didn't have such a respected position, he'd fire me on the spot."

"You're kidding!" Greg turned and looked into her eyes. "I've never heard of anything so outrageous."

Mary shook her head. "He warned me not to try any more probes outside the immediate scope of the study. Jones is definitely playing hardball."

Greg plopped against the back of the bench. "Jones **has** made a 180-degree turn from where he was when he came to **see** me in the hospital and urged me to take the assignment. Something's happened to him."

"Underneath the anger I sensed fear," Mary reflected thoughtfully. "He's always been the knight on a white horse charging into battle. No more! I don't know why, but Jones is under unusual pressure."

Greg stared at the ground. "Allan's never backed off before, even when I turned up some rather scary characters with hit men." He rubbed his mouth nervously. "He's always been there for me. It'd take a lot of firepower to make Jones run for cover."

"He also implied that I was being watched." Mary pressed her fist against her lips. "Not like a threat," she said thoughtfully, "but more like a concerned warning. He sounded like . . .

a terrified parent, disciplining a child for venturing too close to the edge of a cliff."

For several moments Greg pondered her words. "Mary, I've been out on thin ice many times. I'm acquainted with the cracking and popping when things are about to fall in. You're not. I don't want you in the battle zone anymore."

Mary reached for his hand. "I already am. My name is on somebody's list." She turned and looked into his eyes. "It's too late to turn back."

Mary looked bewildered more than frightened. Her eyes didn't signal retreat but concern. When Mary squeezed his hand, he sensed a desire for reassurance, the promise he'd be there. She had gone out on a limb for him. Were they both out there together?

"I didn't mean to get you in this deep." Greg gripped her hand tightly. "But one thing is for sure. I'll do everything in my power to protect you. If I need to go upstairs and read the riot act to Jones, I'll do it, regardless of the cost."

"No. No." Mary shook her head forcefully. "The less he feels we're connected, the better." She smiled. "I just wanted to make sure you were there for me."

Her hand felt small and delicate. He hadn't held a woman's hand in a long time, and the warmth was nice. In fact, everything about her was *very* nice. Greg watched the wind toss her auburn hair to one side. Mary always seemed so completely in control, competent, professional, capable, bright, and totally efficient—but now she was struggling, unsure, vulnerable, and that revealed a different dimension of the superwoman at the top. He liked both Marys, but this one needed him.

"Greg?" She turned to face him. "I'm no stranger to conflict, and I didn't get to the top by playing Pollyanna. In fact, I've seen our government do some rotten things."

Greg studied her face carefully. Her reputation for integrity was justified. It showed.

"I've observed the government intervene on behalf of American corporate interests." Mary became more intense. "I've seen CIA studies proposing the overthrow of other governments so this country could gain access to their petroleum reserves. I know what's going on in Zaire this moment. Because they are floating in oil, our government helped overthrow the national administration to gain control of those fields." She squeezed Greg's hand. "Even now relief trucks with food are being held up until those people buckle to our political interests. Greg, I'm not naïve."

Greg felt pressure building and shook his head to make it go away. "These things really get to me. I began my government career about the time Vietnam exploded. I saw the abuses in that war from our side of the ocean, but I was too inexperienced to know what to do about it." He looked at the long, black stone memorial and felt his stomach churn. "I was sent in to do a geological study to determine whether the jungle terrain was capable of supporting tanks and heavy equipment during military operations. You know what I was really doing?"

Mary shook her head.

"The area turned out to be the site of European rubber plantations and American mining interests. The rubber trees supported European economic interests and made tires for the war machine." Greg began slowly pounding on the bench with his fist. "Guess what? A mountain of titanium was hauled out to support the U.S. aircraft industry. Those American tanks that came rolling in there were to protect our economic interest, not fight the enemy." He felt himself tremble slightly. "That war wasn't about communism but protecting our economy, and I smell the same stench settling around this New Madrid project."

Mary forced a smile. "The naïveté was squeezed out of us a long time ago. Our eyes are open, and we know what's possible." She paused as if choosing her words carefully. "We make a pretty good team, Greg."

The inner tension was escalating, and he began feeling dizzy. "Something's happening to me," Greg mumbled and let go of her hand. The grass in front of him slowly turned white, and he felt sweaty. "Oh, no. One of these attacks is coming on." He felt his mouth go dry and saw images arising before his eyes.

Men rushed back and forth on the floor of the stock market, tripping over mounting piles of ticker tape. They looked frightened and in a panic. People screamed that the market was falling through the floor. Abruptly the scene shifted, and Greg could see piles of money going up in flames. He could smell the smoke. Cars came to a screeching halt, running out of gas. The nation's capital began sinking as all of Washington, D.C. disappeared underneath a sea of black mud.

"Greg!" Mary shook him. "Greg, are you okay?" She kept tugging at his trench coat.

Greg blinked his eyes, and the world slowly came back into focus.

"What's happening?" Mary pulled on his lapels. "You keep mumbling about the stock market going under."

Her face emerged out of the white fog. "Write this down," he mumbled. "Write it while I can still remember."

Mary grabbed her purse and fumbled for a pencil.

"I can see the stock market failing, the national economy falling apart." Greg caught a deep breath. "Our oil reserves drying up."

"Yes. Yes." Mary scribbled on a small notepad. "I'm getting it down."

Greg continued describing his vision. "I hate these episodes."

He rubbed his eyes. "Makes me feel completely crazy." He leaned forward on the bench to get his head lower.

"Are you all right now?" Mary put her hand on his back.

"I think so." He straightened up again, breathing in and out.

Mary looked at her pad. "What do you make of this?"

Greg took it out of her hand. "I'm . . . I'm not sure. Usually these flashes have something to do with what's upsetting me." He looked again. "Maybe big money is behind Allan Jones's strange behavior. The whole thing makes me feel like the two of us are nothing but pawns in a high-stakes chess game."

Mary put her arm in his. "We've got to be careful. Watch each other's backs."

Greg nodded. He shook his head to make sure everything was back in focus. "I'm feeling much better. Yes, it's passed." He stopped for a couple of minutes, then turned and forced a smile. "By the way, I never did take you up on that supper at your house."

"You are the most amazing man I ever met. In the midst of this chaos, you suddenly think about eating?"

"Got to have strength to carry on."

Mary smiled broadly. "We're going to have to be careful about being seen together."

"Sure." Greg stopped and blinked his eyes again. He cupped his hands over his eyebrows, watching a figure disappear behind the black granite monument. "Oh my gosh! I would swear that was Alex Majors standing over there. Watching us. Majors, the CIA agent! Watching behind the black wall . . ."

CHAPTER 21

Sharon thought about the state of the union in their household as she finished her breakfast. She wanted a new and more intimate relationship with her father. Blaming him for everything that went wrong wouldn't get her there. She had to hold up her end of the bargain if things were going to improve. Sharon put the cereal bowl in the dishwasher and went back to the study.

She heard her father come in late Monday night. Concluding he was tired, Sharon didn't say anything. He went straight to bed. By the time she got up the next morning, he was gone again. Usually his pace and the lack of personal contact made her angry, but today she felt a new compassion for the demands of his job. The possibility that they could be under surveillance troubled her. She had to do everything possible to make his life better.

Her unfinished story on messianic Judaism still lay on top of the leather-inlaid desk. For a few minutes, she surveyed her research scattered across the desk. "I need more," she said to herself. "A different angle of some sort." Sharon leaned back in the chair and stared straight ahead. Her mother's face was still watching her.

Sharon picked up the picture. "Okay, okay, I'm 'letting him be' and looking for the silver lining. I'm genuinely trying to make things better. You'd be pleased." She put the picture back in place and flipped on the television to catch the early morning news.

Good Morning America was going full tilt, but the top-of-the-hour news report had already concluded, and an "Up Close" segment was presenting an in-depth look at the current Middle East problems. Sharon pushed her chair closer.

"Conflict in the region is increasing despite concerted efforts by both the United Nations and the United States," the reporter said. Pictures of young people throwing rocks at driving military troops filled the screen. "Special Millennium Unit security forces track potential crazies plotting possible doomsday attacks on Jerusalem holy site, but the anti-terrorist offices are still not offering clues about the bombing." The announcer sounded as if he had turned a page. "The proposed United Arab Republic continues to develop at a rapid pace. Many of the old stumbling blocks have been sidestepped and the infrastructure for political solidarity is coming together faster than any political experts predicted." Scenes inside Egypt's presidential palace showed five Arab heads of state shaking hands amicably and talking enthusiastically. "While these leaders continue to threaten Israel with their missiles, the United States warned that an attack could result in a nuclear response, precipitating World War III. The stakes are high," the reporter's tone conveyed urgency, "and the hour is growing late."

Sharon clicked the television off. "They ought to call it *Bad Morning America*. The Arabs are watching the Jews. The Jews are watching the Arabs. Who knows who is watching our house? The best I can do is watch the television."

She picked up a pencil and doodled on a piece of paper. *First, I want things to be better with Dad permanently,* she decided. *Second, I need more insight and material for my story. Third, I've got to find some help for both problems.* She laid down the pencil and thought about the situation.

Sharon suddenly snapped her fingers. *I can kill two birds with one stone. I know exactly what I ought to do.* She reached for the phone book and quickly found the number.

A friendly woman's voice answered, "Faith Community Church."

"I believe the pastor's name is Wayne Brown," Sharon began. "Is he in?"

"I'm sorry. Not at the moment."

"Would it be possible to make an appointment to see him?"

"Certainly." The receptionist paused as if looking at a calendar. "We have a cancellation this afternoon at 2:00. Would that be acceptable?"

"Sure. Put Sharon Parker in the slot. Thanks."

"See you then," the receptionist hung up.

"Awesome!" Sharon said as she put the phone back in place. "I'll let the pastor tell me about messianic Jews and difficult fathers at the same time."

• • •

The Reverend Wayne Brown proved to be an athletic-looking man in his mid-forties. His casual sweater and Docker pants gave him the air of someone easy to talk with. The pastor had a large toothy grin that left a boyish impression— everyone's best friend.

"Thanks for seeing me," she began.

"Not at all. I noticed your name on our attendance register from last Sunday. I was actually going to call you later this week and thank you for coming."

"Gee, that's a new twist." Sharon settled into the chair across the desk. "Thank me? I certainly appreciate the warm welcome.

Actually, my first visit was several weeks ago when Jacov Palenski spoke. You know, the messianic rabbi?"

"Of course. Jacov is always fascinating."

"I'm working on a story about his position and the people he represents."

"You're a writer?" Brown's voice brightened. "How interesting."

"Yes," Sharon said thoughtfully, "and a daughter. The other reason I'm here is to get help in relating to my father."

The pastor rubbed his chin thoughtfully. "I can give you several pamphlets that will tell you more about Rabbi Palenski's group, but please start on the home front. Tell me about your father."

"Let's see if I can give you a condensed version of our struggles." Sharon quickly described how their being so much alike made for frequent collisions. "You see," she said more slowly, "my mother's sudden death precipitated a crisis of communication. Our tendency to misunderstand each other exploded into full-scale war when Mom wasn't there to smooth things over."

The pastor looked at her intently. "Must have been an overwhelmingly painful time."

"I can't begin to tell you."

"Try."

"Try? Try to tell you what it felt like to have my heart ripped out? To have my soul crushed?" His unexpected probe jarred her, and she felt herself draw back. And then, the door ripped off the hinges and she began crying frantically. "My world exploded in a million pieces," she sobbed. "I thought that I might even die."

"Do you cry often?" the pastor asked softly.

"No." She dabbed at her eyes. "No." She felt surprised realizing how seldom she actually cried.

"Maybe you get angry instead?"

Sharon stared into the pastor's genuine blue eyes. "What an amazing observation. That's exactly right."

"Anger is easier to express than hurt." Brown's voice was steady and soothing. "But usually the primary problem is our pain." He pushed a box of tissues across the desk.

Sharon could see the blurry shape of the minister on the other side of the desk, waiting patiently for her to get it all out. After a couple of minutes, her load lifted. The stained tissue in her hand signaled mascara was probably all over her cheeks. Sharon rubbed frantically and tried to regain her composure.

"Feeling better?" Brown asked.

"How . . . how could you possibly have elicited such an emotional response from me so quickly?"

"When you mentioned your mother's death, a look of pain filled your face. You probably didn't realize that your eyes clouded immediately and your lip twisted slightly. The hurt was obvious."

"But . . . but what happened?" Sharon continued rubbing her cheeks.

"I probably gave you the permission to cry that you don't have at home," Brown offered. "I bet your father isn't able to stand your pain or his pain, and you've learned to stuff it."

Sharon stared. "You are quite the counselor, Reverend Brown. I am flabbergasted. That's *exactly* what's happened! Neither of us ever talks about Mother. We don't touch the subject . . . because . . . I don't think Dad can deal with it out loud."

"And with time you turned into a pressure cooker, waiting to explode with pent-up steam." Brown smiled. "You just needed me to let you know that in this room anything you feel can be expressed and is acceptable."

"I can't believe how much better I feel." Sharon sighed. "That cry was long overdue."

"May I make a suggestion?" Brown asked, smiling. "Perhaps it would be a helpful start if you let your father know that you are comfortable if he wants to express his pain to you. Talk about your mother again. Face the fact out loud that's she gone and don't avoid her as a subject. I believe that would help your father."

Sharon rolled her eyes. "Where have you been for the last several years?"

"Right here." Brown smiled out of the corner of his mouth. "Where have you been?"

"Touché!"

"What about your faith?" the pastor continued. "Have you been sustained by what you believe?"

"We went to church when I was younger, and Mother was a staunch believer. Dad and I tagged along, but we bought the package. Is that what you mean?"

"I mean, did that faith help you when she died?"

Sharon bit her lip. "Everything crumbled," she admitted.

"Maybe you felt God was to blame for her death?" The minister again sounded completely accepting of whatever she might say.

"When I was a child I sorta got Dad and God mixed up sometimes." Sharon carefully chose her words. She felt unsteady, but the path seemed right. "Maybe I blamed him instead of God."

Brown nodded thoughtfully. "So you've displaced the faith that once sustained you?"

"Buried it," she finally answered. "Buried it in the same casket with Mother."

Brown allowed the silence to do its work. Even though he didn't say anything, Sharon could feel his support.

"What do I do now?" she asked timidly.

"We're in the resurrection business." Brown smiled his boyish grin. "Maybe we can help bring your faith back to life."

"Would it help my relationship with Dad?"

"Could it hurt it?"

Sharon looked again. The casualness, the easy manner, the quick grin were a veneer. Wayne Brown was a bright, highly skilled counselor. With a few questions he had stripped away the persona of a savvy, aggressive journalist and laid open the heart of an orphaned child.

She shook her head. "No, it certainly couldn't hurt a thing."

"Possibly we could continue our conversations and see if I could be of assistance in that area as well as working with your father." He reached in the drawer and pulled out several pamphlets. "I believe you'll find some helpful information on messianic Judaism in this explanation written by Jacov. What about talking again this time next week?"

"Yes." Sharon was surprised by how definite she sounded. "I think that's an excellent idea, Reverend Brown."

The minister stood up. "There are other books in the foyer written by Rabbi Palenski. You might want to pick up one of them."

"You've helped me so much." Sharon extended her hand.

Brown shook hands. "Most of the changes in relationships have to begin with us," he observed. "As we make necessary adjustments, the people around us are often released to change."

Although Sharon walked toward the door, she didn't look away. "You are *very* amazing, pastor. I'll do what I can do."

Moments later Sharon found herself in the large gathering

area in the vestibule of the church. She saw a table filled with books and pamphlets. She quickly flipped through the pile.

"Hey, this looks interesting," she said to herself, picking up a book with a fiery red jacket and a yellow setting sun in the center. *"Final Sunset Over Jerusalem,"* Sharon read the title out loud.

"You'd like that one," a voice said from behind her.

Sharon turned and found an elderly lady looking over her shoulder. "I read that a month ago," the gray-haired woman continued as if she were an old friend. "It's a commentary on the book of Revelation."

"Really?" Sharon stared at the woman. "I thought that book was unfathomable."

"So did I, until I read that book." The old lady beamed. "You can leave your money in the basket at the end of the table." She shuffled off as if the matter were concluded.

Sharon looked at her treading down the hall and then at the book's cover again. "This is an amazing place," she said to herself, opening her purse.

After putting a ten- and a five-dollar bill in the straw basket, Sharon stuffed the book in her handbag and walked out to the parking lot. She was on her way home, but her mind lingered on some of the minister's last words. "Most of the changes in relationships begin with us," he had said. "Maybe we can bring your faith back to life."

CHAPTER 22

Helmut Haussman's intercontinental flight landed in Brussels on October 10, two hours before Alex Majors arrived in the city on a train from Paris. Both men had gone to considerable lengths to leave Washington, D.C., without revealing any connection with each other. Majors landed at Charles DeGaulle airport and immediately took a Eurorail express to Belgium. A limousine with darkly tinted windows waited for Haussman at the Brussels International Airport and then returned to the train station for Majors. The basement entrance into the Gent Institute would shield each man from outside observation.

Haussman quickly found himself in an elegant reception room on the fifteenth floor. The marble-walled lounge sparkled in the late afternoon sunlight. Although the ultramodern decor of chrome and leather was striking, the room felt cold. He thumbed through his report while waiting for the big meeting to begin. The presidential aide sank back in the thickly padded recliner chair and looked carefully at each page. During the week that had passed since Parker's assembly in the NSA auditorium, numerous reports had come into Haussman's office. The basic data needed for today's meeting was complete. Haussman smiled. Parker was doing the promised quality job, and Hausman would take home the reward.

"Ah, Herr Haussman," the familiar voice called from the door. "*Wilkommen.*"

Haussman immediately leaped to his feet. "Baron Leestma!" He answered in German. "Good to see you." Haussman extended his hand.

The baron's usual elegant suit lent presence to his stately demeanor. "I trust your flight was not too tiring." He adjusted his silk tie and matching handkerchief in the pocket of his blue-black Italian Armani.

"Not at all. First class on a 747 is enjoyable." Haussman laughed. "You take good care of your people."

"Please sit down." Leestma pointed at a chair and sat down on a matching leather couch across from Haussman. "We can expect Mr. Majors's arrival shortly."

"*Ja, Ja,*" the German answered enthusiastically. "I trust we will meet your expectations."

The baron smiled condescendingly. "Of course. You will only meet with our executive committee. The entire board will not be apprised of the . . . ah . . . more sensitive details until the entire procedure is completely under way."

"Certainly."

A cell phone buzzed inside the baron's coat pocket. "Excuse me." He stood up and walked away from Haussman. "Yes?" He began a guarded conversation, speaking French.

Haussman pretended not to be watching and returned to the file but strained to hear every word. *The baron is more complex than anyone I have worked for,* he thought. *The old tyrant expects flawless reports and demands perfection.* He listened to Leestma's demanding tone. *He makes me nervous.*

"Immediately!" The baron pushed the off button. "Majors is on his way from the train station right now." He walked toward the door. "We begin the moment he appears. I will send a secretary for you shortly." Again he smiled condescendingly and was gone.

Haussman stood up and walked to the window. He pulled back the thin curtains and looked down on the fashionable boulevard. *I've got to make it this time. I won't get another shot at the top. When it's all over, Leestma and his cronies will have the world in their pocket. I intend to be sitting at his right hand. Majors had better prove to be as good as he thinks he is.*

• • •

Baron Leestma walked boldly down the long, highly polished, black marble hall and turned into a small conference room, pausing at the door. *I don't like Yvonne Galla's addition to the executive committee,* he thought. *She manipulated that election right under my nose. Called in all her IOU's. Then again, she's got the assets to command a seat in the inner circle.*

"Good afternoon," Leestma began. "Our agents should be here momentarily." He looked around at the four men and Galla. "They do not know who you are." He cleared his throat. "Only that you are the executive committee. Your identity will not be revealed."

Galla smiled at the men around her and began an impromptu dissertation on how pleased she was to be on the executive committee, as if inclusion was something of a surprise to her. The knit tank dress under a hip-length red jacket had been carefully tailored to make all the right points. The lady in red had their total attention.

The baron gripped the back of the padded leather chair—the only sign that his normally stoic nature was being tested. He thought she was grandstanding before they had even begun and felt the need to watch her even more closely than he'd previously thought.

"In conclusion," Galla's voice was low and husky, "I await this classified report with great anticipation."

"As we all do," the large overweight man across from her effused. "The baron's shared this little secret with only a privileged few."

Leestma nodded knowingly. "Ms. Galla is not the only one who is not fully aware of Project Downfall." He smiled at her politely. "But all things will unfold in due time." The baron picked up a phone on the table and dialed. "Let me see if our remaining guest has arrived."

• • •

Alex Majors stepped out of the limousine and into the elevator. He pushed the button for the seventeenth floor and leaned against the back. *Can't believe I'm actually going to meet these guys face-to-face. Haussman says the Dutch Masters think they're destined to control the fate of Europe. Humph! All I want is a get-rich ticket to big-time retirement. A mansion on an island in the Bahamas. A summer home in Switzerland. At least they pay a whale of a lot better than the U.S. government.*

The door opened and a security man with arms crossed and a plastic earpiece stood in front of him. "Mr. Majors?"

"Yes."

"Please follow me." He turned on his heel and started down the hall.

Majors glanced at his watch. *The only thing I have to beware of is getting implicated as a double agent. Haussman understands. He's been on every side of the line enough times that he should keep his mouth shut. Can't trust a psycho like him, though. Have to hold tight to his leash. That's the trick.*

"Please wait here." The security man left the CIA agent standing in the hall and disappeared behind the large wooden doors.

Majors looked up and down the hall. *The place is pure class. Makes anything in Washington or the Kremlin look like a rec room.*

The door opened. "The executive committee is ready to speak with you." The security man pointed to a chair at the front of the room.

Majors adjusted his tie. *Show time,* he thought. *Let's razzle dazzle the big boys.*

• • •

Haussman sat in the back of the room where the secretary had put him. The executive committee had ignored him as if he were no more than a maintenance man. Being slighted irritated him, but he had no misgivings about the pecking order in an organization of such magnitude. He listened to the small talk around the table and tried to look oblivious to the discussion.

When Majors was ushered in, Haussman smiled at the CIA agent's cocky air. *Thinks he's James Bond ready to charm the high-class broad sitting with the money men. Don't overplay your cards, Majors. These people can see a snow job coming a mile away.*

"The meeting will come to order." Leestma took charge. "We meet today to inform you on the progress of a major initiative that will ultimately destroy America's grip on the world economy, thereby bringing peace to the entire globe." Leestma looked at Galla. "Since some of you are new to the executive committee, you are not fully informed on the status of this top secret project. You will be able to put many of the pieces of the puzzle in place as you *listen.*" He turned back to the rest of the group. "As you know, our purpose is to create a stable, peaceful world where business can flourish without intervention or disruption."

The five executive committee members looked at each other and nodded agreement.

Leestma folded his hands in front of his face and pursed his lips against his index fingers. "Our need for a new business strategy began when we realized the lack of a coherent American economic policy. The statesmanship promulgated by a number of presidents had the potential to wreck our holdings. We realized bad decisions by American planners would soon affect us."

Haussman tried to keep from grinning and looked down at his file. *The old fox has an amazing way of making his diabolic schemes sound benevolent. Whatever he's doing, it's always for the good of somebody else. Just so happens that every time he picks up several million along the way. Leestma's like a doctor who convinces a patient that transplanting his own heart into somebody else is going to be good for both of them.*

"I've asked one of our researchers to give a capsule report of the current dilemma." The baron pushed a button and a young woman entered through a side door. He beckoned for her to stand by him. "Please listen to Ms. Vanderbergger's report."

The small woman with thick glasses looked ill at ease. The severe lines of her black suit didn't soften her appearance. "Dr. Leestma asked for a condensation of my hundred-page report." She looked down at her notes awkwardly.

Haussman scratched his head. *Dr. Leestma? Oh yes. The baron has a Ph.D. in economics. Forgot that one.*

"Thirty years ago the American Council on Foreign Relations decided to neutralize communism by spreading the wealth of industrialized nations to third-world countries," Vanderbergger read slowly and haltingly. "In the sixties and seventies, massive amounts of heavy industry were purposely moved from the United States to these third-world nations. Of course, cheap labor gave additional incentives to companies that made even greater profits. However, the plan had a fatal flaw—the heavy industry they moved had provided a necessary tax base." She paused and laid the piece of paper on the table. "In the Great Depression during the 1930s, America had steel, shipbuilding, railroads, and other forms of industry to provide the taxes to bring the country back. Today these foundations are gone."

Leestma held up his hand to stop her. "Anyone not understand the implications of these facts?" He paused. "The current prosperity that seems to be sweeping across America is a mirage. Like a bridge with limited capacity, the U.S. economy cannot stand significant strain."

Vanderbergger waited for Leestma's cue to continue and started again. "In 2006, thirty million so-called baby boomers will retire and begin drawing Social Security funds. By 2009, an additional forty-seven million will produce additional demands on the already overdrawn system." The woman abruptly looked up and spoke without notes. "Regardless of what the politicians say, no one is prepared for this run on government funds in the midst of a growing national debt. Social Security insolvency will push the government into bankruptcy. America's inability to pay its national debt will be quicksand, sucking their economy— and eventually the world's economy—under."

Leestma again held up his hand. "You see," he paused and raised his eyebrow like an all-knowing professor, "the inability of Americans to practice fiscal restraint and responsibility could seriously jeopardize Gent's massive financial holdings in that country and abroad. Events would spin out of control, and we would be at the mercy of fate."

"And what do you propose to do about it?" Galla interrupted.

Haussman watched Leestma's face for a moment and caught the baron's anger at being interrupted. *This dame either doesn't understand who she's talking to, or she's looking big trouble in the face.*

"That is why we are here today," Leestma said sardonically. "We began answering that question *months* ago."

Haussman studied the woman's response. No sign of rebuke there. Didn't even get the slam dunk. *She's either a dumb broad with a lot of money or calculating like a cobra. Wait till she hears what Majors and I have to say.*

CHAPTER 23

Alex Majors made sure he was among the last to board the Concorde for the return trip to the United States. Once inside, a careful scan around the supersonic jet put his mind at ease. *No more than fifty passengers today.* Only the most affluent can afford the $5,600 one-way ticket, and most are high-dollar business types. *No one looks threatening. The intelligence community seldom flies this high.*

The flight attendant explained the procedures, and Alex buckled up. The woman sitting next to him appeared to be a bit of a twit, jabbering about being thrilled to fly on the Concorde. For a moment, he wondered what persona he should put on for the three-hour-and-forty-minute transcontinental flight. Maybe today he would be a wealthy man of the world.

Once the plane was in the air, the twit turned on again.

"I'm Melissa from Boston," she explained spontaneously. The classic styling of her ankle-length navy dress, buttoned inches above the knee, gave her a cosmopolitan appearance. The designer silk blue, ivory, and brown scarf around her neck added a touch of sophistication that proved deceiving. Ten more words, and the carefully manicured effect was gone. "And where might someone like you be from?" she pushed.

"Every place," Alex reached for a Yul Brenner Russian accent. "And nowhere."

"Oooh," Miss Boston's eyes widened. "A mystery man."

"Not quite the right description. I am an international banker and investor, traveling between so many countries that I don't call any place home."

"My goodness," Melissa exclaimed. "My father's something of that order. He's president of Boston Capital Investments. Mr. Winthrop Brookinghurst."

"Yes." Alex reached for the headphones. *Don't push it too far. Don't want to get into name-dropping. She might trump my cards.*

"You must be about my father's age."

Alex groaned inwardly but smiled thinly. "Never can tell."

"You've been in Paris, working on a new project?" Melissa's distinctly New England accent outdid his.

"A project?" Alex smiled. "Yes. You might say it will be a massive relocation and resettlement by the time we are finished."

"In Europe?"

"Not quite the right description. Actually in the center of the United States."

"You do get around," Melissa noted.

The age comment still stung. The only personal mileage he would get out of the trip had to be in the ego department, and she'd already whacked that one. With such a short flight he probably wasn't going to score beyond that point anyway.

"Have you been concerned with the wild gyrations the stock market's been going through?" Now she sounded over her head and into purely polite conversation.

"The market's always a concern," Alex reached for the distant elitist tone that would eventually take him out of the game and off the playing field.

"I wonder if I'd know your family?" Miss Boston was back again, playing D. A. R. this time.

"Are you acquainted with heraldry or European lineage?" he countered.

"No," she said factually. "I'm simply a New Englander."

"Of course." Alex started adjusting the earphones. So far she hadn't even gotten his first name, although he could have reached into his bag of tricks and come up with a dozen aristocratic family titles that would have dazzled the daughter of the president of Boston Capital Investments.

"Family is everything." Miss Boston was coming through in fine form again.

"Of course." Alex rolled the *r* with the elegance of one of the Brothers Karamazov. He put the earphones on and closed his eyes.

Alex *did* understand the value of family, since his had been nothing but a millstone around his neck. He remembered well landing on the shores of New York City as an eight-year-old without a father. Manhattan's skyscrapers towered over him like prehistoric giants, preparing to devour their victims waiting in the streets. Fear had been his permanent childhood companion.

He thought of his mother, Elsa, struggling to survive on the back streets of the Bronx, the shame and ignominy of growing up in a government-subsidized tenement, the lack of opportunity for becoming anything other than a rough-and-tumble street fighter. Poor Elsa, the little Dutch girl, who had hoped for so much more.

With his eyes closed, Alex could clearly see the one picture his mother had kept in her bedroom for who knows how many decades. Randolph Majors in his U.S. Army air corps uniform; the brave pilot shot down over Belgium in a dog fight with the *Luftwaffe;* her hero who gave her virtually nothing more than a son and misery. Fate and a silk parachute deposited him in a haystack on Grandfather Dekker's farm, where he was hidden until after the Normandy invasion. During those months, Randolph and Elsa developed quite a romance. The American pilot certainly appeared to know what he was doing.

Childhood in the Low Countries had taught Alex the Dutch

and Flemish languages, both of which would serve him well later in life. Randolph Majors, however, bequeathed his son nothing but trouble.

After the war the distinguished army pilot, who also thought himself to be quite an international investor, returned with every intention of making it big in the reconstruction of Europe. He married Elsa, picked up his young son, and set out to be a high-flying American businessman. Elsa always defended him, rationalizing they were nearly rich when he developed Hodgkin's disease and died quickly. Alex could only barely remember his father. Everything went into the grave with him.

The Dekkers urged their war-bride daughter to strike out for the land of promise. Surely more Randolphs had to be waiting on the other side of the ocean. Stories of the land of milk and honey were rife in war-torn Belgium. A year later Elsa settled into the city of steel and strife. Too proud to admit her mistake and call for help, Elsa and Alex Majors walked into the New York City welfare trap. If any living relatives of Randolph Majors ever existed, they never turned up.

A decade later an army recruiter got Alex out of the ghetto with promises of seeing the world, getting an education, and becoming a hero like Randolph. Alex's language ability landed him a place with Intelligence, and he took advantage of every educational opportunity that came along, finishing a college degree and ending up in the recruiting pool for the CIA. Because he would do anything to get to the top, Alex the immigrant soon became Alex the insider. Street smarts had become his strongest asset.

Soft strains of easy-listening music filled his ears and made the pain seem very distant, a lifetime away. The smell of food filled his nose, and he opened one eye. A flight attendant offered a selection of prime rib or rack of lamb with mint sauce. He signaled for the beef. "Champagne, please," he added as an afterthought. Alex closed his eyes again before Miss Boston launched a new round of inquiries.

The good life came with Herr Haussman. The German conniver drifted into his life through a strange set of circumstances. No one inside the CIA knew Haussman to be a double agent—the man was as duplicitous as Stalin. Through a maneuver to make sure the Bonn government played things straight up in a prisoner exchange with Russia, Alex first became involved with Haussman. One thing led to another, lots of money went under the table, and through a series of maneuvers Majors never completely understood, Haussman ended up working in the State Department. A presidential election catapulted him into the White House. Alex now perceived Gent had been behind the entire operation.

The flight attendant spread a small, white tablecloth over Majors's tray and placed a china cup and saucer before him. The aroma of beef galvanized his appetite. He kept the earphones on to negate the possibility of conversation with sweet little Melissa.

Actually, his dual citizenship with Belgium had opened the doors to the Gent Institute. Friendship with Haussman paid off in dividends as large as striking it rich on the stock market. He squirreled away every penny in a Swiss bank account for the day he'd leave the United States forever and be what his father never was in Belgium. No sudden lavish spending that might tip off a supervisor at the CIA! Of course, should a leak develop, he'd claim to be nothing more than a business consultant to Gent. No one would buy it, but the ploy might give him enough time to get out of the country before the ruse was fully exposed.

He looked out the window at the blue Atlantic far below him. How deceivingly peaceful the calm sea appeared, not unlike

Helmut Haussman. Through CIA contacts, he'd pulled Haussman's file from State Department records. The psychologist who tested the German recommended not hiring him under any circumstances. Someone at the top obviously pulled strings. The tests said Haussman was a character disorder case, a sociopath with homicidal tendencies, a man with the capacity to kill without conscience. He would discount the value of human beings and act on his own best interest regardless of the expense to others.

Well, yes, thought Majors. *That's what makes Haussman so lovable and helpful.*

"Wonderful champagne," Miss Boston interrupted the music. "How's your lamb?" she persisted, raising her voice slightly.

Alex removed the headphones and forced a smile. "Again, not quite the right description," Yul Brenner answered. "The *beef* was excellent."

"Oh? Didn't notice." Melissa only paused. "As a businessman are you concerned with the current foreign policy of the United States as it relates to global stability?"

"You sound like a diplomat."

"I'm working on an MBA at Harvard. My father is not very complimentary of current international practices by our president."

"Your father is a wise man." Alex sipped the champagne. "Perhaps he has his own political aspirations."

"Dad?" Melissa Brookinghurst giggled. "Never. He's far more interested in following the graphs and statistics. Sits up in his top-floor office and shuffles funds. You look far more the type to be a mover and shaker in the political world."

Alex raised an eyebrow. "Mover and shaker? Yes," he said slowly. "My dear, you have no idea how accurate *that* description is."

CHAPTER 24

October was quickly slipping away. Pumpkins and Halloween decorations decked the houses up and down Greg's street. The initial crunch of meeting the White House deadlines had passed, and the pressure seemed to be subsiding. Greg pulled into the driveway and waited for the garage door to open. Sharon's car was already parked there. He certainly wasn't going to be late for supper again.

"Dad? That you?"

He closed the door from the garage behind him. "Yeah. I'm here."

"Don't dillydally," she called from the kitchen. "I'm putting food in the bowls. You're late."

The aroma of supper hit him full force before he was through the door. "Wow! Smells great in there." He set his briefcase against the wall. "You've certainly pulled out the stops tonight."

Sharon gave him a quick peck on the cheek. "If I remember right, roast and mashed potatoes are on the top of your list." She looked at him out of the corner of her eye. "On those rare occasions that you come home on time."

Greg grinned. "You got me dead on target. Right on the mark."

"Wash your hands." She sounded like her mother. "And make it snappy."

Greg laughed and ducked into the half bath off the kitchen. *Couldn't possibly blow this one like I did last month,* he thought. *Sharon's really trying. Time to be on my best behavior. No 'big dad' stuff tonight.* He dried his hands and hurried out.

Greg stopped and stared. The overhead lights were off. Two candles cast long shadows over the table and sent a warm glow around the room. Sharon stood behind her chair, anticipation in her eyes.

"Oh, kitten, the table is lovely." Greg walked around and hugged his daughter. "Just superb." He pulled out her chair for Sharon to be seated. "Everything looks wonderful."

"I hope everything is still hot enough."

Greg slid into his chair. "You've really outdone yourself." He passed the potatoes and reached for the meat. "The garden salad looks scrumptious."

"I'd like you to say a little prayer like we did when I was a child."

"Sure." Greg bowed his head. "Lord, thank You for being with us through these past years of transition and struggle. And thank You that we are together tonight. Please bless this food. Amen."

"Amen," Sharon echoed.

"Hey, we've still got the touch to do these things."

Sharon smiled and began filling her plate. "You haven't been here for supper in quite a while." Sharon sounded like she was teasing. "Not sure why," she sounded tentative, "but just who is this Mary Morgan? She seems to have wrapped you up these past few weeks. You keep saying she works for the NSA, but it sounds to me like she's an even bigger workaholic than you are. Or . . . or, there's more to the story."

Greg shrugged. "We've had an *unusual* amount of work to get out of the way."

"Strange." Sharon kept her eyes on her plate. "You once came home exhausted from the office, but today there was a spring in your step when you came in. Interesting."

"Mary's a very nice person." Greg fumbled for words. "A good friend." He cleared his throat. "Actually she's been a . . . a . . . very . . . a . . . helpful to me and . . ."

"Dad." Sharon laid her fork down and looked up with a grin on her face. "You don't have to explain a thing."

"But I want you to know that . . ."

"Dad." She raised an eyebrow and took on a parental air. "Your change shows."

"What?"

Sharon laughed. "Dad, nothing could please me more than to see you return to a normal life. Truly, it's fine with me if you've come up with a lady friend." She pressed her lips together and suddenly looked pensive. "You have to go on with your life."

"Sharon." Greg reached for his daughter's hand. "No one could replace your mother or what she meant to me . . ."

"I understand that," Sharon stopped him, "but that time in our life won't return. During the last month, I've had to face how both of us allowed her death to shut us down emotionally. We loved her so much, and she was the glue that kept everything together." Sharon seemed to be fighting back tears. "When she was gone, we came unglued." Sharon sniffed. "But a lot of time has passed since then. The time has come to go on."

"Thank you." Greg struggled to say the words. "Sharon, in the last several weeks I've also thought about 'going on' for the first time since her death. I don't know that I'm there yet, but . . ." Greg swallowed hard, "I'm at least trying to get to that place."

"I really didn't mean for things to get this heavy so quickly." Sharon pressed her hands against her lips. "But here we are."

She smiled. "I want you to know that I recognize my part in creating much of the tension we've had through the years. I'm going to do better."

Greg felt a lump rise in his throat. "I don't know what to say . . . I guess 'thank you' sounds too small."

"More than enough." Sharon dabbed at her eyes. "My, haven't we gotten overwhelmingly serious. Do roast and mashed potatoes always have this effect on you?"

Greg laughed. "See the power of a little home cooking?" He squeezed her hand.

"Well, I haven't seen any strange cars on the street lately." Sharon started eating again. "You think that situation is better?"

"After I had our house searched, I made plenty of noise at the office and sent memos all over creation. Maybe that took some of the pressure off. I think our phones here are okay. I never know about my office." He grinned. "By the way, whether you know it or not, you've had protective surveillance for the last month."

"You've got to be kidding!"

Greg chuckled. "You didn't notice any strange people around?"

Sharon rocked back in her chair. "I don't know whether to laugh or cry."

"Let me give you some idea of what we're still dealing with." He set his fork on the edge of the plate. "Wide angle and pinhole lenses with night vision equipment and supermagnification can maintain twenty-four hour surveillance in a full-circle radius. A car doesn't have to be parked down the street to know who comes and goes from our house."

Sharon stared at him.

"Infrared radar can detect activity not only in the darkness, but behind walls," he continued. "Virtual interactive policing and computerized face-recognition software are linked into hundreds of cameras that feed into central networks. A monitor can scan a crowded street and within seconds cross-match your face with a million others and spot you. Getting the picture?"

Sharon shook her head in disbelief.

"There's a new program over at the CIA that also identifies faces by taking into account head orientation, skin color, makeup, jewelry, facial expressions, hair, and aging. If they want to watch us, they will."

"Dad, you are scaring me!"

"Sharon, this thing is far from over. Maybe now's the time to move back on your own. As soon as you get out of here, you won't have to worry."

Sharon inhaled deeply and then pushed her plate back. "When I came back from Israel, it was because of that, heaven help us, awful sense of duty you put in me." She forced a smile. "And we've certainly had a few tiffs during the past two months trying to get things back together, but I've experienced a great deal of healing as well. I wouldn't have missed it for the world." She reached for his hand. "We're in this thing together, and I couldn't think of leaving until the whole matter is behind us."

"Sharon . . ." Greg knew it sounded like he was reprimanding a little girl and stopped.

"And besides, I want to know who this Mary Morgan is." She looked over the candles, returning the parental posture.

Greg opened his mouth and started to say something, but the words weren't there.

"Enjoy the roast beef." Sharon winked just as Alice used to. "I won't be making supper like this very often."

She sounds exactly like her mother. He shook his head in defeat and started eating again.

• • •

For the next hour, father and daughter talked like old friends, but supper was over, and they had to press on. Standing by the cabinets, Greg helped put the salad bowls into the dishwasher. "You can't say that I don't leave things better than when I started."

"Indeed!" Sharon flipped on the garbage disposal and rinsed the last of what she had in a large bowl into the drain. "Thanks for the help. I think everything looks good enough. We're just about done."

Greg folded his towel and stuck it back in among the other towels. "You've certainly done your part with excellence!"

"Dad . . ." Sharon turned slowly and looked intently at her father. "I've been thinking about sitting down and talking over another matter." She pulled his towel out of the drawer and hung it from the rack on the stove.

"What?"

"I got this book on Revelation at the church I visited," Sharon explained, "and I've read the thing a couple of times." She put the last piece of china up in the high cabinet. "This book explains what's coming. The big problem is that we're not in it."

"Huh? I don't think I'm following you."

"Dad, the most powerful, wealthiest country in the history of the world is not mentioned in Revelation. In other words, America's gone."

Greg scratched his head. "I hear what you're saying but, . . ."

"You see," Sharon slowed down, "that's the point. The United States has nothing to do with the end times. We simply aren't in the story."

Greg frowned and looked at Sharon out of the corner of his eyes. "What's your point?"

"My point is, we have nothing whatsoever to do with how the world's story ends." Sharon bounced her fist on the table's top. "Get it? We're gone!"

Greg rubbed the back of this neck. "Well, yes," he fumbled, trying to find the right words. "I realize that."

"America is completely and totally gone." She leaned over the table. "We have left the entire scenario. But why? What happened to us?"

• • •

Lying in his bed and staring at the ceiling, Greg thought about their conversation two hours earlier. Sharon said quite a few profound things, but she also put her finger on the heart of the problem. Somehow in the near future America would no longer be a world power. They would be gone.

He rolled over on his side and pulled the pillow under his head. Outside, the tree branches bobbed up and down, spreading fingers across the backyard, covering the sky, and letting the scenery peek through. He stared into the night and wondered.

Could he really let everything out? Describe what he saw out there on the horizon line? Sharon's problem was far from simple, and he couldn't tell her what he thought . . . but the book of Revelation's description of the end times was right. America could well soon be gone.

He thought about the good experiences that had happened with Sharon. Her old combative attitude was gone. Things had become again like they were a decade earlier, but even better— much better. She didn't push him for answers. She asked. She explored, but she let his explanations be what they were, incomplete.

Greg pulled the sheet up around his neck and stared out into the black emptiness. Above the top of the house, he could see the shape of other houses and, off in the distance, the skyline of downtown. The night loomed dark and was filled with black shapes. The horizon line felt empty.

Everything was orderly; everything awaited destruction. Everything was poised for another hundred years; everything was waiting for the last moment. And when would it come?

"Our Father," he began slowly, "who art in heaven." He hadn't prayed for a long time. "Hallowed be Thy name." The rest of the prayer came out much easier. "Thy Kingdom come, Thy will be done on earth as it is in heaven . . ."

CHAPTER 25

Halloween came and went, and the first of November reminded Greg that Thanksgiving wasn't far behind. Winds abruptly shifted, and the cold north gales found their way into Washington, turning everything into winter. The sudden early onslaught of ice and snow seemed to say that the cold season would be long. Greg barely got to work on time on Wednesday because he slept late. Too much work was catching up with him.

At 9:00, the team assembled in the NSA auditorium for a second major discussion of the issues and facts their explorations had gathered. Moments before the meeting began, Mary dropped a note on top of Greg's files. He didn't look until she was seated at the back of the large table, then he took a quick look at the simple one-page sheet.

"Mr. Alex Majors is now officially on the team through the appointment of the office of Mr. Helmut Haussman. Vice-chairman of the CIA."

Greg froze, looking at the paper in front of him, his heart racing. For a few moments he breathed heavily but kept staring down at the paper until slowly his heavy breathing subsided. He glanced at Mary and found her staring straight at him. Without flinching or indicating any emotion, he saw a message in her eyes that only the two of them would grasp.

Get ready, she seemed to be saying. *Be prepared. Don't panic or get shook.* Mary didn't look different, but the fixed stare was clearly intended to reassure him. *Don't let Majors get under your skin*, she said only with her eyes.

Greg slowly scanned the room but saw no unexpected person until he turned the last corner in the back. Alex Majors sat next to another man Greg didn't know, but he was there, although somewhat cloistered.

Greg felt his mouth go dry, and he slipped down into his seat. The pressure of business closed in on him, but for thirty seconds Greg was somewhere else. His mind had taken the tunnel down to the center of the past.

He was in a gray bathroom and felt hot and claustrophobic. A man was bearing down on him, but Greg would not be an easy target. "You want the bottom line?" Greg stepped forward. "I've watched you operate for a long time, you greasy slime." He reached for the man's gray coat.

Alex Majors grabbed Greg's lapels and swung him back into the rest room stalls. The small door exploded behind him, and Greg knew he must move quickly. Metal crashed against metal, and Greg grabbed for the door handle, but Majors shoved him backward into the side of the stall. Greg swung wildly, but Majors ducked and stepped back. A terrible pain filled Greg's head, and he felt almost paralyzed. He felt Majors going for him, and the dark picture faded into blackness.

For several seconds, Greg couldn't hear anything. Slowly other sounds from the auditorium pushed in again, and he knew the episode had lasted only a few moments. But that was long enough for him to know exactly what Majors had done. Greg felt dizzy, but now he knew that Majors had sent him to the hospital.

After an entire minute of staring at his pile of folders, Greg slowly allowed himself to come to grips with what he had to do. Without looking at Majors, he called the meeting to order and started the business of the day by receiving a report from the NSA Department of Commerce. A secretary read the data and placed the information as part of their record. Most of the time Greg stared down at the table.

Greg appeared to be making notes, but he was carefully positioning himself. *Got to appear normal,* he thought. *If Majors thinks I don't remember the experience, I've got an edge.*

"In conclusion," the secretary finished, "the facts are obvious. We are not economically prepared for an earthquake of this magnitude in any shape or form." She sat down.

"Thank you, Ms. Cochrane." Greg stood up. "We recognize that this information is considered confidential and will deal with the details in that manner." He made a quick survey of the room, not pausing when his eyes swept past Majors. "Is Roger Mills here?" He kept looking around the room.

A middle-aged man in a gray suit slowly stood in the middle of the room, raising his hand. "Mills," he answered slowly. "I'm here to respond."

"I believe you have a report for us, sir."

Mills stood up hesitantly and, after a stumbling beginning, was soon into a heated discussion of the meaning of the Cochrane report. Greg appeared to be listening intently, but his mind was elsewhere. Majors was always the man to watch. Greg didn't have the whole thing completely in his mind, but he had enough. Majors was the one person to avoid.

Mills slowly turned his report into an attack, coming on finally like a Mack truck, slipping in and out of the center lane of traffic, maneuvering to make his points, and yet heading straight up the middle toward poor little Ms. Cochrane. He seemed to be both defending Ms. Cochrane's points and attacking them at the same time—a bit confusing but fascinating to watch.

Moving carefully in the director's chair, Greg kept Majors in the corner of his eye. His mind went back to the events of 1994. *I've got to get this issue as straight as I can,* he thought. *The San Onofre Nuclear Reactor was too close to the San Andreas fault. I remember that well enough. We were concerned with what might happen if the reactor was compromised in some way. Everything starts there for sure.*

Greg's attention returned to the present as he heard the speaker summarize, "Therefore, I believe that Ms. Cochrane's report has problems." Mills pulled his papers together as his voice trailed away. "However, we can trust this report in terms of its general conclusion." He quickly sat down.

Immediately a number of hands filled the air. Greg mechanically pointed to the first hand he saw. *Mary is caught up in this problem. She put in my hands a suggestion that a warning be sent throughout the area twenty-four hours before the Northridge quake. We've both gotten stung!*

The questioning went back and forth for nearly ten minutes. Greg felt his own sense of confidence rising with the discussion. He determined not to fall apart and realized, much to his own surprise, that he was in control.

"I believe we have another report," Greg interrupted the ongoing discussion, checking his agenda. "Let me see . . ."

"Yes," a voice in the back of the room broke in. "I have the report on the latest technology in relieving tectonic pressure between the subterranean plates." Alex Majors stood up and waited to be called forward.

Greg looked blank for a moment. "Of course," he said slowly. "Please feel free to begin."

Majors came forward quickly, nodded politely to Greg, and launched into his report. "Let me review one of three systems that has been kept secret until this moment," he began slowly. "The approach received significant testing in the Rocky Mountain Arsenal outside of Denver, Colorado."

Greg looked at Mary. Her face was stoic, but her eyes stared at him. She was saying, *Pay attention. Get this material down.*

For the first five minutes Greg kept his eyes focused off in the distance as if only partially listening, yet he indelibly recorded everything Majors said. *Good heavens!* Greg thought. *He is describing the government's attempts to dispose of industrial lubricants by pumping them into a deep aquifer! This action has never been reported by anyone anywhere.*

"To the surprise of the agencies involved in the secret expulsion," Majors continued both reading and explaining, "the vast amount of material lubricated the plates under the city of Denver so that they functioned quite effectively, moving smoothly over each other. This caused about fourteen hundred tremors before the government stopped the project. I suggest that this method will be of value in reducing the potential tension between the plates in the area between St. Louis and Memphis."

Greg tapped his files several times with his ballpoint pen. *Majors is offering us a way out of the dilemma,* he thought. *Doesn't fit what I expected from him. Something's not right in his report.*

"Therefore," Majors cleared his throat and took on a more exalted posture, "it is possible that a potential threat could be reduced and consolidated by completing at least four wells and saturating the area with a lubricant material."

"But," Greg suddenly broke in, "what if the lubricant doesn't relieve the pressure and actually precipitates a quake?"

"What?" Majors said with an astonished look.

"Isn't it possible for imprecise geological data to actually create a quake?" Greg repeated. "I have a report from Dr. Jack Forbes, a NASA scientist, raising questions about reliable data."

Majors looked stunned for a moment. "If your people guarantee the geological data, I will guarantee the results," he fired back. "Regardless of the speculation, it is preferable to attempt a controlled event rather than simply wait for an unavoidable disaster." Majors smiled condescendingly. "I *can* manage the proposal."

"Thank you for your report," Greg cut him off.

"But . . ."

"We have completed our time for today." Greg abruptly stood up but reached for the switch that allowed the moderator to control the microphone ten feet away from where the CIA agent had been speaking. "Thank you again, Mr. Majors." Greg nodded politely but hit the off button on the microphone to prevent any exchange. For a moment Majors looked surprised but quickly gathered his papers and prepared to retreat. "We will return to this report at a later date. In fact, if you will turn in your complete statement, we will make sure that papers are distributed to all members of the team." Greg smiled professionally and immediately turned back to the larger audience. "Our time has now concluded. Thank you for being here today. Our discussions will help us to come to a more quickly defined sense of purpose." He smiled broadly and waved a dismissal.

Mary stood with all of the people on her row; she looked at Greg and motioned upward toward her office. He nodded slightly and then launched into a conversation with his own secretary.

Fifteen minutes later Greg slipped through a side door that took him into the back of Mary's office. She was waiting by herself. "Something happened down there, didn't it?" she began at once.

Greg nodded. "I'm sure Majors attacked me and sent me to the hospital. You and I are the only ones with that conclusion, but I believe that's what really happened."

Mary looked shocked and shook her head slowly. "We must watch our backs!"

"Our backs?" Greg laughed disconcertingly. "The time is here to watch *everything*."

CHAPTER 26

Greg thought about Mary all the way home. The quick bite they had caught in an obscure restaurant shouldn't have put them in the all-seeing watchful eye of Director Allan Jones . . . or hopefully anyone else. She listened to him the way Alice always did. No sense of being a superior. Everything about Mary felt right, good, and promising. If ever he needed her, the time was now.

But tonight Greg also needed to talk with Sharon.

Mary's face wouldn't go away. Always strong and more than capable, she still left a warmth and compassion. In the last several weekends, his feelings for her had grown. Mary's eyes stayed with him. She looked natural, alive, deeply caring. As Greg drove the winding road into Virginia, Mary almost seemed to be sitting in the seat next to him.

He thought about how much had changed in his life since Sharon had returned home. Between her and this new project, Greg had been pushed into a new world of problems and people beyond anything he'd known for a decade. Sharon had taken him back to where they'd lived years ago. And she caused him to get back in touch with the things he believed, the issues that were the most important to him.

For the first time in years, Greg remembered the Methodist church he had gone to as a boy in the hills of Kentucky. The small, white structure was tucked away in a grove of trees in the

Cumberland Mountains not far from Laurel River Lakes. In the fall, the beauty of the trees and mountains bathed in a thousand colors touched the depths of his soul. All the beauty of the tree-covered mountains had come to rest in that little church one Sunday evening in the fall.

At fifteen, Greg was skinny, tall, and awkward. Old Brother Henry, the pastor, had rounded up an even dozen of the town kids and hauled them into the wood-floored sanctuary for a "come to Jesus" meeting. Not that the call to the altar wasn't expected, but the occasion was more than a little scary for Greg. Brother Henry had launched off on one of his "talks" that could very well last for an hour. The kids pretty well knew what the parameters would be, but on that evening something was different. Skinny Greg listened in a way that he'd never done before. Brother Henry seemed to have him at the end of his gun barrel.

The preacher only talked about thirty minutes when he called each of the dozen teens to accept Jesus and ask Him to come into their lives. He described how Nicodemus heard the call as well as Peter and Paul. Their only hope was to say yes and kneel at that rickety old altar with Henry.

Greg was never sure just how many kids went forward because he felt a powerful inner urge to kneel with Brother Henry and get his way to heaven taken care of. He could remember tears running down his cheeks and the feel of the wood pushing into his knees. Greg prayed as hard as was possible for a solid twenty-five minutes. When he looked up, only six of his friends remained around the long narrow communion rail. The others apparently left, and not one of the group ever talked about the evening again.

Years later Greg remembered how that one evening had determined the direction of everything that followed. Brother Henry told him how important it was to be honest and sincere. He was supposed to live out this faith that was now deep in his heart.

"Yes, sir," Greg told Brother Henry hesitantly. "I promise to do my best."

"Now you listen here," Old Brother Henry answered. "Twenty years from now when I hear about what's become of you, I expect it to be good. Don't never want to hear of anything funny happenin'. Understand?"

"Oh yes, sir!" Greg nodded his head.

"You've made an agreement with the La-ord!" Brother Henry waved his fist over his head. "The deal is done!"

"Oh, yes, sir-ee!" Greg gritted his teeth as he thought about that evening.

He carefully turned the curve that would soon take him to his home. His old '89 Pontiac held the road well. He grinned. "Twenty years?" he said to himself. "It's been forty years ago, I guess."

He slowed for the cutoff to his home. *Brother Henry must have died years ago. He was probably sixty that night in the little church. God bless him.* Greg drove on, consumed in thought.

When Greg arrived at the house, Sharon had eaten earlier and was working in the study. For several moments, he stood in the kitchen and watched her on the other side of the living room, typing on the computer. She seemed alone, distant, completely absorbed in what she was doing. Sharon and the number two at NSA had many similar characteristics yet were completely different. In a strange way, she and Mary were the two bookends that held his life together.

"I'm home," he called from the kitchen.

Sharon looked up, a surprise wrinkled across her face. "It's after 7:00."

"7:30 or so." Greg came into the hall. "I'm actually doing better than usual."

Sharon got up, walked out of the study, and crossed the living room, meeting Greg in the hall. She kissed her father on the cheek. "Not much. Glad you're home anyway though."

"Let's go into the kitchen for a bit." Greg beckoned for Sharon to follow him into the kitchen. He sat down at the table. "Well, our little project at the office seems to be chugging along quite well. I think we're going to meet our deadline."

Sharon smiled thoughtfully. "Good."

"That's all you've got to say. Good?"

"Good job." Sharon raised her eyebrow slightly.

"I'm totally overwhelmed." Greg went to the refrigerator and took out a small container of milk. He reached for a glass and sat down at the table. "I'd hoped for a little more enthusiasm than I usually get at the NSA, but not too much more." He smiled at his daughter's distant demeanor. "You're certainly an encouragement."

Sharon sat down on the other side of the table. "Dad, let's put the kidding aside. I've actually been thinking about several important things before you got here." She looked thoughtfully out the window. "You know, I came home from Israel simply to take care of you. Nothing more." She smiled again. "But time has gone by and things have happened. Know what I mean?"

Greg laughed. "Yeah, I sure do."

"Suddenly you're home and everything is fine."

"Really think so?" He drank the glass of milk.

"No, Dad. I don't." Sharon didn't smile this time. "I think you're in over your head."

"Ah-h yes, yes. My, my, where are you going with this little message?" Greg laughed. "You don't see me doing quite as well as I'd hoped."

Sharon reached for his hand. "Things really aren't going so well at the office, are they?"

Greg got up from the table and put the milk back in the refrigerator. "No." He put the empty glass in the sink. "No, things aren't running well at all, as a matter of fact."

"Just as I suspected. I knew you weren't telling me the whole story."

Greg leaned back in the kitchen chair. "You think you can help me put everything back together, huh?"

Sharon smiled. "Maybe I can." She settled against the table. "Dad, I want to tell you more about the book that I started reading several weeks ago. One I picked up at the church when I was running down material on messianic Jews." She stirred nervously. "I've mentioned the material before but haven't said that much about the book in a week. Yet it's made a tremendous difference in how I see everything happening to us right now." Sharon leaned over the table. "I think you need to read it."

"Okay." Greg conceded. "If it's good enough for you, it's got to be great for me."

"No, Dad. The book is much more profound than anything we've dealt with in this whole mess you've stirred up. It explains the meaning of the book of Revelation. I want you to consider every line carefully."

"I promise." Greg held up his hands. "Why don't you give me a little sense of what it says . . . just a tiny, teeny taste? I've got something to tell you too."

Sharon frowned. "Dad, I'm serious. The chapter titled 'The Woman and the Dragon' describes all of the experiences that the world will go through just before Jesus Christ returns. Remember our discussion the other night, about how America isn't a world power at the end of time?"

"Yes." Greg's voice changed, and he didn't sound cute anymore.

"Well, I've been thinking more about that. I read the book three times and worked hard to be sure I understood what the author was saying. Edlow Moses tells the story like it is."

Greg squinted at his daughter and said, "Why don't you lay this out in a little more detail? I don't usually give as much time as I should to biblical matters."

"Dad, I've checked out the plan of action that Edlow Moses describes in this book. It's clear that something extraordinary is going to happen in the United States, removing the entire country from involvement in the final exchange between the Jews and their enemies."

Greg felt his chin. The usually soft skin was covered with stubble and felt rough. He rubbed the corners of his mouth for a moment. "You're talking about something that will happen years and years from now. Right?"

Sharon shook her head slowly. "I'm getting the idea that this scene could happen in the very *immediate* future." She paused for a moment. "Like next week. Next month. Next year."

"Next week is a little early, isn't it?" Greg said. "How about in another century or so?"

"No. I'm telling you that we're looking at a problem that could happen any time—and this entire country will be gone from the scene of world power." Sharon reached for his hand and held it tightly. "The final countdown could start momentarily, but we're not going to be in the story."

For a moment Greg looked at his daughter's hand holding his. "Sharon, I'm not sure of all the reasons that this book has affected you like it has, but I *do know* you're a very thoughtful person. Not easily sidetracked by something wild and woolly." He stared at her hand. "Obviously, we could talk about these matters all evening, but I've got something important that I came home specifically to talk about. As important as what you're telling me, the truth is, I need your help more today than I did a month ago. Things are heating up at the office, and you could make a tremendous difference in what happens to me."

"What are you suggesting?"

"I'd like to have you assist me as a confidential aide, to help me face a big problem that I'm going to have to handle in the next several weeks."

Sharon withdrew her hand and leaned back in her chair. "Dad, I'm not sure what's happening here. I start out telling you about a book, and you're suddenly talking to me about a very different matter."

Greg shook his head. "I'd hoped for a more simple approach to all of these problems, but the truth is that something happened today that has affected how I see and hear everything that is occurring right now."

For several minutes Greg talked about Alex Majors showing up at his hearing and what he said. Greg described as clearly as he could why he thought Majors attacked him in the rest room. Sharon listened intently, saying nothing.

"Oh wow! This is heavy," she finally said. "Sounds to me like Majors and Haussman have got something big going on together. Right?"

Greg nodded his head. "I think these boys are closer to the heart of my problems than I've recognized. Something big is unfolding, and I'm about to see it come to life under my nose."

"But that's just what I'm trying to tell you. If this gigantic earthquake came off, where would we be?"

Greg watched his daughter's eyes. Nothing slick or gimmicky

there, he knew. Just a good kid asking the most important question in America today.

"Let me put the matter another way," she said. "Where would we be if a gigantic earthquake broke this country apart?"

"Out of the game."

Sharon leaned back in her chair. "We *are* talking about the same problem."

Greg folded his arms over his chest and pulled at the bottom of his chin. "Yes, Sharon. We're talking about the same problem, and I need your help. We can make things big and complex or simply hit the bottom line. We are dealing with a problem that could be at the heart of what Revelation warns us is coming."

"And I want to help you," she said simply. "Really help. We may be looking at things from different viewpoints, but I believe that the heart of this matter has to do with God. We've spent years out on the edge of the branch because we couldn't face Mother's death." She caught a deep breath. "Well, Mother would ask, 'Why in the world haven't you gone on with your lives?'"

Greg nodded his head slowly. "You're right, Sharon. We haven't talked about these religious things very much." He stretched out in his chair. "The time has come for me to get real about where we are spiritually."

"I hadn't faced my spiritual needs since her funeral either," Sharon said. "I don't want to live that way. Okay? We both need God in our lives. That's our most pressing reality."

Greg reached for his daughter's hand. "Maybe you've already done much more than I have, but the truth is that half the time I seem to be operating on some high-level system of knowledge. The other half of the time I feel like a yo-yo for some guy named Haussman about whom I know virtually nothing . . . except that I don't like him." He squeezed her hand. "I really want to be more effective, and I need you and God to help me. Would you consider being the confidential aide I need?"

"Only if you're willing to pay the price I'm putting on the table." Sharon scooted forward. "I want to do everything I can to help us come into the full relationship with God that we once had and shared. Is it a deal?"

Greg looked hard at his daughter. Sharon had her mother's sense of honesty. She played things straight up the middle, and she wasn't kidding today. There wasn't anything more important to her than this one dimension right now. There wasn't anything more important to him either.

"Is it a deal?"

Greg reached over and hugged his daughter. "You bet it is."

CHAPTER 27

Greg leaned over and turned his car radio on. "November 2!" the radio news reporter blasted across the car. "Another great morning in the most powerful city on earth!" Greg grimaced at his daughter on the other side of the front seat. "I don't think I need one of those early morning explosions today. I got up at sunrise highly aware of where I work." He turned the radio off.

"Dad, you really think this is the right way to go?" Sharon looked out the car window at the thick clump of trees whizzing past. "I mean . . . do you think they are just going to let me walk around your building?"

"Yes," Greg answered firmly. "I think that your old man has enough firepower and past accomplishments to pull off hiring you to work for me. I'm going to tell the people over in personnel that you're coming on board to help with this new assignment, and they're going to say, 'Hurry, sign her up.'" He looked at his daughter with a firm glance. "The main item we must obtain this morning is an ID tag for you to wear. Got to get you past our security system in the NSA offices without any problems. I think we can push that one through in a few hours. We've got plenty of money to hire you."

Sharon rolled her eyes and exhaled forcefully. "I don't know."

"You are now Alice Mathewson. That was your mother's maiden name. Eventually it will turn up on the computers. If there's a problem, we should be done by the time the security people work everything through in a week or so."

Sharon shook her head. "I don't usually function like this," she answered. "But then again, I don't fly at your altitude very often."

"Oh, really?" Greg feigned surprise. "We're talking Ms. AP reporter here, right?" He poked her with his elbow. "We're jawing with the woman who marched into the explosion on the Temple Mount and got the first pictures of the big hole going all the way down to China. Is this the person I'm having this conversation with today?"

"Well, yes, but . . ."

"But what? I'd say your father is lucky to have you on his team."

Sharon grinned. "You know what I mean, Dad. We're talking about me being involved in a truly wild scheme. You're getting ready to mess with the security of the United States government."

Greg grinned and raised an eyebrow. "By the way, that's another change." Parker swerved around the car in front of him. "From now on, it's got to be Dr. Parker and Ms. Alice Mathewson. While we can't hide everything, we don't want to broadcast the depth of our relationship." He gave her a quick look and then focused his eyes back on the traffic. "Got me?"

"Yes sir, *Dr.* Parker."

"Good. That'll keep the boys on the team downstairs happy, and not suspicious."

"Fortunately, I don't look like you at all." Sharon looked out the window again. The outskirts of Washington, D.C. were not far ahead, and the city was coming into view. "Not many people would assume I'm your daughter. Particularly, if I use mother's last name . . . that *you* came up with."

"Got a better one?"

"Actually I like Smith. Just plain Sharon Smith."

Greg shook his head. "You've got to be kidding."

"No, I like Smith."

He shook his head again. "Man, that would give the boys in security something to work on. Unfortunately, they'd figure out a Smith alias in about thirty seconds."

"Really think so?" Sharon sounded completely unsure of herself.

He looked out the side window and stepped on the gas. "Absolutely."

• • •

Dr. Parker glanced at his watch. 11:00. He'd been in the building three hours, and by this time Sharon should be on her way up to his section of the building. He'd leave getting her geared into the program in Mary's hands. She'd do it better anyway. He hurried up the fire escape steps to Mary's office and entered through the back door.

"Hey, what's happening?" Greg called in from the back hall. "Are you in here?" He came around the corner into Mary's office.

Mary's secretary looked startled.

"Oh, excuse me." Greg froze in the hall. "I didn't know anyone was here."

"Thank you, Ms. Jones." Mary sounded professional and looked distant. "I think that will take care of our business for now." She turned in her chair. "Hello, Dr. Parker."

The secretary smiled broadly at Greg, winked, and hurried out the outer door. She turned at the door for a moment and winked again.

Greg looked at the ceiling and shook his head. "Oh, no."

"A little phone call helps take the edge off these things." Mary raised an eyebrow.

Greg looked chastised. Mary stood up at her desk. "Wouldn't you say, *Duke*?"

"I know better," Greg apologized. "Didn't think anyone was in here."

"Got caught, didn't you?" Mary grinned impishly. "So what's on your mind this morning?" She dropped down on a small couch across from her desk. "Sit down and let's talk."

"I have a new employee that I need you to help me train," he began and sat down at the other end of the couch. "The sort of business you'd be quite good at doing this morning."

Mary crossed her arms over her chest. "This morning? Listen, I'm already swamped. I haven't trained people in, maybe, oh say, ten years." She looked skeptical. "You've got a little angle you're playing today?"

Greg smiled. "You might put it that way. I have a young woman named Alice Mathewson whom I need to help us at the highest levels. I think you could do well with her."

"Alice Mathewson?" Mary frowned. "Who in the world is *that*?"

"Actually," Greg cleared his throat, "her full name is Sharon Parker, and she's actually a journalist full time."

"Your daughter?" Her jaw dropped slightly.

Greg put his index finger to his lips. "Shh. We don't want to wake up some of the people on our little team."

Mary shook her head. "Dr. Parker. Would you like to fill in some of the blanks for me? This sounds like a Duke deal to me. Like John Wayne is flying the airplane this morning."

Greg leaned back into the overstuffed couch. "I'm not sure what's going on in this entire scheme that Haussman and Majors are pulling off, but I had a strange experience yesterday evening." Greg put his hands behind his neck and looked up at the ceiling. "Sharon and I had a good talk last night. Worked out some details that I've been thinking about for a long time. Personal things, but this time we touched some of my deeper, hidden buttons."

"I don't have any idea what you're talking about," Mary interrupted.

Greg looked straight at Mary. "And then I went to bed," he talked even slower. "I had one idea in mind but was still feeling a little on the agitated side." Greg took a deep breath. "Then, I had one of those attacks . . . those strange visions that hit me when I seem to be upset about something."

Mary nodded her head very slowly. "Yes. I know well."

"I can't exactly tell you what happened to me, but Majors was making the speech he made yesterday again in this sort of vision experience." He shook his head. "It was as if the afternoon was being replayed exactly as Majors gave his speech, but as I listened, much of what he said shifted from what he said before. Turned into a different speech. I lay there in bed and heard this CIA meathead make a completely different speech. At the end, Majors walked away, and I was in a straitjacket." He rubbed his head nervously. "After that I simply went to sleep, hammered to the bed."

"How strange." Mary rubbed the side of her face. "But *exactly* what was different in his speech?"

"That's the big problem. I remember being completely absorbed, listening to Majors detail the other side, but I can't remember what he said. I saw the details, the shape and form of their plan . . . but now it's gone. Like the whole thing went up in smoke."

"You didn't get anything?"

"One thing." Greg leaned forward. "I got one thing that's enough. Remember Majors talking about drilling four wells?"

Mary nodded her head.

"I think he was telling us in my vision that the wells are already drilled."

Mary stared. "You've got to be joking." She shook her head more emphatically. "Aren't you?"

"I don't think so." Greg squeezed Mary's hand. "I'm afraid I've seen something that I can't quite put together but is an essential ingredient in what is going on behind the scenes. Majors is already completing what he described."

"You're sure that was the message?"

Greg rubbed his chin. "Yes. I can only make a guess, but we'd never have had a clear idea of exactly what Majors is doing without my strange experience. We simply wouldn't know." He scratched his head. "At least, that's what I'm feeling right now. I believe my vision has opened a very important door. You know emotion hasn't been my strong suit in the past several months."

Mary smiled for the first time. "Feelings, huh? Now that's a new twist." She patted the top of his hand. "Don't worry, Greg. We'll get this thing worked out one way or another. We obviously need to find where those wells are."

"That's where Sharon comes in. I'm going to need her to help me run down this angle. We don't have much time, but my vision gave me the necessary clues about where to go."

Mary stood up and walked back to her desk. "Yes, you're right. We don't have *any* time even if you're half right." She sat down behind her desk. "Okay, bring in the young lady as soon as they process her papers and give her an ID tag. I'll get her into gear."

"Thanks, Mary."

"I think it might be better if she worked for me," Mary said thoughtfully, turning around to the bookcase behind her desk. "We could put her up here on this floor."

Greg smiled slightly. "An interesting idea."

Mary stopped and slowly turned back around, looking straight in his eyes. "You set me up!"

CHAPTER 28

By evening, Sharon was signed into the NSA as a member of vice-coordinator Mary Morgan's staff. She had received four hours of careful instruction and had a small office in Mary's staff suite. The kid, as Greg called her, was signed on with Washington's insider organization.

Through her office door Sharon watched the clock across the hall. In five minutes, the large hand would touch twelve and it would be five o'clock. The first day done.

The young woman leaned back in the small desk chair and deeply exhaled. Never had Sharon experienced such a whirlwind day. From the moment she had walked into the personnel office, the hiring process happened quickly. Some people who had tried for days to get to that level of hiring glared at Sharon, but Alice Mathewson only smiled back kindly. She looked out the side window over the landscape of Washington, D.C., and the land rolling down to the Potomac River. Sharon shook her head. At least she still seemed to have fingers and toes.

"The place is a killer," a woman said from the door.

Sharon whirled around. Mary was standing in the entry.

"You're telling me." Sharon lifted her tired hands. "I don't see how you and Dad . . . I mean Dr. Parker . . . survive your jobs."

Mary laughed. "I guess we get absorbed into the NSA machinery like a couple of pieces of driftwood floating down the river. One thing leads to another and here we are, up to our necks in a big-time mess."

Sharon studied Mary. She had proven more attractive than Sharon expected. Clever. Articulate. Mary Morgan had to be extremely intelligent and perceptive. Up to this point everything they said had been on a business basis with little spare time for personal thoughts. Maybe things were about to change.

"NSA can be a grinding machine." Mary walked in and sat down in a small corner chair. "Feel like someone's been working on you just a bit?"

"More than a little." Sharon tried to be casual. "And I have no idea where everything is going. I feel completely out of place, like an empty sugar bowl on a restaurant table."

"Let me encourage you." Mary sounded professional but not distant. "We can be forthright in this office because I know it's clean, but you must be very careful when talking on the phones. Assume they are bugged." Mary smiled and shook her head. "I didn't think your father could pull so many strings and get you into this office by this first afternoon, but the Duke did it. Did you know we sometimes use that name for him?"

Sharon laughed. "I've heard his Duke stories through the years."

"Well, today you witnessed the whole thing happening first-hand. You're here in this office because Duke Parker made it happen. That's the bottom line."

Sharon smiled but watched Mary closely. The older woman seemed genuine. Nothing negative there. Obviously, she could be a mother type, but she was trying to reach Sharon where she lived. The openness felt good. She could learn to like her a lot.

"I'm glad to be here," Sharon said.

Mary smiled. "I'm glad to have you here. It will be my pleasure to get to know you well." She started backing away. "Call me if you need anything." Mary waved casually. "I'm not far away." Then she was gone.

Sharon stared at the empty door. Mary Morgan was, indeed, much more than anticipated. The woman was both inviting and intimidating. Everything she'd done that day was helpful and gracious.

Mary definitely had a strong interest in Sharon's father. And that was good but it created a new context, a different environment that added a skewed social setting. Sharon wasn't sure what to do with the new world, but she was there to learn and would figure her place out sooner or later.

After the big hand slipped past 5:00, Sharon called downstairs. "You there?"

"Well, how are things up there where the big boys play?" Greg answered.

"I doubt if they're one tad faster than down there in your offices," Sharon fired back.

Greg laughed. "Feel like you're getting to know my world better? Did Mary say anything about the phones, Alice?"

"Good grief! This place is wild. Excuse me! I take back whatever I once said about this place as pure understatement." Sharon caught her breath. "Yes, I understand that we could have . . . problems with the phones."

"Is this repentance I hear?"

"Dr. Parker," Sharon paused a moment, "whatever I said in the past was a vast understatement. This place operates like a machine gun firing range."

Greg laughed again. "Welcome to our little piece of the world called the NSA. I'm glad you understand the importance of keeping a sense of propriety in what you say anywhere around this place. Are the people leaving your offices up there?"

Sharon looked out the door again. "Looks like most of the staffers on this floor are long gone. Mary is probably still here."

"Yeah, she is. I'll be up there in just a couple of minutes."

"Whatever you say, *Duke*." Sharon hung up before he could respond. She smiled and stared at the phone. "Oh, yes. The big man will be here very quickly. I'll just wait patiently for his eminence to come sailing through the office door."

Sharon leaned back in her chair. Three minutes later her father still hadn't come through the door. She looked at both the hall clock and her wristwatch. Five minutes passed and she worried. Maybe he'd had another one of those strange attacks. She started to call again. The phone rang.

"Yes."

"Alice, would you please come back to my office," Mary asked professionally.

"Sure. I'll be right there."

Sharon paused at the door, hoping to see her father and then went down the hall. She opened the door and stopped. Greg was standing next to the large window, looking down on the people pouring out into the street.

"Dr. Parker!" Sharon shut the door behind her quickly. "How did you get in here?"

"Osmosis." Greg turned around slowly. "Sometimes I go through the walls. Sometimes I use the ceilings."

Sharon caught her breath and shook her head. "I obviously don't know anything about this place."

Mary came around the corner, her arms filled with files and papers. "I guess the time has come for us to get down to business," she said. "I think I have everything we need."

"Good." Greg pulled a chair up to the small worktable. "Let's see if we can put this thing together. We can speak frankly in this room. I know everything checked out last week. Want to watch, Ms. Mathewson?"

Sharon scrutinized her father and Mary as they began sorting out the pile of materials as if they knew exactly what they were doing. Little was said as papers and files were quickly put in different stacks.

"Excuse me," Sharon finally said. "Maybe I ought to go back to my office until needed."

"No, no." Greg pointed at a chair without looking up. "Pull up here with us. We'll show you what to do in a moment."

Mary moved quickly, putting materials in neat piles while Greg methodically lined up his portion of materials. Sharon stared, unsure of even what to say.

"You see," Greg began after a couple of minutes, "you're going to set up flight plans for us in the near future." He looked at Sharon for almost the first time. "We don't know exactly where we are going, but you're going to help put the other pieces in the puzzle together tomorrow."

"Wait!" Sharon held her hands up. "I don't have the slightest idea what you are saying or doing. Let's stop this process, and one of you give me some idea of why I am in here watching the two of you play out this little game."

Mary blinked several times and looked across at Greg. For a moment Greg looked blankly at his daughter. "Hmm." He rolled his tongue around inside his cheeks. "I guess we haven't really told Alice what we're attempting to do. You do remember that I'm a pilot?"

Mary raised an eyebrow and shrugged casually.

Sharon watched her father lean back in the chair so far that only two legs were on the floor. "Sharon, I need to tell you about a piece of this story you haven't heard before." He cleared his throat and looked out the window. "Lately I haven't had nearly as many of those strange visionary experiences that came after my stroke, but I had one incident that continues to haunt me. During a committee meeting, I thought I saw some wells being drilled and a lubricating substance pumped into the earth from those sites. It was one of those hallucinotory experiences. Mary was there. Remember?"

Mary nodded her head solemnly.

"For a long time I couldn't decide what the experience meant, but as other data came in, I came to the conclusion that I was given a special insight into the problem that NSA is struggling to solve in the New Madrid fault zone.

"I don't understand, Dad." Sharon scooted closer. "Be more specific."

Greg took a deep breath. "I believe that a CIA agent is drilling wells somewhere in a region that runs from Missouri down to the Mississippi. His goal is to lubricate areas in the Reelfoot Rift that will cause a shift in the New Madrid fault. The end result would cause an earthquake of enormous proportions."

Sharon's eyes widened. "You've got to be kidding!"

"No, unfortunately I'm not. "If I'm right, our task is to locate these wells and identify them before that are able to set off an earthquake."

"And that's what I'm here for?" Sharon's voice raised. "You're going to give me the job of researching through two, three, maybe up to five states looking for several wells?" She shook her head. "I'd say that's a little on the other side of finding a needle in a haystack!"

"Not quite." Greg shook his head. "I think we've got the data a little more precisely in this material that Alex Majors used."

"Majors!" Sharon bolted forward.

"Afraid so." Her father returned to the materials in front of him. "Remember, the White House shoe-horned my little friend into our research team."

"What exactly does his inclusion mean?"

Greg didn't look up as he quickly searched through the papers in front of him. "My old buddy is with me as a representative of the CIA. Because he was forced in as a member of my secret research project by Helmut Haussman, I have come to the conclusion that he and Haussman are in some way linked. Because of that tie, everything that I do must be done on a top secret basis."

"Just a minute." Sharon stood up and abruptly put her hand in the middle of the pile between Mary and her father. "I want the bottom line on what we are doing here after 5:00? Okay?"

Mary smiled. "Sharon, your father believes that Majors is on our research team to use our findings in a way that could hurt many people. Your job is to help us locate the places where this may be happening and get us there to check out the drilling sites."

Sharon raised her eyebrows and took a deep breath. "Oh. I thought this was something really complicated, but now I see. I'm supposed to help the two of you go through heaven knows how many acres of land until we find several wells doing something or the other about which I don't have any idea."

Mary put her hand on top of Sharon's and gave her a gentle squeeze. "I understand how difficult this is today, and what we're doing can't make much sense, but I think your father is going to show us where those wells are. He's the key to this mystery."

Greg worked without looking at his daughter. "Sharon, I don't know for sure that Majors is drilling wells, but I think I have an angle that's going to tell us what we need to know. The location is where the Reelfoot Rift crosses a major crack in the New Madrid area. Mary has compiled information today in the areas that Majors alluded to in his talk yesterday. We have charts and lists of oil wells and water wells, all special projects that must be filled out and registered within the states. All we have to do is find two to four of these wells that were started in the same period, and we may be on to what we're looking for. Your job is to piece these together, using your computer. Without a computer the project would be tough; with one, things should work out quickly."

Sharon shook her head. "I guess I'll figure it out in the morning." She stood up and ran her hands through her hair. "Dad, when do we go home?"

"After supper." Greg was back in the pile.

"I'd hoped for a little time to talk," Mary said quietly. "Just the three of us." She turned back to the table.

Sharon looked at her father, a man she knew well, and Mary Morgan, a mystery woman, working together quickly, precisely, methodically. They had invited her into their world, but no one was making Sharon say yes. The matter was her decision.

Sharon finally said, "Yes." She cleared her throat. "Yes, I'm here for as long as is necessary."

"Good." Greg Parker didn't even look up. He just kept rummaging through the files.

CHAPTER 29

Mary watched Greg talk to his daughter while they ate supper at Dante's, an Italian restaurant about three blocks from the office. Hot spaghetti tasted good on a cold evening. Far from having problems, the two traded jabs and asides with casual ease. Their pace moved along quickly and neither gave any ground, but Mary sensed Sharon was also watching her with more than a perfunctory interest, not with hostility as much as a strong desire to figure out what made her tick. She would be under a microscope for the evening.

"Sharon, you can see why we needed you." Greg said. "I've *got* to find out what Majors is doing, and you're the one to tell me exactly where to look."

"Sure." Sharon sounded disinterested. "Consistent casting. My job is to show up at the last minute and save everything just before the boat goes under in the big fire."

"I don't believe that is what I just said," he corrected her as if he were a politician answering questions during a television interview.

"I'm describing what's going to happen." Sharon flipped back. "Just a simple detailing of how I'll save this project from sheer disaster."

Greg looked at Mary. "Can you do anything with this woman who's such a mess?"

"Is that a nice way to talk about me?" Sharon smiled and took a bite. "I just don't understand what's happening here."

Mary broke into laughter. "Oh, brother, the two of you are worse than a couple of little kids arguing over which one ate the most Wheaties for breakfast."

Greg shook his head. "As I was saying," he spoke to Mary, "Sharon is going to finish first thing in the morning. After all that we clarified a few hours ago, the task shouldn't take long."

"Don't try that angle on me," Sharon pushed. "I've been on your payroll for about six hours. You can't possibly expect me to know what to do with this huge problem."

"I think your father is trying to tell us something," Mary broke in. "Am I right, Greg?"

"Maybe." Parker smiled confidently.

Sharon feigned a glum look. "You have *another* little surprise?"

"I'm waiting." Greg held on.

"This is the nonsense I live with day after day." Sharon spoke to Mary as if Greg wasn't there. "Do you have any idea how maddening he can get?"

Mary watched Greg, enjoying the repartee and grinning. He had Sharon in a bind. He probably knew exactly where the oil wells were but wouldn't tell Sharon until the last minute. It was the sort of game Greg liked playing occasionally. He was the big fisherman, and Sharon was on the hook.

"Let's see if I can get things back on track," Sharon bore down. "Maybe if I looked at those sheets of paper you put in your inside coat pocket back at the office, I would be able to tell you how long it would take tomorrow morning to get the thing lined up."

Greg's mouth dropped slightly. The big fisherman had become the fish.

"You didn't think I saw you put those figures in your pocket," Sharon persisted. "My hunch is that it will take about fifteen minutes to get this project wrapped up tomorrow."

Greg looked completely dumbstruck.

Sharon's thin smile slowly spread across her face. "Gotcha! Right?"

"Well, I wouldn't make any quick judgments." He sounded as if he were in full retreat. "These things aren't satisfied by a simple flip of the wrist."

Sharon held her hand out, palm up. "The papers."

"In all my years with the NSA, I've never seen anyone successfully complete an end run around Greg Parker." Mary shook her head. "But the kid won this round, Dad."

Greg suddenly laughed. "Not bad, Sharon." He reached inside his coat. "Here's what I think will eventually prove to be the four wells." He laid the plans on the table. "Think you can figure this out?"

Sharon picked up the sheets of paper and looked at them for a minute. "Sure. When do you want to go?"

Greg grinned sheepishly. "I really didn't think you'd get this one so fast. Okay. You win, Sharon. Not bad."

"Dad thinks I'm going to function like I did in the tenth grade, Mary. I don't know why, but I win every time." She gave him a got-you-last look and then picked up the dessert menu.

Mary watched Sharon's self-satisfied look. Being friends was certainly much easier than she first thought. Sharon didn't lose very often, and when she did, it would be twice as hard to prevail next time. She would do well to keep that fact clearly in mind.

Sharon closed the menu and looked seriously at her father. "I can set up a flight the day after tomorrow," she said factually. "We can leave whenever you wish."

"Good." He took a deep breath, nodding his head slowly. "We must see what Majors has done so far, and it may not be so easy. Probably ought to leave around 8:00 from Dulles Airport. I'm sure that no other reports have gone into the states on these proposed wells." Greg turned to Mary. "Can you go up with us?"

Mary's continual analysis of their ongoing supper conversation was scattered. "Can I go?" she asked herself aloud. "I suppose I should check with my secretary in the morning, but if I don't have something unexpected, I'd be glad to go."

"I'd like you to be with us." Greg seemed to be thinking out loud. "I don't know what to expect, but your observations will be important."

"You want me?" Sharon asked.

"Of course. You will be doing a number of things, including taking pictures."

"Oh, is that right?" Sharon answered sardonically. "If I remember, you had nothing but bad comments about the college courses I took in photojournalism. If I remember correctly, you said . . ."

"Thank you, Sharon." Greg shut her down. "We *all* get the picture."

"Just reminding you," Sharon countered.

"As I was saying," Greg turned to Mary, "I want Sharon to take pictures if there's anything to record, and you'll be there to take notes. Okay, Mary?"

Mary looked at Sharon. "Sound acceptable to you?"

"Sure." Sharon finished her salad. "Whatever the big boss says is fine with me."

Mary started to say that she was the big boss but didn't. The truth was that Greg called the shots, and he should be in charge, at least in Sharon's eyes.

"Okay!" Greg crossed his arms over his chest. "We've got this one settled. Tomorrow Miss Calculator will arrange for a private airplane. Mary will make sure she can go, and then on Saturday we fly off in the clouds with the flair and skill of people going around the world in eighty days. Everyone agreed?"

Sharon gave him a thumbs up.

Mary smiled agreeably and leaned back in her chair. Sharon and Greg broke into a conversation about the right company to use for the flight and were quickly lost in the details. Mary watched the young woman. Few people in the NSA would or could stand toe-to-toe with the Duke like Sharon. She was strong and not giving him an inch.

Mary watched a few sparks burst into the air and fall to the table. *Don't want to offend Sharon. I've got to try to make her into the best friend I've got. A promising task.*

CHAPTER 30

The roar of the departing airliners only a few feet away shook the much smaller airplane. Greg edged out onto the runway with the DC-10s and the 747s. Even though the inside of the two-engine plane was warm enough, everything felt stark and limited, but that didn't bother Greg. He flew often enough to pay little attention to the sound of the huge airplane engines. The roar and the flurry of activity around an airport excited him. Sharon sat next to him with a number of maps in hand and seemed without a care in the world, but Mary looked out the rear window, much more apprehensive.

"Beech N235D," the tower operator advised. "You are cleared for take off."

"Roger you," Greg answered. "Beech N235D cleared for take off." He pushed the throttle forward, and their airplane roared down the runway. Moments later they were off the ground and well on their way south. Greg smiled and settled easily into the cockpit seat. He soon reached the best altitude for the trip and headed south.

"We've got a bit of a ride before we zero in on our targets," Greg spoke out of the side of his mouth. "Hope you ladies can sit back and enjoy the flight."

Sharon turned in her seat and glanced at Mary, who was looking a bit grim. "You okay?"

"Sure." Mary forced a smile. "Just don't fly in these smaller airplanes that often." She tightly clutched the arm support next to the window.

"Let me help you get a tad more relaxed." Sharon turned in her seat. "You don't have to worry. Dad's been flying me around the countryside for a hundred years. Why, our family . . ." She stopped and bit her lip. Sharon started again. "We've flown everywhere since I was a child. Don't be nervous. The old man always gets us there and back in great shape." Mary kept the resolute look.

Greg paid little attention to the conversation going on beside him. He kept his eyes on the horizon and thought about the job they needed to complete before sundown. The first leg of the trip would take time, but because the airplane was smaller they could set down in a more remote area. They were prepared to spend the night if necessary. In a way he could not completely describe, Greg knew the trip was crucial. He was soon lost in his thoughts about how to proceed if they did find anything.

Four hours later the airplane landed in St. Louis, and Greg waited outside while a crew refilled the fuel tanks. In record time, they were off the ground and on their way again.

"We've got to watch carefully from here on out," Greg told the women. "We can't be too far from our destination. Sharon, you got the maps ready?"

"Sure do."

"Okay." Greg gently lowered the nose. "We need to keep checking the coordinates and maintain a sharp eye. If we don't find anything on this run, we'll have to try another route. We're going to have to watch the trees. They get thick in this area."

"I've got confidence in you, Dad. You fly the plane, and I'll keep us on track." Sharon started unfolding the maps.

Mary pushed forward and talked over the seat. "What can I do?"

"I want you to watch the ground," Greg said. "We're going to need all the help we can get to identify the possible location of these derricks Majors put around the countryside. You know what to look for?"

"Think so," Mary answered. "I presume we'll come down fairly low."

"You bet," Greg reassured her and stopped lowering the airplane.

"I'll do my best." Mary settled back in her seat and looked out the window apprehensively.

For the next thirty minutes Greg flew silently over the heavily wooded area. Little was said as they crisscrossed the rolling countryside and wound through valleys. Woody terrain increased and the area became more dense and rolling. Houses poked up here and there, but most of the area appeared to be uninhabited.

Sharon abruptly reached for her father's arm. "We can't be too far from the first place. At least, if this compass and map location are accurate."

Greg slowed the airplane. "I'm going to take a run up that valley. We're not that far from the Mississippi River either." He pointed to the left. "The area has the appearance of everything we're looking for." The airplane dropped several hundred feet.

"Look!" Mary pointed toward the ground. "There's something at around nine o'clock. See the cleared area down there?"

"Where?" Greg pulled back on the throttle and tilted the airplane slightly. "I'll have to maneuver some to get over there." The airplane's wing dropped, and they began a slow circular swoop over the area.

"I can see the place much more clearly," Mary urged. "Look

down on your left! See? Looks like a derrick sticking up through the trees."

"Sharon, get your camera out!" Greg pulled the airplane level. "I want shots of this site."

"Bank the plane to my side," Sharon answered. "I need a little more space off the wing. Just dip a bit more."

Greg responded immediately, allowing the airplane to go downwind, and then prepared for a turn back over the site.

"I don't want to be too obvious," he said. "We've got to get the evidence on film and move on."

"You aren't going to be happy," Sharon added, "but I can see plenty of action down there."

"What do you mean?" Greg asked his daughter.

"We'll have to study the film, but I'm sure that I saw a rather large derrick with some type of storage tank beside it. Looks to me like the job is done."

"Must be the wrong place," Greg grumbled.

"Nope." Sharon sat her camera on the floor and held up the larger map. "If our signals are even half right, that's a well down there, and it looks like it's ready to pump . . . or *is* pumping."

"Can't be," Greg objected.

"If I'm looking at the same place you are," Mary leaned over the seat, "I saw a derrick too."

"I'm not sure what to make of this." Greg scratched his head and nervously ran his hands through his hair. "I don't think we can risk making another pass. You sure you got the pictures?"

"You know I do." Sharon held up her camera.

Greg shook his head. "All right. I don't know what to do with this scene. Let's see if we can find the next place." He pushed the throttle forward, and the airplane rose several hundred feet.

Ten minutes later, he slowed the plane down, taking a gentle run over another area heavy with trees. "Time to pay careful attention," he said. "There's a good possibility of another derrick in there somewhere. Keep your eyes open. I'm going a bit lower so we can see better."

"I think we need to look up that creek area at about two o'clock." Sharon pointed ahead. "My map says the next place is adjacent to a stream like that one running into that woody area. If there's anything down there, we're going to have to get closer to the ground."

The right wing dipped abruptly, and they started a sharp descent into the area. The hillside was thick with small oaks and large cottonwood trees. The absence of houses left an Appalachian look of remote barrenness. A lone road wound around the hillside. Moments later Greg leveled the plane out and started his first run up the valley.

"Hey!" Sharon whirled around in her seat. "I think we just flew over the place."

"I didn't see anything," Greg objected.

"This place is really covered," Sharon said. "We're going to have to come back over slowly. Can you do that?"

"Maybe once."

"Okay, Dad. Here's your chance for the big time." Sharon picked up her camera. "I'll be ready."

Greg slowed the airplane down to the point of stalling and then started into a shallow bank at a very low altitude just above the treetops. Moments later he came back through the area from the opposite side and then flew straight up. Once the airplane was back at the normal flying speed, Greg leveled out. "Did everybody see the same thing?"

"No question about it," Mary answered. "I saw people drilling and running in every direction. They have some storage containers nearby."

Greg turned to his daughter. "Well?"

"Mary hit the nail on the head. We've seen two wells, and both are pumping."

Greg shook his head. "I can't believe this."

Without saying anything else, Parker added power, and the airplane climbed to a safer altitude and turned south. He flew over the ridge and started up the opposite side of the Mississippi River. In five minutes he was scanning down the other side.

"I think we're a couple of minutes from the next place." Sharon studied her map. "After we hit this one, the last drilling site is only eight or nine minutes away from us."

"I still can't believe these derricks are already going full tilt."

"You've got that one right," Sharon insisted. "Each of these locations is fully operational. I don't know what's happening, but these guys are down there pumping away like there's no tomorrow."

"May not be a tomorrow at the rate they're going," Greg snapped.

"What do you think, Greg?" Mary asked and leaned over the seat.

"I don't know. I'm going to have to think about this quite a while before I have much to say."

"We're just about to the next place." Sharon pointed to her left. "Can you make a slow pass through that valley?"

"Hang on." Greg dropped the wing, and the airplane drifted in a large circle toward the ground. At a thousand feet, he leveled the plane. "Here we go. Have your camera ready. The rig can't be far in front of us."

Sharon pushed her camera against the airplane's window and watched. Without a word, she began snapping pictures.

"I don't see anything," Greg objected.

"You aren't on my side," Sharon quipped.

"Absolutely," Mary added. "No question about it. I've just seen number three in full operation."

Greg gripped the controls tightly. "You're sure?"

"Yes," Mary answered. "If our maps are right, they are either drilling or long past that stage and are now pumping some kind of substance into the ground. Did you see the large trucks down there?" Mary asked. "Looked like gas trucks or something similar pulling long containers."

Greg brought the airplane up and banked to the right. "If there's anything at the next place, it's going to be hard to avoid an inevitable conclusion that Majors is far ahead of us."

"I'm sorry, Greg." Mary leaned over the seat. "But it seems your vision was right. He's put you in a straitjacket. The problem is far more serious than I thought . . . and I was worried *before* we left Washington."

"Start preparing to slow down." Sharon pointed to the left. "The last well isn't too far away. My maps suggest we've got to get beyond the other side of that rise, I think. Shouldn't be another five or ten minutes, at the speed you're going."

Greg nodded. "I think one or two passes over the area won't create a problem. On the other hand, these people may have surveillance equipment. If they do, they'll know in a hurry that we're on to them."

"We're going to have to work faster than I would ever have guessed," Mary concluded. "We thought we were in the first quarter, and these people are working in the fourth."

"Hang on," Greg lowered the airplane and began reducing speed. "I'm going to get a look at this next drilling unit myself."

"Then you'll have to drop the wing and come back around," Sharon argued. "I won't get good pictures shooting over your face."

"No problem," Greg answered. "This time the first run is mine. You be ready when we come back around."

The airplane dropped toward the ground. As they came over the small ridge, Greg lowered the wing but kept the airplane on a vertical plane. A minute later he looked to his left. The last site was by far the largest. Tractor trailers were lined up down the road. Men looked up as they flew over. Without ground cover, the rig was obviously working. One glance was enough. No question about what was happening. The crew was pumping something into the earth.

"Get your telephoto lens on," he barked. "I don't want to come down that close again, and you can get shots from higher up. I think we've seen enough."

CHAPTER 31

Greg Parker landed the airplane at Dulles International Airport shortly after 8:00 in the evening. A bedraggled Mary took her car home while Greg and Sharon left in theirs.

Sharon drove and Greg looked out into the night. "Dad, what do you think is happening?" Sharon asked halfway home.

"I don't know."

"What do you *think*?" Sharon persisted.

He started to tell her to knock it off because he was tired but remembered Sharon was far from a little girl. "I'm thinking about it."

"That's not an answer. You can do better."

Greg turned to his daughter, realizing his mouth was already open. He caught a deep breath. "A bit on the fresh side, aren't you?"

"No, I'm supposed to be your aide." Sharon looked at him with an eyebrow raised. "Don't I get your deepest thoughts before the rest of the team hears them?"

Greg shook his head. "Looks like my hallucinotory experience was right on target. You've got to get your pictures developed first thing in the morning, but . . ."

"I'll do them myself tonight. I learned how before I went to Israel."

Greg shook his head in wonder. "Great." He started over. "What I was going to say was that I want to see what you've got. I need blow ups, close-ups. Anything that will get me on top of this problem. Then, I'll tell you what I think."

"Good." Sharon pushed harder. "You'll have pictures before you go to bed tonight."

Greg shook his head again and then looked back out into the black night.

• • •

The last news report of the evening had finished, and the meteorologist was launching into a full-scale description of what to expect through the entire month of November as Greg drifted away in his large bed. He looked up at the light on the end of the bed and was debating about turning it off when a gentle knock stopped him.

"Sharon?"

"Yes, it's me."

"What is it?"

Sharon opened the door and came in. "I have something I promised you before you go to sleep."

"What?" Greg lazily pushed himself up in bed. "What are you talking about?" He yawned.

"Mary Morgan would be disappointed if she could see the great man right now."

Greg blinked several times. "It's been a long day."

"Yeah, and you quit an hour ago." Sharon dropped down on the end of his bed. "But not me. I have a little surprise." She opened up a black hardback folder. "Here are your pictures."

"You're kidding." Greg straightened up in the bed.

"Here's the first set." Sharon handed him three large pictures. "Take a careful look."

Greg studied the scene for several minutes before speaking. "No question about it. That well is fully operational." He held the picture up to the light. "Notice what they're doing." He traced all the edges of the pit and the drilling system. "Those boys appear to be pumping *into*, not *out of*, the ground."

"That's about what I thought." Sharon reached for the next pile of pictures. "Take a long look at well number two."

Putting the first pictures aside, Greg took the second pile. He shook his head as he studied Sharon's work. "Same thing. This drill is pumping into the earth."

Sharon smiled. "You'll be bored with the other two sets of pictures. Simply the same results."

"Let me see them!" Greg's sleepiness disappeared as he reached for the other stacks.

Sharon handed each pile separately, and he looked carefully Finally, he sank back against the head of the bed. "I am astonished. Majors has four wells pumping industrial lubricants into the earth right now."

"So, what's your conclusion, Dad?"

"The only reason anyone would do such a thing is to intentionally trigger an earthquake. I can't imagine any other reason."

Sharon leaned back against the end of the bed. "Then we've certainly uncovered a very serious problem today."

Greg ran his hand through his hair. "About as serious as it gets."

"What do we do next?"

"That's the second most important question anyone could ask. The most important question is why and who has the most to gain from this event, and we don't have much time to find out."

• • •

The next morning Alex Majors's secretary walked briskly into his office in the CIA headquarters and dropped a note on his desk. Majors didn't look up or respond but kept working on his computer. At that moment, Ian Blackmoor walked in.

"I say, old chap, how are things?" Blackmoor smiled broadly.

"What's on your mind?" Majors shot back.

"You sound a bit uptight," the Englishman began slowly. "Hope I'm not bothering you." He rubbed his long narrow chin. "Just dropped by to chat for a bit."

Majors bounced his pencil on the desk several times and then cursed. "What do you want, Ian?"

The Englishman grinned wryly. "How are things going with *the Duke*?"

"What do you want?" Majors repeated himself but tried to speak without revealing any emotion.

"Just asking questions." The statuesque ex-soldier slipped into the chair in front of Majors's desk. "That's my job, you know."

"You're not getting any answers here. Either state your business or breeze on down the hall."

Blackmoor laughed again. "Actually," he leaned over Majors's desk as he talked, "I'm interested in how you are functioning as part of Greg Parker's team."

"You and who else?"

"Me and the head of this entire organization." Blackmoor's voice took on a menacing edge.

"Tell everyone up and down the street that things are just fine." Majors lit a cigarette. "Yes, yes, I know, forbidden to smoke in the building." He tapped the cigarette on the edge of an ashtray. "Anything else you want?" He blew smoke at Blackmoor.

"Just checking." Blackmoor stood up. "Maybe, we can get together when you have a bit more time."

"Let me know." Majors turned back to the material on his desk and didn't look up again.

"Remember," Blackmoor sounded grim, "keep me informed."

"Sure." Majors didn't glance up as the Englishman left.

As soon as the door closed, Majors raced around his desk and locked the entrance. He returned to his desk and pulled out the briefcase, quickly opening the combination lock on the side. He took out the cellular phone used only for one purpose and dialed the international number.

"*Oui*," a receptionist answered after the encryption system kicked in.

"The falcon is calling," he said in French. "I must speak to the baron."

"*Oui.*"

After a minute, Baron Leestma asked abruptly in Flemish, "Is there a problem?"

"Yes and no," Alex continued in Flemish. "I was making sure that nothing has occurred that I don't know about."

"Nothing," Leestma answered abruptly. "What is your problem?"

"I've been checking on some pictures that came in late yesterday and was concerned," Majors answered slowly.

"Don't call me unless you have information. You're responsible for correcting any issues that are amiss in your operation. I am in an important meeting."

"Certainly."

The telephone clipped off. Alex closed his own system and then dialed the number on the paper in front of him.

"Helmut Haussman," the man answered.

"Alex Majors. I checked with our foreign department a moment ago, and everything is apparently fine in Europe."

"Fine?" Haussman's voice rose. "You are sure?"

"No. I'm telling you what I heard."

Haussman paused for several moments. "I have no idea what's happening. I depend on you to make sure everything is occurring on time."

"To my knowledge, it is, but I have concerns."

Haussman took a deep breath. "Keep your eyes open on every detail. We're getting near the end of this game."

"Think I don't know where we are?"

"Of course, but don't call me if you don't have something to say."

"You know who you are talking to?" Majors clipped.

"Listen . . ." Haussman took a second big breath. "It's my job to make sure that nothing goes wrong. I'll do that any way that works."

"Good," Majors sounded disinterested. "See you around." He hung up first.

The CIA officer leaned back in his chair with his arms crossed over his chest. *Everybody's getting uptight.* He suddenly leaned forward, grabbing a nut from a small bowl on the corner of his desk. With one swift thump of his hand, he cracked the nut. *Is something going on here that I'm missing?* He slowly ate the kernel and threw the pieces of the husk in the trash.

CHAPTER 32

Sharon sat behind her new desk in Mary's office suite and thought about her conversation with her father the night before. Things were beginning to escalate in a way that didn't feel good. She looked across the mountain of data that had come in during the short time she was with the NSA. How could she possibly be of much help in the midst of the daily avalanche of research and material floating in from a thousand places?

For a few moments, she leaned back in her chair and thought about the special task her father had given her. In some unique way that only heaven knew, Alice Mathewson was supposed to help Greg "Duke" Parker cut through all the minutiae and solve this problem. *I'm supposed to make some dramatic decision and take action to straighten everything out!*

The pressure to do something right felt like a giant flat iron descending on a pair of wrinkled pants, but Sharon wasn't sure the pants were straight on the press. If she wasn't careful, Sharon Parker would come out of this problem permanently bent. Not at all what she had in mind.

Sharon took a steno pad from the bottom drawer and laid it in the center of her desk. "What should I do?" she wrote across the first page and put a number one on the next line. For a couple of minutes, Sharon looked at the page before she picked up the pen again and started writing. "I am here to help my father recognize the basic issues he may fail to see."

She put the pen down and stared at the page. *If Dad has a problem, it's that he occasionally misses the obvious. He gets so caught up in a thousand small details that he overlooks the fundamental problem. He's done that forever.*

Sharon remembered when she was eight years old and her communications book disappeared for a couple of days. With considerable reluctance, she finally asked her father for help. For thirty minutes he questioned her about everything going on in their home, down the block, across the street, in the alley, and at the school. Like a tired caterpillar going up and down a tomato plant, Dad asked her to think about everything under the sun . . . except *exactly* where the book was last seen. Eventually Sharon went back to her bedroom, plopped down on the bed and rolled over next to the wall. To her surprise, the bed was several inches away from where it normally was. Reaching down the edge, she found the book where it had slid off the bed. Par for the course!

Pushing the steno pad away, Sharon thought about the circuitous path she had traveled to this point in the journey. How had she changed her rather jaundiced attitude toward everything happening in her father's world? Why had she become interested in his problems? What touched her life? At that moment Sharon remembered the book, *Final Sunset Over Jerusalem,* found at the church.

The little commentary on the book of Revelation had been like a key opening a lock around her heart. Even more than she earlier realized, the book was the major factor in everything she had done during the last fifty days. Each detail made a tremendous difference in how she saw her father and what he did. The little book had been of tremendous importance!

And what had she learned? One powerful, simple fact. When the final battle came in Israel, the United States would not be on the playing field. Something terrible would have reduced national capacities to nothing. And the discovery frightened her.

That one idea changed everything Sharon perceived was true about what her father was doing . . . and his very personal struggles. Even though he didn't see his work involved in a massive international struggle, the possibility was very high that he hadn't wrestled with the singular problem that could render the United States a broken machine in God's heap of defeated nations.

Someone in the White House, a person at the highest levels of American government, was working hard to destroy the potential of the country to make a difference in the world. Even as she thought about the problem, she knew that she must make sure her father kept that fact squarely in front of his eyes.

• • •

One floor down, Greg spread Sharon's pictures across his desk in his office. With a high-powered magnifying glass, he inspected every detail of each picture again and again. Now and then adjusting the desk lamp, he detailed the pictures.

"There's only one reason Majors is pumping some form of industrial lubricant into the earth," Greg said to himself. "He couldn't have any reason except to set off an earthquake. He's attempting to initiate the very thing we have been exploring as a future possibility. But why? Why would he subvert everything we are working on?"

Greg bent down and went back over the pictures again, looking for any possible detail he might have missed. On a notepad he kept a detailed list of what he had already observed. Slowly, painfully, he kept adding small but significant details. Each time he went back over the pictures, something new was added.

After thirty minutes, Greg laid the magnifying glass down and stared at his pages of notes. Only one conclusion was possible. Majors was preparing to move the ground in a way that would create a major earthquake. Only one more detail was needed.

Greg crossed his arms over his chest and stared at the paper. At some time during nearly every day of the last month, he had thought about Alberto and Maria Martinez and their six-month-old daughter, all killed in the earthquake in Northridge, California. The pressure of the business at hand had pushed the Martinez family into the back of his mind, but they were no less significant, and his memory forced them forward.

Once again, Greg could see them standing at the far end of his office. Alberto, a man of medium height, and Maria, just barely shorter, standing next to him. She carried the baby today. Small. Quiet. Sleeping. The family stood in the corner watching Greg work. They said nothing. Just watched what he did.

For a moment Greg flinched. He rubbed his eyes and looked again. They were gone. The corner was empty. Greg thought about the Martinez family in another way. What would they tell him? Was there a particular message they came to offer him? They had to know something he had missed.

Suddenly Greg saw the entire picture. What occurred in the Northridge earthquake flashed before his eyes. Alex Majors was far more clever than he'd recognized. His dislike of Majors had caused him to minimize the man's capabilities. Alex Majors knew *two* things. In addition to discovering what caused an earthquake, Majors had learned how to *set one off.*

Greg stared at his desk in shock. A cold sweat broke out on his forehead. California had been merely a dress rehearsal for Majors's plans in mid-America. He was staring at the detailed strategy of how the United States would be destroyed financially.

Greg's hands began shaking. He could see exactly what this devious but very bright man was planning. But who would believe him? Sharon? Mary? Greg shook his head and stared at the floor. The details were too strange and extreme. The NSA's number one man, Allan Jones, couldn't even be given a hint of such an idea. Jones would lock him up in the basement of their building!

Greg stood up and began pacing in front of his desk. He had to find some angle, some unique approach to minimize where he stood in this bizarre arena of events. He paced back and forth in front of his desk, seeking an idea, an action, anything that would switch the balance of power. For thirty minutes, he walked in circles with his telephone turned off. One facet of the formula kept coming back. Secrecy. *How could anyone deal with what was the biggest secret in the world?*

Five minutes later Greg called the *Washington Times*, the city's number one paper. "Greg Parker with the National Security Agency," he began.

"Oh!" the man answered, "What can I do for you, Mr. Parker? This is Jack Benz."

"My records indicate you're still one of the paper's editors."

"Something like that. I'm responsible for most of what comes out in your morning paper."

"Would you be interested in a major story on someone in the government attempting to cause a major earthquake in the center of this country?"

"Are you kidding?" Benz's voice rose. "Of course."

"Good." Greg cleared his throat. "Listen to what I have to tell you."

CHAPTER 33

Ian Blackmoor walked briskly into Alex Majors's office and shut the door behind him. Without saying a word, he pulled a small black device from his pocket, flipped it on, and walked slowly around the room.

Majors rubbed his chin. "I've already scanned once today for bugs, Blackmoor. The room is clean."

Without responding, the thin Englishman took several more steps around the room before clicking the machine off and sitting down across from Majors. "I want you to listen carefully to this request that came in a few moments ago from the *Washington Times*." He hit the button on a small recorder he took out of the other pocket.

"As I was saying," the man on the tape coughed and caught his breath, "this is Jack Benz, and I need confirmation on some confidential information I received."

"If I can, certainly," Blackmoor's English accent was clear.

"I've had a man named Parker claiming to be from the NSA call me and tell me that he's got an insider story on someone attempting to set off an earthquake in the New Madrid fault zone south of St. Louis."

Majors immediately reached over and clipped the machine off. "What's going on here?"

Blackmoor stuck his aquiline nose several degrees higher in the air. "That's my question for *you*."

Majors cursed violently. "Don't give me your nonsense, Blackmoor. I want the straight story on what this is about."

"Don't play dumb with me, Alex. Greg Parker called Benz with the story of an earthquake being set off in the center of the country," the Englishman sounded hard. "It's your turn to explain the incident to me."

"I don't have an explanation."

"Listen to me, old chap." Blackmoor's eyes narrowed. "Your job was to keep us informed on every detail of what Parker is doing. No one has the slightest idea of your doing one thing more. Am I correct?"

"Of course," Majors snapped back. He could feel the heat forming on the back of his neck. Blackmoor looked dangerous and sounded unpredictable. "You tell me what this recording is about."

"Don't try any of your little tricks with me," Blackmoor hissed. "I'm the one asking questions. Not you."

Majors slowly crossed his arms over his large chest and leaned back in his chair. He watched Blackmoor's eyes. The old Englishman was not going to be taken in by anything Majors came up with at this moment. The situation was thick, tense, and dangerous. "Then ask what you will," Majors concluded.

"I want to know what this tape is about."

"Don't have the slightest idea."

"Listen, you imbecile." Ian Blackmoor rose in his chair until his face was only inches from Majors. "You know exactly what's going on, and I want an answer."

Alex Majors knew his face betrayed nothing. He was the master of no response and could hang onto the same look all day. "I told you once that I have no idea what this *strange* story of yours is about. I suggest you tell this Benz character that."

"Except that I don't believe that's all there is to this account."

"Want to take a private trip with me to find out if there's more to it?" Majors quipped. "You tell me where you want to go, and I'll fly you there at your convenience."

"Really?" Blackmoor, caught off guard by the proposal, slowly withdrew.

"Really."

"Let me think about it." Blackmoor settled back in the chair. "I'll let you know shortly."

Majors watched the Englishman for a moment. No hint as to what he thought. "Better yet, find out from your friend Benz where this alleged activity is taking place, and I'll take you there."

"Is that a fact?" The Englishman picked up the recorder. "If you'd listened to the tape, you'd have gotten the exact location."

"You tell me right now, and I'll have an airplane waiting for us out at Dulles." Majors slowly leaned across the desk as he talked. "You want to find the place? I'm ready."

Blackmoor sank back in his chair. "You don't mean it," he finally concluded.

Majors reached for a hat and put it on his head. "You ready to roll?" He stood up. "Let's take the back stairs right now."

Blackmoor eyed him suspiciously. "Okay," he said slowly and stood up. "Let's go take a look."

Majors leisurely adjusted his hat. *Got to get this worthless Brit out of the building first. The car is the best route. Need to take a little walk.*

"I'm waiting," Blackmoor said.

"Follow me." Majors walked decisively in front of Blackmoor

and then stopped. "Why don't we first call Benz back and tell him the whole thing is a ruse?"

• • •

Jack Benz watched the fax come in on the credenza behind his desk. He pulled it out of the machine and read the substance before turning to the telephone on **his** desk. "Standifer?" he roared into the phone.

"Not so loud," the calm voice at the other end answered. "What do you want?"

"I just got an insider's response on this earthquake story, some guy who said he's at the NSA called in. The people at the CIA say it's nothing but nonsense. We can toss it."

"How do you know the CIA isn't lying?"

"Come on," Benz barked. "I'm talking the real CIA here. The Central Intelligence Agency people. I got contacts out there. They don't lie."

"Who says?"

"Drop the story. Forget it." He hung up and turned back to coverage of a story coming out of California.

• • •

Two hours later Alex Majors returned to his office. He came up the emergency stairs and went down the back corridor that allowed him to enter without his secretary seeing him enter. He stopped for a minute at the file system and randomly pulled out a file from the first cabinet he saw. After several minutes of carefully scrutinizing the office, he opened the door and called loudly enough so everyone in the front corridor would hear him. "Mrs. Schultz, would you please come in here for a moment."

Thirty seconds later, the secretary came in. "Excuse me," she began apologetically. "I didn't realize that you were working during the noon hour."

"Working? What else would I be doing?"

"I know you've been under a lot of pressure, and I assumed you had left to eat elsewhere."

"No problem," Majors snapped.

"Of course, of course," Mrs. Schultz sounded regretful. "I simply wanted you to know that I didn't put calls through as you indicated."

"Good." Majors picked up a file from his desk. "Would you please return this file to the materials section for me and get me the next file in the series?"

Mrs. Schultz looked mystified. "The next file in the series?"

"Yes. The one behind this material. Thank you."

The secretary quickly walked out of the room, looking puzzled.

Majors lit up a cigarette and watched the woman disappear down the hall. *Got to make sure everyone believes I stayed here. So far so good. The woman has no idea why I'd be working with those files.* He chuckled. *Neither do I, since I just got through pulling it out at random.*

Majors blew a big puff of smoke back into his office and shut the door behind him.

CHAPTER 34

Greg looked at his watch. Six hours had passed since he called the *Washington Times*. Nothing had happened. Not one single reporter called him back. Benz hadn't taken him seriously. Probably had written him off as a nut. The offices would close in a few minutes, and he didn't have much time left. He grabbed his coat and started upstairs.

Three minutes later, Parker entered Mary's office from the regular hall entrance and asked to see her.

"Greg?" Mary walked down her own hall, smiling. "You want to see me?"

"If you have time."

Mary frowned. "Have time? Are you kidding? Come in."

Greg closed the door behind him. Mary turned around slowly with an eyebrow slightly raised. "My, Greg, aren't we formal this afternoon."

Greg hesitated and rubbed his chin. "Mary," he spoke low and slowly, "I've got to talk with you about a difficult conclusion." He stopped and took a deep breath. "You'll think I've lost my mind."

Mary studied his face for a moment. "Greg . . . what's wrong? You look troubled."

"Please sit on the other side of your desk." He pointed to her chair. "And I'll sit on this side like I should."

"Really?" Mary sounded surprised. "Whatever you say."

Mary walked behind her desk and sat down.

"All day I've been working on the pictures Sharon took yesterday. I've studied every angle of her shots, and I'm sure where this whole thing is going." He watched Mary's eyes. She looked troubled.

"Go on," Mary said.

Greg took a big gulp of air. "I don't know why they are doing it, but I believe that Majors, and probably Helmut Haussman are immediately preparing to cause the New Madrid fault zone to enter a trauma sizeable enough to set off a major earthquake, which may well accomplish everything our team feared could happen to the entire United States."

Mary blinked several times.

"At any moment, Majors has the capacity to start an earthquake as he did in California. I believe he will act in the very immediate future."

"You're telling me that in two weeks . . . one week . . . tomorrow . . . today . . . Majors could set off the earthquake?"

Greg nodded his head. "That's my conclusion."

"You've had a vision . . ."

"No." Greg looked down at the floor. "Strange, but it's been a while since one of those episodes hit me. They seem to be leaving me." He looked up into her eyes. "I'm telling you what I deduced from my studies both from Northridge and our recent findings."

"Okay," she said factually. "Go on."

"I am convinced that I cannot stop Majors if it is his intent to set off an earthquake in the next few hours . . . or even the next couple of days. I recognize that you may have come to a very different set of conclusions." He watched her face again.

No hint of what she was thinking. "However, I must personally do everything in my power to stop Majors and Haussman. I must act quickly. I will understand if you wish to distance yourself from me."

Mary stood up and walked to the window. For a moment she looked down on the few people hurrying out of the NSA offices to the parking lots. "People are starting home," she turned around as she spoke. "Everything looks very normal, natural. Cars fill the streets. Exactly what anyone would expect this afternoon."

"Yes." Greg nodded his head. "Probably."

Mary walked around her desk and sat on the edge. "What's our next step, Greg?"

"Mary, I've just told you one of the most frightening hypotheses imaginable. Do you understand? We could be on the verge of watching this country experience a catastrophe."

"I understand. I saw the wells." Mary held up her hands. "I've seen the evidence. Remember? If this is what this material means to you, then I am able to accept your findings as readily as in every other area."

"But I'm telling you something very . . ."

"Extreme," Mary completed his sentence. "The issue is, what we are going to do with this problem?"

Greg stared at her and rubbed the sides of his temples. "You have taken the words I was going to say and, and . . ." Greg's voice drifted away.

Mary stood up. "I think we need to get busy." She walked quickly behind her desk. "We don't have much time."

Greg nodded his head mechanically and watched Mary sit down. "Clara," she said over her intercom system, "please come in here as quickly as you can."

• • •

Baron Wilhelm Leestma walked into the small executive committee room, nodding to each person. He smoothed the side of his impeccably maintained Armani suit. Today it was important to be flawless. He glanced at Yvonne Galla, wearing sunglasses as she always did when she wasn't sure of what was happening. The woman was intelligent, but today she had entered a land of which she knew not.

Leestma smiled at her professionally. *Madame Galla is in this operation way over her head. She has no idea what I'm about to say. It will be interesting, very interesting, to watch her response after I speak.*

For a moment, Leestma arranged the material in his file. He glanced at his watch. The second hand was ten seconds away from 10:00 A.M. He waited until it was precisely the hour. "Good morning," he began in English. "I have several very important announcements to share with you." He paused to collect his exact thoughts.

"I don't see an agenda for our meeting," Galla interrupted. "What are we doing today?"

"Listening to me," Leestma answered instantly.

"Oh?" She smiled.

"Please be quiet," Leestma said firmly. "You will know what we are doing when I am through speaking." He looked harshly at the woman and then began again. "In our last meeting, I discussed the problem that retiring baby boomers will present the United States in the years 2006 and 2009. I asserted that the United States is unprepared for the impact this retiring force will place on their economy." He picked up a sheet of paper. "My exact statement was, 'Social Security insolvency will push the government into bankruptcy. Inability to face national debt will be quicksand, sucking the entire country under.' I indicated the necessity of moving our accounts out of their system and making certain significant social adjustments to guarantee our investments. Correct?"

Leestma watched each person's face. Galla's indignant posture didn't conceal her complete lack of knowledge of what he was about to say. The rest of the group of eight men smiled, nodded their acknowledgment, and implied their consent. Even though Galla hadn't discovered the movement of opinion, she was already negated.

"To stabilize our situation, I presented to you the overall projections for Operation Downfall," Leestma continued. "While I did not give you all the data, I indicated that we were pursuing an aggressive plan that would put the Gent Institute at the top of the world's economy." He again smiled politely and took a second hard look at the group.

Even though each person oversaw a vast amount of money, Gent's executive committee looked to Leestma for most of the final decisions. No one had said anything more than what appeared to be an all-accepting trust of anything he said. With the exception of Galla, each man had gone through many months of experience, training, specially-crafted events which brought them to this place of complete and total acceptance. Unfortunately, the woman spoiled what would otherwise be the perfect apex of the meeting.

"Therefore, you should be ready for the final moment in our plans," Leestma began again. "Within the next few hours, a massive earthquake will rip through the center of the United States. Just as we blew away The Dome of the Rock Mosque in Jerusalem. The country is totally unprepared to respond. We are moving our assets out of the country, and their stock market will discover the transaction later in this day. No one will pay attention to this destructive transfer, as their country will be so completely caught up in trying to survive the massive earthquake." He cleared his throat. "However, in somewhere between one and two weeks, their stock market will crash because of the earthquake."

Galla abruptly took off her sunglasses. "You are saying that a massive earthquake is about to hit America?" her voice was barely audible.

"That is *exactly* what I just said."

"An earthquake caused by us?" Galla's voice was higher.

Baron Leestma looked hard at the woman. "Do not interrupt me again or I will have you removed from this meeting."

Galla's jaw dropped.

"And it will happen instantly!" The baron snapped his finger. Silence fell over the room.

"In a very short time, we will return Europe to the glory of Louis XIV!" Leestma began again. "The splendor of the days when the Dutch and the Spanish ruled the waves! Gentlemen, the Arabs did exactly what we thought they would do. They moved their armies next to Israel and left their oil fields unprotected. We only have to use our influence to have NATO troops move in as a peacekeeping operation, and the oil fields will be ours." He beamed uncharacteristically. "With the passing of the Americans as a world power, the Jews will soon vanish!"

The group suddenly exploded in enthusiastic applause. Galla stared at the wall, her mouth still partly open.

CHAPTER 35

The November night air forced the two men hidden beneath the large trees to turn up their collars against their necks. Haussman and Majors huddled behind the tree where they could see everything happening around Greg's house.

"What do you think?" Haussman asked Majors.

The CIA officer looked at his watch. "It's 8:10. I know Parker's daughter is upstairs, but I have no idea why he's not here."

Haussman wrapped his scarf more tightly around his neck and ears. "You *said* they'd be here early tonight."

Majors looked through the bushes at Greg's house again. "I'm an agent," he said brusquely, "not God Almighty. Parker will be here soon. Don't push me *or* your luck."

Haussman tucked his hands under his arms. "Look. I don't care if it's only around the middle of November. I'm cold. How did I ever let you talk me into this nasty ploy?"

"You and I are all there is," Majors hissed. "We're the only people who can take such dramatic action. The rest of the players are in Belgium. You've been in on hits in the past. Shouldn't be a big deal for an old pro like you."

"Don't toy with me, Alex. Assassinations have never been my thing, and that was a long time ago. I'm an important person now."

"Not so important that you can't help me finish off this guy. The rest of the plans are already in gear. We don't have much time, and after it's done, no one will be paying attention to something this small."

"Killing people is never small," Haussman growled.

Majors watched the house and raised his eyebrows.

"You get what I'm saying?" Haussman pushed. "Standing out here in the pitch black of night doesn't fit."

"Keep your mouth shut and watch." Majors cursed. "The action will start shaking soon, and then there's nothing to do but wait for the money to roll in."

"I don't want to get caught in some wild-eyed scheme to shore up a few loose ends at the last minute," Haussman grumbled.

"Then shut your big mouth. We've had this same conversation for the last twenty minutes."

Haussman fumbled around in the dark for several minutes. "You're sure no one is home in this house behind us?"

"See any lights?"

The German shook his head.

"Watch out. Looks like Parker's '89 Pontiac coming down the street."

Both men dropped to their knees behind the bushes. Greg's car rolled into the driveway, waited for the garage door to go up, and then drove in.

"If his daughter is in the house," Haussman began before the door was completely down, "then he's got a new woman in the car."

Majors looked at the German out of the corner of his eye. "You're bright, Helmut."

"I don't like it."

"We kill all of them."

Haussman shook his head. "We didn't plan to go this route."

"Well, here we are." The CIA officer turned to face the German. "Now, you've got two choices. You do it my way, or I'm ready to go back to the office and wait for you to come up with a better alternative." He leaned into Haussman's face. "Got me?"

"Okay, okay. I know time is of the essence. Let's go in there and do it. We'll make it look like a burglary and get on our way."

"Exactly." Majors nodded toward the back door. "Give me precisely five minutes, then you walk over there and ring the front door. When that door opens, I'll be coming in the back. Shoot everyone as quickly as possible." He started down the hedgerow and then stopped. "You're with me? *Right?*"

Haussman's head bobbed up and down, but he was looking carefully at his watch. Majors watched him for a moment and then continued. He walked carefully and quietly through the shrubs and bushes until he got to the end of the backyard of the house next to Greg's place. Because the thick hedge served as a fence, it was not difficult to cut across into the backyard, but the maneuver took time.

Majors silently worked his way back up the hedgerow until he came to the garage. Pausing to listen for noises, he started across the rear end of Greg's house. He heard a door open inside the garage and hit the ground.

For what seemed like forever, Alex Majors listened to confusion and noise coming out of the garage. He reached into his coat and pulled out his .38 Model 10 Smith & Wesson revolver. He reached back into his coat and pulled out a silencer, which he quickly and quietly secured to the end of the two-inch barrel. Carefully pulling his coat cuff up, he looked at the luminous dial of his watch. One minute and fifteen seconds until he had to be at the back door. Less time than he planned.

• • •

Greg hurried in the back door and called for Sharon. She came downstairs quickly.

"Mary!" Sharon bolted. "What are you doing here?"

Mary hugged her. "My, my, so much is happening so fast." She hugged her again. "I think your father had best tell you where we are right now."

"Just a second," Greg pointed to the garage. "I've got a map out there that I want you to see as I tell you what's happening at this very minute."

"This minute?" Sharon blinked several times and shook her head. "Whatever you guys say." She started toward the kitchen. "Let me get you a cup of coffee."

"Great idea." Mary took off her coat and hung it over the back of a chair. "I need a little something inside to warm me up. We've been going strong since five o'clock."

The door to the garage slammed.

"I'm glad you could come this evening," Sharon said as she reached into the kitchen cabinet. "And it's no problem with me, but I didn't see but one car come up in the driveway."

"That's right." Mary sat down at the kitchen table. "I'm afraid I'm going to be around through this evening and until who knows when."

"Really?" Sharon's voice rose. "I'm all ears. What's going on?"

Mary looked at her hands for a moment and then closed them tightly. "Like I said earlier, I think your father should tell you the details. This story is more his baby."

"Okay. Sure." Sharon looked puzzled but took cups out of the cupboard.

"I don't think I want any sweetener tonight. Black is fine."

"Gotcha covered." Sharon set a steaming cup in front of Mary and sat down. "I'm sure you know that you've got my total attention." Sharon put a teaspoon of sugar in her coffee. "You *really know* what's going to happen next?"

Mary looked straight into Sharon's eyes and saw innocence lurking in the corners. How would she deal with her father's story?

"I've never been a part of anything like the adventure that started about the time I went to Israel," Sharon continued. "You know, that trip to the Middle East was truly awesome." She stirred her coffee. "Never was a part of anything like that in my life."

"I'd give anything just to have a trip to the Holy Land," Mary answered, reaching for her cup. "I can't imagine what it must be like to step in the exact places where the people of the Bible walked."

"Simply amazing." Sharon shook her head. "I can't tell you how wonderful it was to . . ."

"The doorbell?" Mary frowned at Sharon.

"I'll get it." Greg came out of the garage and hurried through the kitchen. "Must be a neighborhood kid."

"Be careful," Sharon said as she stood up. "No one ever calls here in the evening."

"I'll get it for you." Mary hurried out of the kitchen for the front door.

"No problem. I'm in here," Greg called from the living room.

• • •

Haussman stood in front of the large blue door, his hand in his pocket with his knuckles tightly clenching his Model 36 Chief's

Special .38-caliber pistol. He waited very nervously for the door to open. He had already twisted the porch light off. Helmut knew he'd pushed the doorbell hard enough that someone should be there quickly.

The door opened.

"Helmut Haussman!" Greg stood in the doorway. "What are you doing here at our house?"

"I must speak to you." Haussman knew he sounded upset.

"Tonight?" Greg opened the door wider.

Haussman walked in.

"Somebody's coming in the back door!" Sharon suddenly yelled. "Look out!"

Haussman instantly jerked his gun from his coat pocket to shoot, but Greg grabbed his hand and forced him against the door.

"No, you don't." Greg growled and pushed Haussman's gun hand against the wall. Haussman swung with his other hand but missed Greg's head. Suddenly they were swinging around together. Out of the corner of his eye, Haussman saw Majors coming in the kitchen door with a gun in his hand, but Greg kept whirling him. He wasn't sure where his gun was pointed until he felt something metal pushing into his chest.

The gun went off. Two more explosions filled the room with smoke. Suddenly Haussman's back stiffened, and then his whole body went limp as he slumped to his knees. Haussman looked up and realized Parker was standing above him, his hand on his shoulder. Everything was fading to black . . .

• • •

Greg Parker felt the bullet hit his shoulder and sensed it had gone on through his body. The impact pushed him back, and he bounced off the wall. Somehow he was holding Haussman's gun. He tried to raise it but his arm wouldn't move. He looked into the face of Alex Majors, still standing in the kitchen door.

Majors's mouth dropped slightly, and he simply stood there. Only then did Greg see two increasingly red spots in the center of Major's coat. His face froze. For a moment, Majors stared at Greg, his glance fast becoming more distant. Majors tumbled over backward into the kitchen.

Greg realized he had sunk to his knees. He fell facedown on the carpet.

CHAPTER 36

Greg felt the carpet brush his nose and knew he was still alive. For a minute, he heard sounds above him and was more out than in, but slowly everything returned. "What's happened?" he mumbled, feeling like he was back in the hospital.

"Dad, are you okay?" Sharon shouted from above him.

"Yes," he said slowly. "I think . . . I . . . got hit in the . . . shoulder." He blinked several times. The room was coming into focus.

"Don't move," Mary ordered. "I've just called the police and an ambulance."

"Okay. What happened to Majors?" Greg sounded bewildered.

"I shot him," Sharon whispered. "I had a gun hidden in the kitchen." Her usually strong voice faded.

"You what?" Greg moaned.

"I expected an attack in our home . . . sooner or later," Sharon explained slowly. "I put . . . the gun in a safe place behind some cookbooks. I kept it where I could grab it in a matter of seconds." She rubbed her forehead and looked at the floor. "I knew nobody respectable would be coming to our house at this hour of the night. As soon as Mary left the room, I got the gun out . . . I had it in my hand when Majors came in the back door, holding a gun. I was ready and fired . . . twice."

"Oh, geez," Greg groaned and stirred. "I can't believe it. Mary, are you okay?"

"I'm all right . . . yes . . . okay."

"I think . . . I need . . . to sit up against the wall." Greg pushed against the carpet. "Man. Did I ever grab the tail of the dragon this time."

"Are you sure you're okay?" Sharon asked, agonizing over her father.

"I need to sit up." Greg rolled over to his good side. "Help me up."

"Be careful." Mary got next to his side. "We'll assist you." She and Sharon slowly pulled Greg up against the wall by the front door.

"Sharon," Greg said softly, "I promise never to doubt you again about anything." He took a deep breath. "Maybe now . . . I've done . . . something to avenge the deaths of Alberto and Maria Martinez."

"Who?" Sharon leaned closer.

"Don't worry," Greg answered. "They are people who were killed in an earthquake." He felt his shoulder carefully. "A long time ago."

"Dad, I've watched how you operated for every year I've been alive. Just observing you taught me to be ready for the unexpected. I simply did what I've learned from you. I went down town and bought this 9-millimeter pistol. I knew it needed to be powerful. I don't know," her voice trailed away, "I guess I never thought I'd *really* have to shoot it." She stopped and looked away.

Greg shook his head and felt his shoulder. "I'm sure I will be okay." He looked at the two men lying on the floor. "I wonder how soon the police will be here?"

"Shouldn't be long," Mary said and looked away.

"Are you sure you're okay?" Mary asked Sharon. "I mean . . . shooting someone . . . and . . . just everything."

"I don't want to talk about it." Sharon ran her hands nervously through her hair. "I knew if I put a gun in the house, one day something like this could happen." She took a deep breath, stopped, and forced a smile.

"You saved our lives." Mary reached out for Sharon's hand.

Greg's head fell back against the wall, and he looked up at the ceiling. "I don't ever want another one of these adventures. This one's been enough for the next twenty years."

Sharon held her father's hand tightly. "Don't worry. I'll do everything in my power to make sure we don't go down one of these wild roads again."

Greg shook his head. "I don't believe it. We seem to walk into these wild escapades without even half trying." He looked down at his bloody shirt. "This one really got out of control."

"Don't kid yourself," Mary added. "If I have anything to do with it, you can bet I'll put a brake on the next wild ride." She pressed a covering from an overturned end table against Greg's wound to stop the bleeding.

Greg flinched and looked at the light fixture in the center of the room. The brass light hung on the end of a chain with a wire running down the center. It started to swing slightly and then gradually increased. "Look at the chandelier!" He nodded up. "The thing is moving."

Sharon stared. "Good heavens. The fixture is swinging!"

The floor began to shake slightly, and the light swung in a larger circle.

"The earthquake!" Greg shouted. "I think they've started the earthquake!"

Sharon and Mary huddled next to Greg. "God help us!" he prayed.

The house groaned and cracked. Then, the noise stopped. Greg didn't move.

"It's over," he finally said.

"For us to have felt anything in this suburb means it was big," Mary concluded.

"Very big," Sharon gasped.

"What do you think?" Mary asked Greg.

"I don't know but I'm afraid of what Majors has created." Greg pulled his legs in. "Maybe we slowed down the quake . . . maybe we didn't. I think I should stand up. I've got to get on my feet."

"No, Greg." Mary said firmly. "We've got to get you to the hospital."

"I'm feeling better now. Get me into a chair to sit down." Greg leaned on Mary as Sharon pushed from the side. "I'm getting there," he groaned.

With the help of the two women, Greg got to his feet. "The feeling is starting to come back to my shoulder, and it certainly doesn't feel good."

Off in the distance a siren wailed. "They're coming," Sharon observed. "Got to be here in just a minute."

"We need to get these two men out of here." Greg dropped into the large chair close to the door. "I didn't think we'd be attacked quite this soon."

"Look." Sharon stood in front of her father. "I want to know what is going on west of us. Level with me before the police come and everything goes crazy."

Greg opened his mouth, but words wouldn't come out. His head fell back on the chair.

"Sharon, I think your father's going into shock!" Mary ran

her hands up and down his wrist, feeling for a pulse. "I can't find anything. Get out there and wave that police car down!"

Sharon ran for the front door and burst down the steps, shouting "Police! Police!" She kept yelling. "Police . . ." Her voice faded off in the distance.

Greg partially opened his eyes. "Things keep turning white on me," he muttered. "I'm having a hard time."

"Just take it easy," Mary urged. "Sharon and I are right here."

"I know that I'm losing blood."

"We're doing everything we can to slow it down, dear." Mary stared at the red oozing from Greg's shoulder. "You're going to be okay."

Sharon burst back into the living room. "They're here! An ambulance is pulling up with the squad car."

The siren suddenly stopped in front of the Parker's home.

"Thank the Lord that they're here," Greg muttered to Sharon. "I think you saved us."

"None of that kind of talk." Sharon walked to the door and waited. A car door slammed in their driveway. She turned and looked at Greg and Mary. "We each simply did our part."

Greg looked at his daughter. "I love you, Sharon. I couldn't have survived this thing without you."

Sharon kissed him on the cheek and looked at Mary. "If this isn't the final big disaster, then we've got other important matters ahead. If it is, then we know what God wants from each of us. Regardless, this catastrophe is the prelude to a new beginning, and we're going to make it *together*."

• • •

Experts in the Washington, D.C. Earthquake Prediction Center hurried back and forth between the rooms, pumping out the seismographic printouts and their office desks. A few men were trying to get a public television response while others made frantic calls across the country.

"I don't get it." The geologist stared at the long printout. "One minute everything is normal. The next we get the biggest event any of us have ever heard of in the New Madrid zone. "I don't see any evidence of tectonic subterranean plates bumping together, and yet this thing is the biggest earthquake any of us have ever measured in that area."

"I'm deeply concerned," his administrative advisor answered. "If this earthquake is as big as all evidence indicates, we're looking at a tremendous disaster."

A computer operator hurried into the room. "The people over at the National Security Agency knew what they were talking about. We're in the midst of exactly what they were concerned would happen someday. This quake has really smacked the middle of the country."

"I don't think we got any damage around here," the Prediction Center's spokesman said, "but they must be in big trouble over in Memphis and down the Mississippi River valley. I'm not getting any telephone or television response."

"Okay, boys," the geologist said, "you know what to do. If there ever was a time to pull out those emergency instructions, it's now."

The men nodded.

"Let's go," the spokesman said. "Going to be a long night." He stopped and turned around. "And maybe a longer tomorrow."

CHAPTER 37

Sharon stopped pacing and glanced at her watch. Twelve hours had passed since the ambulance had taken her father to the hospital. She had waited until the surgery was over and finally gone home at around 2:00 in the morning. Mary stayed at their house, and they ended up sleeping longer than either intended.

"You can come in." The nurse came out of the room and shut the door behind her. "He had a few rough moments last night but he is definitely improving. I think your father is doing fine."

"Oh, wonderful!" Sharon grabbed Mary's hand. "Let's go." She smiled bravely and pushed the door open slowly.

With the overhead light off, the room was dim. Dr. Greg Parker lay in the bed with his eyes closed and seemed to be asleep. Clean white sheets had been pulled up around his neck, and a large bandage covered his shoulder. He looked shaved and like he had been bathed not long ago.

"Dad?" Sharon asked quietly.

"Hmmm," Greg groaned but didn't open his eyes.

"Are you awake?"

Greg slowly opened his eyes slightly. "Sharon?" He blinked several times. "Sharon? Is that you?"

"Mary's with me."

Greg opened his eyes wider. "You're both here?"

"Yes," Sharon answered. "We came to visit our injured gun slinger."

Greg laughed gently. "Feels worse than last night. Turn on some light or open the blinds."

Sharon flipped on an indirect light. "Hurting quite a bit?"

"Worse than last night." Greg smiled. "Guess that's just par for the course." He looked around the room. "Have you seen the news on television? I'm worried about the effects of the earthquake."

"Only once," Mary said. "Things are fairly rough out there, but only two of the wells went off to start the quake. Apparently Majors's crew released enough lubricant to create significant trouble, but we did make a difference in how much damage occurred."

Greg smiled. "We tried hard enough." His head dropped back on the pillow and stared at the ceiling.

Sharon pulled a chair over near the bed. "Look. I want to know what the two of you did before you came home last night. Obviously you took some very significant steps. Level with me. What did the two of you do?"

Mary and Greg exchanged a quick glance and smiled.

"Think we can let an outsider in on our top secret work?" Greg feigned indifference. "Our investigation is completely confidential." He looked away as if unconcerned.

Mary laughed. "I don't think that one will fly, Greg. You hired your daughter to work for us."

"Yeah, Dad. I'm one of the insiders now. Remember?"

Greg shook his head. "What can I say? Outflanked by the press again." He winked at Mary. "I suppose we can share maybe, oh, a few clues."

Sharon beckoned with her fingertips. "Come on, Dad. Tell me the *whole* story."

Greg sighed. "I guess I can tell you a little bit." He grinned.

"Here's what happened. Just before the NSA offices closed, I went to see Mary and told her that your snapshots convinced me that Alex Majors was going to set off the quake in the very near future. I thought Haussman was part of the problem but never in terms like what, well, what we . . . experienced last night." He glanced down and then looked away quickly. "I wouldn't ever have expected Haussman to come to our house, intending to kill us, but when I saw him, I knew something was terribly wrong. On the other hand, Majors wasn't a surprise."

"Your father shared some of his suspicions with me earlier," Mary confirmed. "By the time he came in late in the afternoon, everything he said made sense to me. Greg, tell Sharon the basic story."

"All right," Greg said. "Mary and I started trying to get my conclusions to our team at five o'clock yesterday." He grimaced. "Ow, my shoulder hurts! You tell her some of the story, Mary."

"Your father leveled with me. Told me exactly what he thought would happen quickly." Mary rubbed her forehead. "And it occurred just as he projected. Your father felt that we might not believe him." She managed a smile. "But I'd seen the wells. Of course, I knew he was right. So, we first contacted everyone we could get on the phone who was part of the NSA research team. We instructed them to call people and agencies from oil refineries to state departments of safety. In fifteen minutes most of our team was on the phone calling key people up and down the Mississippi River basin. An hour later we were in touch with everyone from governors on down. Our team did a significant job getting the message out."

"Our telephone contacts knocked out two of those drilling wells," Greg added. "We called many, many people, and put other officials to work implicating some of the initial decisions our team has been preparing over the last several months. I don't know how bad the results of this earthquake will prove to be in a week, but we've done everything we could to make sure some preparation was made before the big rumble hit."

Sharon nodded her head slowly. "At least the two of you started the plans that, maybe, just maybe, kept this earthquake from doing fully what Majors intended."

"Before I left our offices last night, I even talked with the head of the CIA," Greg added. "At this moment, they are working on, in, and everywhere Majors has been this year. They will find out the rest of the story." He coughed and held his shoulder. "Sharon, the big issue is what the earthquake has done to our national economy. We won't know for possibly twenty-four hours, but we must pray that the country economically survives this terrible quake."

"I watched a television report this morning," Sharon said. "Things aren't good up and down the Mississippi River, but apparently your staff callers got some of the natural gas lines turned off before the quake hit. What I got from the news reporter seemed to indicate that two of the oil wells didn't function. Part of the earthquake's tremor went east toward Washington, D.C., but the oblique angle didn't create the damage that Majors must have intended. Some of the big bridges and highways escaped the terminal damage our old friend had in mind."

"That's what I heard, Dad," Sharon added. "Looks like catastrophic economic damage to the country may have been averted."

"It'll take a day or two before we know just how bad the effects will be, but I think the two of you are about to become national heroes." Sharon grinned at Greg and Mary. "Looks like the two of you are going to be famous."

"Hey! Let's not let things get out of hand," Greg protested.

"I can see it now." Sharon acted as if she were drawing a picture on the wall with her finger. "The president of the United States hanging a Distinguished Service Cross around each of your necks. The band is playing. The Rose Garden lawn packed with senators and representatives gathered from across the nation."

Greg laughed. "Tell her the story, Mary. Peons like us only get the time off stated in that national medical policy our health insurance allows. That's the only reward we receive."

"I don't think so," a deep resonant voice said from the door. "We can do better than that scenario."

Everyone turned and looked at the door. NSA head Allan Jones stood in the doorway. He nodded and came into the hospital room.

"Last time I was up here, Greg, you were having strange visions or whatever those unusual experiences were. Everyone thought you'd had a stroke."

"Allan! I can't believe you're here!" Greg reached out and then flinched.

"Turns out you were actually in a big wrestling match with a CIA agent." Allan shook his head, talking as he walked around the room. "My . . . a . . . private investigation indicates you've been fighting worse enemies than any of us even guessed were out there."

Greg looked at Mary with a dumbfounded stare. "Private investigation? What are you talking about?"

"I got bad vibes the first time you and I talked with Helmut Haussman. Remember that day?" Allan smiled at the ladies. "I contacted a couple of my close friends at the White House, and we started our own top level inquiry. Unfortunately you stayed about two steps ahead of us, Greg." Allan sat down in the chair. "I'm sorry, but I had no idea that Majors and Haussman would try an assassination attempt. No one saw that twist coming." He looked down at the floor. "When I heard about the earthquake, I tried to call your house. One thing led to another, and shortly I knew you were here. Sorry that we didn't do a better job protecting you."

"I can't believe my ears, Allan." Greg's head dropped against the pillow. He closed his eyes. "You were watching this situation from the shadows all the time."

"Apparently not well enough." Allan patted Greg's arm under the sheet. "But I think we'll do much better next time." He turned and smiled at Sharon. "I think a presidential recognition of some sort is an excellent idea, Sharon. Would you stand next to me at the ceremony?"

Sharon beamed. "You call me, and I'll be there."

"Good." Jones grinned. "Excellent. Greg, if you need anything, you just let me know, and it'll be here in maybe fifteen seconds." He got up and walked to the door. "I'll be watching to make sure they treat you like a king."

"Thank you, Allan," Greg said. "Thank you for coming. How do you think the country is making it after this shake?"

Allan looked thoughtfully out the window. "Hard to say at this moment, Greg. Obviously such a major earthquake is going to affect how people live. The worst-case scenario is that the financial markets are severely affected and even Social Security may take a big hit. I don't see it in the cards, but the country could be run by executive order or through FEMA if the devastation proves significant enough." He stopped and rubbed his chin. "My hunch is that we're not at that point, but the insurance industry is going to be in big trouble. They may have to sell such a volume of stock that the Wall Street market is affected. We're going to have big trouble keeping the auto industry from nearly collapsing." He abruptly looked tired.

"Got to get you out of here and back at the NSA to help us solve these problems."

Greg winked. "I think you'll do fine until I get there."

All walked toward the door. "The two of you take good care of my top man." Allan waved and was gone.

"I told you, Dad. You're going to be a famous person."

"Nice to have my daughter think good thoughts." Greg nodded soberly. "But what I like most is what I heard you say last night just before the policemen came in. Remember?"

Sharon blinked several times. "I'm not sure?"

"You said that we were on the threshold of a new beginning. Whatever happens in the future, we'll face it *together*." Greg looked at Mary. "I like that promise best. All of us facing tomorrow *together*."

About the Authors

Robert L. Wise, Ph.D., is the author of twenty-three books, including the best-sellers *The Third Millennium, The Fourth Millennium,* and *Beyond the Millennium,* and *The Secret Code.* His most recent book with Thomas Nelson is *The Jerusalem Scroll,* coauthored with Mike Evans. Dr. Wise is a bishop in the Communion of Evangelical Episcopal Churches and is the founding pastor of Church of the Redeemer in Oklahoma City.

William Louis Wilson Jr. is currently employed by an agency within the Department of Defense. As a member of the Defense Acquisition Corps, he has initiated and participated in federal investigations that exposed fraud and waste at the highest levels of government.

Don't miss this exciting book by Robert Wise

The Jerusalem Scroll

When Musah Salah, a Palestinian archaeologist, discovers an ancient golden scroll in a cave, the document seems to hold the key to Jerusalem's past—and its future. Though he cannot decipher all five languages used in the scroll, Musah can read enough to conclude that the scroll records the Donation of Melchizedek—the gift of the city of Jerusalem to the son of Abraham. But which son is it—Ishmael or Isaac?

As Salah tries to translate the text of the scroll with the help of two other experts, Leah Rosenberg and Father Michael Kelly, it's clear that many people will have a vested interest in the scroll's content. Though the three go to great lengths to conceal the scroll, news of its existence soon hits the newspapers, and violence begins to escalate around them.

Even as speculation about the scroll drives events in the city, outside Jerusalem powerful forces—the Islamic Revolutionary Front, OPEC, and even the United States—are turning their focus to the ancient city for the last great political battle of the millennium.

0-7852-6915-0 • Hardcover • 352 pages